THE DEAL

ARRANGED BOOK ONE

STELLA GRAY

ABOUT THIS BOOK

On my eighteenth birthday my father, the senator, gives me the gift he thinks every little girl dreams of.

The man of my dreams, and the wedding to match.

Stefan Zoric is heir to an elite worldwide modeling agency. Practically a prince.

My arrangement is simple, as far as sham marriages go.

I give him my virginity, behave as the perfect wife and he'll pay for the college degree my father found irrelevant.

But I don't want to be the perfect wife.

I want him to want me the way I want him.

I want him to confide in me.

But Stefan has secrets that he holds close, dangerous secrets.

And soon I'm wondering what kind of devil have I made a deal with?

PROLOGUE

STEFAN

I'm the kind of man who lives for control.

From the office to the bedroom, domination is my instinct—and I show no mercy when it comes to getting what I want. Because if there's one thing I know, it's that when I take charge, I always close the deal. And I never hear any complaints.

Not from my employees and sure as hell not from my women.

Tonight would be no exception. The handshakes, the easy grins, the raised glasses of high-end booze: it was all a means to an end as far as I was concerned. One more move on the chessboard, and one step closer to controlling KZ Modeling, the company my father had founded. The company he still controlled.

For now.

I leaned back in my chair, taking in the room. My father's penthouse was luxury defined, and his private office was expansive, its richness accentuated by polished wood paneling and antiques. Never-read first editions lined the walls. Every object, down to the Waterford paperweights, was costly and rare. Just like everything my father treasured.

I checked the time on my Patek Philippe. "He's late."

"He'll be here."

Behind his desk, my father—Konstantin Zoric—poured himself a scotch. Macallan 25 Year, because in our world, image is everything. He cut an imposing figure in his signature monochrome charcoal. People said I looked like him, but most of the men in our family had the same dark hair, square jaw, full lips and olive skin.

He gestured toward me, offering me a glass. I took it but didn't drink. Normally I'd go through the motions, act like I was one of the boys, but I needed a clear head going into this.

"Ah, here he is," my father said as he stood to greet our guest.

An athletic, middle-aged man with ice blue eyes and gray streaks at his temples had been ushered into the office. His suit was well-made, cleanly tailored to his body. His tie was red. His lapel pin was an American flag. If I didn't already recognize him from television, I still would have assumed he belonged in politics. The self-satisfied smirk was the cherry on top.

"Senator Lindsey, this is my eldest son, Stefan," my father said, making the introductions.

"Welcome," I said, already standing. I shook the senator's hand, matching the strength of his grip. "A pleasure to finally meet you in person, Senator."

He gave me a long, assessing look.

"Indeed," he said, revealing nothing. "Glad you could make it."

"Sit, sit! Let's raise a toast to our joint venture," my

father said, passing a glass to Lindsey. "And to Stefan, entering fully into the family business at last."

"And what a business it is," the senator said. He eased into the plush leather. "You've got quite the little operation going. And KZM's support is gonna go a long way toward securing—"

"The company is hardly small," my father interrupted. He affected good humor, but I caught the edge in his voice, saw the way his shoulders drew back. "Tell me, Senator, can you name *any* other agency in the northern hemisphere that even comes close to the number of—"

Diplomacy has never been my father's strong suit. "*Živeli*," I cut in, raising my glass.

They lifted theirs, echoing their cheers, and we drank, the tension dissipating.

"Nice scotch," Senator Lindsey said, after downing half his drink. "Macallan?"

My father grinned. "None other, my friend."

"I usually prefer an American brand," Lindsey went on, swirling the liquor around in his glass, "but what the hell." He drained the rest and flashed his teeth at us.

I smiled back, put on a good face, but I was assessing the senator on my own. Looking for any signs of hesitation, a crack in the brisk façade.

What kind of man agreed to a deal like this?

Then I remembered that *I* was the kind of man who agreed to a deal like this. In fact, I was at the center of this deal, even if it hadn't been my idea. But there was no other way.

"I think you'll be very pleased with the terms of our agreement, Stefan," the senator said smugly as my father poured him another drink.

3

"Oh, I will," I said. "I'm sure we'll all be coming out on top."

We all shared a laugh at the innuendo. It was exactly the kind of talk that disgusted me. But I knew how to play the game.

"My son is very eager for this *merger* to take place," my father added with a wink.

"No doubt. Keeping his eyes on the prize." Lindsey turned to me. "Trust me when I say, you won't regret this. And neither will I, I hope."

I took a hard swallow of my drink. "We don't deal in regrets here."

"Only success!" my father added, gesturing around the lavish room like it was proof that he'd never tasted failure. "One conquest after another."

"That's what I like about you, Konstantin," the senator said. "Always confident."

"Always right," my father corrected.

They exchanged the grins of men who had no qualms when it came to breaking out the Machiavellian tactics. Even if that meant manipulating the people closest to them.

Was I really any better?

Suddenly the room felt hot and small. Ridiculous considering the total square footage, and the fact that the temperature was always set at a cool 65 degrees. Still, I fought the urge to loosen my tie, reminding myself that the terms I'd agreed to would be worth it in the end.

I wasn't a man who could afford to have second thoughts.

After all, this deal was the only way I'd convince my father to hand over the company. Even though I wouldn't have full control, not yet—this was just my opportunity to step in as his right-hand man. A job I should have had years ago, after I got my MBA.

Frustrated, I took another gulp of the scotch in my glass. One drink wouldn't hurt. It might even take the edge off.

My father could have put me in charge of KZM right out of grad school. I knew the business inside and out, and I finally had the degree from U Penn to back it up. Instead, he'd shuffled me from one management role to the next, the executive positions just out of reach, making promises he never kept.

Until now. When he needed me to make a sacrifice for the greater good.

But now that a leadership role would be officially mine, I could start making moves. And once I was in charge...

I drank, not wanting to get ahead of myself. First step: Finalizing this deal.

"Cigar?" my father asked, pulling out a box of hand rolled Cohibas.

"Certainly." The senator retrieved one, taking the time to smell it. Savor it.

Cigars had never been my thing; my mother had always hated the smell. It was one of the few things I remembered about her.

My father and the senator clipped and lit their cigars, reveling in the richness of it all amid talk of local politics. I topped off my scotch and took another drink. A long drink.

"...don't you think so, Stefan?" my father was saying.

I grinned easily. "Without a doubt." I was never this distracted. I had no idea what I'd just agreed with him on, and my collar felt too tight. Impossible, since my suits were custom made to fit me perfectly.

Morality be damned. I'd been working for this far too

long to back off now. My dreams. My goals. My control. They were all within my grasp.

Even if people got hurt in the process.

"To our...mutually beneficial partnership," my father said, getting up to refill our glasses.

"To a powerful union," I added. I stood with my drink raised. Committing fully.

Clearly not wanting to be outdone, the senator said, "To the start of a beautiful relationship." He winked at me as he rose from his chair.

I forced a smile. True to form, this meeting had devolved into a dick-measuring contest.

"To KZ Modeling," I said.

"To family!" my father threw in, insistent as always on having the last word.

The senator laughed. "Indeed. To family." We clinked our glasses and he clapped me on the back so hard I almost stumbled. "Welcome to the family."

TORI

CHAPTER 1

onight I felt like Cinderella. My Marchesa dress
matched the cool blue of my eyes, the full skirt
embellished with silk flower petals and subtle
embroidery that gleamed in the light. Thanks to some last-
minute tailoring, it fit me like a glove. Such were the benefits of having a wealthy, influential father who wanted me to
look my best for my eighteenth birthday party.

Even if it was a little hard to breathe.

The outfit, the whole presentation, was an homage to
the rags-to-riches story my father loved to trot out for all his
campaigns—how his family had come from nothing,
working their fingers to the bone to give him the opportunity to make a difference. His own male version of the
Cinderella story. So here I was, an emblem of his success
and power. Freshly eighteen and ready to take on the world.
I hoped I'd live up to his expectations. And my own.

I took one last look in the mirror, practicing my smile as
I adjusted my tiara.

"*Carpe noctem*," I whispered. "The night is yours."
That, at least, was true.

I headed downstairs toward the murmur of voices, the tinkling of glasses, and the soothing sounds of the chamber orchestra. It was almost like a royal ball. And it was all for me.

At first, I hadn't been excited about the event. The only 'parties' my father had thrown at our luxurious Springfield home over the years had all been fundraisers for political races. Hopelessly boring despite—or maybe due to—the fact that I was fully capable of keeping up with the guests' endless political discourse.

My father had promised tonight would be different.

"And if you do well, there will be a big surprise in it for you," he had told me.

I knew I was too old to be excited about birthday surprises, but I couldn't help the anticipation building inside of me. Was he finally going to give me the tuition money I needed to attend the University of Chicago in the fall? Their prestigious, uber-competitive linguistics program offered classes I hadn't seen anywhere else, and I'd be able to study Old Church Slavonic, Turkish, and Greek. It was my dream.

"Prosciutto-peach canapé, miss?" a bow-tied server asked as I descended the final curve of the Calacatta marble staircase.

"No thank you," I said with a smile. The truth was, I was too nervous to eat.

The day I'd gotten my acceptance letter was the best, and worst, of my life. I hadn't partied away my senior year like everyone else at my private, all-girls preparatory academy, and it had paid off. UChicago was awarding me a partial scholarship, based on my GPA and a passionate personal essay I'd spent weeks writing. But it turned out my father was too wealthy for me to get a full ride—and he refused to pay the rest of the tuition. My own savings didn't even get me close.

"No one wants to marry a woman with a snooty degree, sweetheart," he had reasoned.

I hadn't given up, though. I had subtly—and not so subtly—been singing the praises of the program, and its real world benefits (diplomatic functions, ease of traveling, better conversations at cocktail parties, etc.) for months, hoping to change my father's mind.

Maybe it had finally worked.

I scanned the ballroom with a sinking heart. I didn't see my father, nor a single other face I recognized. The party was fancy and glamorous, of course, but looked to be solely attended by guests my father's age, or older. Just like always. That was what happened when you spent your formative years working your ass off to stay permanently on the honor roll. Zero social life. I'd invited Grace, my SAT study partner and only friend, but she was on a ritzy vacation in Spain.

"There's the girl of the hour," a soft, feminine voice crooned from behind me. I grinned. I'd recognize that southern accent anywhere.

My stepmother, Michelle, was gliding over with a champagne flute in her hand, smiling as she led a stooped older gentleman toward me. He looked like the crotchety old grandfather type. In contrast, Michelle was blonde and buxom, impeccable in her skirt suit and Jackie O. pearls—always the perfect image of a politician's second wife.

"Woman of the hour," I corrected. These things mattered. *Words* mattered. "Soon to be heading off into the world on my own. Because I'm an adult now."

"Of course you are," she groaned. "And that means *I'm*

getting older. Couldn't you have just stayed six years old forever? I'd better buy up stock in Botox."

We all laughed.

I loved Michelle. My mother had passed when I was young, too little to remember much about her, and Michelle entered my life soon after. She'd never attempted to replace my mother, which I appreciated, and we'd always been more like friends than stepmother and daughter. She was a southern belle, through and through, and had taught me the importance of appearances in all their forms. Especially when it came to my father.

"Victoria, I'd like you to meet Congressman McDonnell," Michelle said by way of introduction. Using my full name was code between us: she didn't know him well and it was best to keep up my guard. "We just met, over a champagne tray."

"Happy birthday, and congratulations on your recent graduation," McDonnell said. He leaned closer, a gleam in his eye. "I plan to persuade your father into supporting a new environmental proposal by getting in your good graces. Do you dance?" He held out his arm.

"How devious of you," I responded, warming to him instantly. "And of course I do."

McDonnell was surprisingly light on his feet, and I found that I was actually enjoying myself.

"I heard you were VP of your school's Latin club. Blessed with beauty and brains, eh? I believe the phrase is '*quidquid Latine dictum...sit altum videtur*'?" he said with a wink.

I laughed. "'Anything you say in Latin sounds profound,'" I translated delightedly.

I'd been obsessed with language—its history, its influence—since I was little, and as the daughter of a politician

I'd seen firsthand how words could be used to change people's minds. My father was an expert at it. In fact, my logophilia—my love of words—came from him. From a young age, he was always quizzing me on vocabulary. Always urging me to choose my words carefully.

Suddenly, though, I found myself speechless.

Across the ballroom, in a shawl-collar tux that looked like Tom Ford had made it just for him, was the most attractive man I'd ever seen in my life.

Raw, animal magnetism seemed to emanate from him. He was dark and handsome and strong-jawed, the sleeves of his jacket hugging broad, sculpted shoulders. His posture was both laid-back and confident. When he threw his head back to laugh, I felt a tightening in my gut. I wanted nothing more than to be in on the joke.

"Victoria?" the congressman broke in. "Are you alright?"

I'd stopped dead in my tracks.

"Sorry," I said, realizing I had been holding my breath.

We resumed, dancing closer to the mystery man. He seemed to be focused on the gentleman in front of him—an older, leaner, grayer version of himself. I couldn't tear my gaze away, desperate for the younger man to look in my direction.

Finally—finally—he looked up. His eyes were green.

Not just any green. A pale shade, like sunlight through leaves, a color you'd call...viridescent. From the Latin *viridis*. So striking against his warm skin tone.

And then our eyes caught.

I felt my pulse quicken under his gaze. I wasn't usually one to bask in the attention of strangers, but amid the sea of black and white eveningwear, I knew I was impossible to ignore.

In my shimmery blue dress and diamond earrings, I was meant to give the impression of an American princess, down to the tiara in my upswept hair. My skin glowed, my makeup natural except for a dark red lipstick; a concession from my father. The lipstick made it clear that I was a woman now. I hoped the green-eyed man had noticed.

Over McDonnell's shoulder, I could see him still looking my way. My skin tingled.

Who was he?

Feeling bold, I murmured an apology and pulled away from the congressman mid-step, making my way toward the man even as I tottered a little in my silver satin heels. There had to be a way to meet him. He was here for a reason; my father never invited people to events like this unless he needed something from them.

Across the room, the man abruptly turned his back to me as his companion grabbed his arm in emphasis. I halted in the crowd, my pulse still pounding in my ears.

How was he having this effect on me? It wasn't as if I hadn't been around attractive men before. As a politician's daughter, I'd rubbed elbows with celebrities of all sorts—actors, musicians, artists. None of them had ever made me breathless the way this stranger did.

I'd had crushes, too—fleeting moments of infatuation with the older brothers of school friends or the college-age baristas at Starbucks—but this felt completely different. The source of those previous crushes had been boys. Whoever this guy was, he was a *man*.

I shivered.

Forcing myself to act casual, I feigned interest in the orchestra. The last thing I wanted was for him to look back and discover I was still staring at him like he was my birthday cake. I might not have been very experienced with men, but I knew they appreciated a chase.

"There you are!" Michelle said, sweeping up behind me to take my arm. "Daddy needs you."

I spotted my father as we headed over. As always, his posture was upright, his presence commanding. The gray streaks in his hair gave him a look of authority and experience. We had the same steel blue eyes, the same headstrong nature. Of course, I kept mine hidden beneath a veneer of docility. I'd learned from a young age that if I really wanted something, I had to play the good girl. Make my father think it was his idea all along.

We came upon him speaking with a colleague, and I presented my cheek for a kiss.

"And the princess arrives," my father announced. "Are you excited about your gift?"

"Very much so," I said. "I can't wait."

He smiled at me, and I felt a rush of joy and pride. Our arguments about college lately had been dredging up all the old fears: that I wasn't the kind of daughter he wished he had. But in that moment, things between us felt exactly right.

"First things first," he said, turning me to face his guest. "Tori, my dear, have you met Congressman Ellis?"

"It's an honor." Ellis took my hand and placed a kiss on top of it. His gaze however, remained fixated on my cleavage.

"Nice to meet you," I said politely.

Enduring Ellis's roving eye was all part of the job.

He and my father picked up their conversation where they'd left off—something about a new committee they were both serving on. I tried to tactfully drift away, but Michelle held me fast. It was also part of the job to smile and nod.

I loved my father and I knew he was doing good, important things. If dressing up and being polite helped him win elections, then I was happy to play my part. But I still dreamed of breaking free, of doing something more with my life.

College would give me a chance to get out into the world, and beyond the opportunity to nerd out on linguistics to my heart's delight, I'd also, finally, be able to explore other currently-uncharted territories...of a more personal nature.

That's why I was so anxious about my gift. It could change everything.

Unable to help myself, I glanced back across the room at the dark-haired man in his perfect tux. Yep. Still gorgeous.

He was looking at me again, too. His eyes were like flames, flickering and hot. Everything inside of me felt like it was on fire in the best possible way.

I might have been a virgin, but I wasn't a prude. I had a vibrator. I'd paid attention when Grace or the girls at my lunch table had gossiped about their sexual exploits. And I knew what it felt like to steal kisses, even if they'd only been from the prep school boys that were invited to our chaperoned dances by the academy's principal. But up until now, all of my experiences had been exploratory. They didn't mean anything except a little fun for the moment. Though it wasn't like I was missing out—I'd never met anyone in real life that inspired the kind of reckless, aching *want* that I imagined was possible.

Not that I would have been allowed to pursue those feelings even if I *had* felt them. My father had a strict no-dating policy, one I was planning to challenge now that I was eighteen. An adult, I reminded myself again. My own woman. And if I was away at college, there'd be no stopping me.

"Are you enjoying your party?" Ellis asked, jarring my thoughts with a hand to my arm.

"Ah, yes. My father has been very generous with me." I didn't love that this guy was touching me, and his stare made it obvious he thought I looked good enough to eat. When I tried to inch away, he moved in closer. My father, meanwhile, had turned to speak with someone else.

"I hear you're quite the little dancer," Ellis said.

"How lovely of you to say!" Michelle cooed, edging in next to me and pouring on a fatal dose of the southern charm. "By the way, have you spoken with Congressman McDonnell tonight? His head is just bursting with ideas about alternative fuels and I don't know what."

"That man is uncivilized," Ellis said sourly.

"Then we'll have to challenge him to a duel! Isn't that him, over by the punch?"

She took his arm and made to drag him away, shooting me a conspiratorial wink. Michelle was very good at this.

"Actually," my father said, stepping in to block Ellis, "I'm sure Victoria would love to dance with you first."

"Wonderful!" Michelle chirped, shooting me an apologetic look.

"Of course I would," I said, accepting the hand Ellis offered. I knew what was expected of me. And I'd done this before. Forcing a smile, I let him lead me back out onto the dance floor.

He was a passable dancer, but his eyes stayed glued to my chest even as we made small talk. I couldn't help wishing, just once, that a man would ask me to dance because he wanted to get to know me better, not just ogle me. And I knew exactly which man I'd wish for.

I craned my neck, looking for him in the crowd, but the congressman kept twirling me every time I thought I'd caught a glimpse.

Beyond that, I was completely distracted by nerves. What if I was wrong about my big surprise? It could just as easily be a new car, or a posh vacation. Not that I wouldn't be grateful...but those things wouldn't help me build a life. I loved my father, but I knew he didn't understand my obsession with studying linguistics. Nobody did.

"Those classes are going to be *so* boring, Tori. And you know you'll never do anything with that degree, right?" Grace had constantly ragged me during our study sessions.

But she was wrong, on both counts. I'd never get bored in a class that explored the link between language and humor, or one that broke down the difference between 'bullshit and lies' (I'd read all about it on the UChicago website). And who wouldn't be interested in learning about the culture of the Deaf community, or psycholinguistics? Plus, while the degree was something I needed on a soul level, I was also considering a career in academia—so it's not like my studies would be totally useless. Grace was set to inherit a billion-dollar designer handbag empire someday, but I wanted to forge my own path. Politics may have been in my blood, but they weren't in my heart.

Finally the congressman led me off the dance floor, his hand pressing at the small of my back, a little too close to the curve of my rear. He dropped that hand the moment my father came into view, though. He was still standing with my stepmother, but someone new had joined them.

The mystery man.

My heart jumped into my throat. Up close, he was even more striking—those green eyes sharply intelligent and assessing. This was a man who missed nothing. But what did he see when he looked at me? I was so captivated that I barely noticed Ellis departing from the group.

"Victoria, darling," my father said, taking my hand between both of his. "Remember how I told you I had a surprise for you this evening?"

I nodded distractedly, my attention still fixated on the man. He had the most incredible lips, full and sensual. They were set in a firm line, though. One that made his expression inscrutable. I had no idea what he was thinking.

"Well. Here it is," my father said, gesturing expansively with one of his arms.

"Where?" My eyes darted around the room, but I saw no UChicago banners in white and maroon, no cake with a tuition check popping out of it, not even a scrap of wrapping paper. I looked back at my father. He was grinning broadly.

"Right here," he said, clapping the mystery man on the back. "This is your present, Tori—meet your future husband, Stefan Zoric."

TORI

CHAPTER 2

I found myself unable to speak, temporarily struck aphonic—from the Greek *aphonos*, without sound. Words had always been my salvation and now...nothing. All I felt was the blood draining from my face, my mouth falling open as I tried to process what my father had just said.

Husband?

Husband?

There was no possible way I had heard that correctly. It had to be a joke.

I forced a small laugh, but no one joined in. Everyone was staring at me, their faces expectant. My father was still grinning. The handsome stranger—my new *fiancé*, ostensibly—wasn't smiling, but he wasn't frowning either. He looked...inquisitive. Like he was gauging my reaction.

But he didn't look surprised.

In fact, no one did. Instead, they all seemed to be waiting for me to say something.

"My...husband?" I somehow managed.

"Congratulations! And happy birthday!" My father put his arm around me and gave my shoulder a squeeze.

I gaped at him.

"Mitch." My stepmother stepped closer to both of us, then lowered her voice to a respectful whisper. "You didn't *tell her* first? What were you thinking?"

Finally, someone else was as shocked as I was.

Except, not for the same reason. Michelle had known what was going on. They had all known. All of them except for me. The person who was supposed to be getting married.

"I was thinking it would be more fun this way," my father said, sounding a little put out. "It's a *surprise*."

Michelle's frown was brief and just for us. And then immediately it was gone, the furrow between her brows smoothed out, and she turned to my new fiancé with a warm smile.

"Welcome to the family, Stefan," she said, reaching out toward him.

"Thank you." The handsome stranger took her hand and bowed slightly as he clasped it between his own, his bearing as regal as a fairytale prince. Even in my shock, I couldn't help but be charmed. Just a little.

Then he turned that charm directly on me.

God, was I in trouble.

His smile made my knees literally go weak, those full, gorgeous lips curving into a secret promise of...something. Something good. Then he took my hand firmly in his, drawing it toward that tantalizing mouth, and pressed a kiss to my knuckles.

His lips were hot, their warmth spreading through my entire body as his eyes met mine. When he turned my hand over to place another kiss on the soft skin of my inner wrist,

I had to drop my gaze. It was like I could feel that kiss between my legs.

"Victoria Lindsey," he said softly, finally releasing me. "A pleasure to meet you."

Was it just my imagination or had he put a small emphasis on *pleasure*?

I shivered. I'd been overwhelmed by surprise and shock, but now I felt arousal, too. Bodily, chemical attraction, beyond the initial appreciation of his face and figure from before. It hit me hard, and I found it difficult to look away.

Stefan. Even his name sounded exotic and like the promise of something new. Something different. It was also familiar. Or at least, his last name was.

"Zoric—are you related to Konstantin Zoric? The owner of KZ Modeling?"

Something shifted in his gaze, but Stefan nodded. "My father. It's a family business."

Of course I'd recognized the name. KZ managed some of the hottest models in the country, possibly in the world. The company was in the headlines frequently.

My head was spinning. I stood frozen, a Barbie doll, stiff and still in my gown.

"Stefan, will you excuse us for just a minute?" Michelle cut in, wearing her perfect hostess smile. "I think we could use a moment alone."

"Of course," my fiancé said. *My fiancé.* It gave me a shock just thinking the word.

My father frowned at her. "They're just now getting acquainted. It can wait."

"I think you and Tori need to have a little father-daughter discussion first? In private," she said, subtly shooting him a look. It was one she rarely used—as she never contradicted my father in public—but it worked.

"Please, go. I'll be waiting." Stefan gave a discreet nod and backed off, giving us space.

Taking my elbow, Michelle led me to the small parlor adjacent to the ballroom. My father followed. It was quiet and secluded, and my stepmother furtively pressed a glass of champagne into my underage hand before shutting the door so the three of us could be alone.

I sipped the drink, then downed the rest in one gulp. Reality was beginning to sink in.

My father had arranged a marriage between me and Stefan. A man I had never met before. *That* was my birthday surprise. Not college. Not tuition. Marriage. I was being given away.

The heat that had spread through me at Stefan's touch had dissipated, and now I was cold. Goosebumps rose on my bare arms and I resisted the urge to shiver. I wanted to wrap my arms around myself, but I knew the body language would make me look like a bratty little girl throwing a tantrum, and I wanted my father to take my next words seriously.

"I thought you'd be pleased," he said. He spread his hands, looking genuinely baffled. "You knew this was coming."

"I did, but..." How did he not understand that I'd been completely blindsided by this?

"He's handsome enough, isn't he? Rich. Well-connected. He has an MBA from an Ivy League school, for god's sake," he continued.

"He is an exceptional young man," my stepmother agreed. "I think Tori was just taken off-guard by the arrangement." She gave me an encouraging look. "Weren't you, darling?"

I managed a nod, knowing that Michelle was doing me

a kindness in helping me navigate this confusion and surprise with some grace.

Because any fleeting hope I'd had that this was a joke was long gone now. Even though Michelle had stood up for me, rescuing me from the humiliation of having this discussion in public, it was clear that she wasn't going to contradict my father's decision about my future.

Except, it was *my* future. I was eighteen now. An adult. I didn't have to marry Stefan.

Did I?

I had to admit, I was completely dependent on my father for everything. I'd never had a job beyond my volunteer work and community service, had never earned money of my own. Everything I had came from him. I'd always known there were strings attached.

I just hadn't realized the strings would be this major. This life-changing. This soon.

"Why Stefan?" I asked. "He's not from a political family. This doesn't make sense."

"It makes perfect sense. These are exactly the kind of people we need in our inner circle," my father said, tugging on his cuffs, as he did when he was feeling impatient.

"How so?" It was obvious he didn't want to explain, but I needed him to. Surely he had his reasons. He never did anything without endless hours of planning and decision-making.

Michelle cleared her throat. "Tori, the Zorics are wealthy and generous, and they have a vast network of influence. The bond your marriage will create between their family and ours will be essential for your father at reelection time next year. Do you understand?"

I nodded my comprehension, feeling numb. Of course.

It all came down to hefty campaign contributions and securing the maximum number of votes.

I shouldn't have been surprised. My father was facing a tough batch of rivals next year and needed all the help he could get. This was the help he was turning to. No doubt the Zorics would be an invaluable asset.

"You should consider yourself lucky," my father said. "This guy's a catch! Men like Konstantin and his sons are surrounded by beautiful women every day. Stefan could have chosen any number of brides, but he agreed to marry *you*. He's making a sacrifice too."

That stung.

"This is all just...happening so fast," I murmured. "What if it's a mistake?"

"Don't be childish, Victoria," my father snapped, losing patience. "I saw the way you looked at him. You were practically undressing him with your eyes. You're clearly halfway in love already. This is a win-win."

It was a little embarrassing that my father could read my interest so plainly. Still, I couldn't shake the feeling that I was missing some piece of the puzzle. Even if I was intrigued by the possibility of being married to a man like him—powerful, confident, with a jaw that could cut glass— what did Stefan stand to gain? Our fathers' interests were more than clear...but what about my fiancé's?

"I still don't understand what he's getting out of this."

"Oh, Tori," Michelle said, shaking her head. "You know how men are about shiny objects. But just think—this is someone who can take care of you. Give you security."

"What more could you ask for?" my father added. "He'll be able to give you everything you want."

"You have no idea what I want!" I said, shocking myself. I never talked back to him.

But I still had dreams of my own. Dreams I'd assumed I would get to pursue before settling down with someone. And now my college plans were off the table. Because my father needed me to drop everything that mattered so I could be a trophy wife to the son of his ally.

"Is this about your little underwater basket-weaving degree? You still want that? Well, guess what. Your new husband can afford it," he said.

I pressed my lips together, gazing out the window while I collected myself. He had a point. This situation could benefit me. My father would get what he wanted, and maybe I could, too. Plus, he wasn't wrong about Stefan being good looking. And I'd be his.

At least until I got my degree. Four years, maybe eight if I decided I wanted my doctorate.

I could stand to be married to a man as handsome as Stefan for a few years. Couldn't I? Sharing a home, a life...a bed.

My head was swimming.

"This was always the plan, Tori," my father said. "This man—his family—can provide you with anything you could possibly dream of. I'm offering you the chance to have a life of luxury and ease. You should be thanking me for finding you such a match."

"It's just...so much to think about," I said, my temples suddenly throbbing.

"Then stop thinking!" my father ordered.

Michelle put her hand on his shoulder. "Mitch. You catch more flies with honey."

"I don't know what to do," I whispered. "I feel trapped."

"Dance with him," Michelle suggested, turning toward me. "Go back out there and take a turn around that ball-room and see how it feels to be in his arms. Then you can decide what you want to do. I know you'll make the right decision."

"I suggest you take your stepmother's advice," my father said, a warning in his voice.

I nodded my acquiescence. Michelle's words had been kinder than his, but the implication was clear—you can dance with him, but in the end you're going to marry him, no matter what.

I guess I did know something, after all. I knew I had no choice.

CHAPTER 3

"The princess returns," Stefan said, flashing a devilish smirk as I approached.

I had marched back out to the ballroom with my chin up, determined to approach this proposal with an open mind. Now I was standing in front of my maybe-fiancé, trying to reconcile his flirting with the formal, gentlemanly front he'd put up when my parents had been standing there.

I liked him better this way.

"I thought you might've run away with a stable boy or something," he teased. "Not that I would have blamed you. You looked shell-shocked. Though I'll admit, this whole situation is..."

"I believe the Latin term is '*insanus maximus*,'" I blurted, then immediately regretted it.

But Stefan just tilted his head and laughed, in the same full-throated, infectious way I'd seen earlier. This time I joined in, and when we shared a smile afterward there was an undeniable spark of heat between us. This was good. Chemistry. Attraction. And he'd enjoyed my

Latin joke. Whatever lay ahead of us, we would at least have that.

"You are...not what I expected," he said. "It's a pleasant surprise."

"And I hadn't expected this at all," I said.

At the end of the day, I knew I was lucky. My father could be trying to marry me off to someone like Congressman Ellis—wealthy, well-connected, but several times my age. Instead, he'd found me a young, handsome man with devastating green eyes and a laugh I already loved.

It still didn't feel real.

"I think we may have gotten off on the wrong foot," Stefan said as the orchestra began to play a waltz. "In the interest of starting over, may I have this dance?"

"You laughed at my nerd humor, so I guess you've earned it," I said with a smile, and took his hand.

He was a good dancer. Incredible, actually. As I fell in step with him, a hum of electricity seemed to buzz between our bodies, his palm hot against mine.

"Your dress is stunning," he said as we spun around the dance floor. "You look like a fairytale princess. My sister Emzee's favorite when she was little, I think. The one with the mouse friends and the missing shoe..."

"Cinderella," I murmured, suddenly struck shy again. His voice was low and soothing, his breath warm in my ear, giving me goosebumps.

"Right. The one with the carriage made from a squash. Completely impractical."

I laughed, missing one of the steps. "It was a pumpkin, actually."

"Ah yes," he said, guiding us back in time with the music. "I've always liked pumpkins. They're the spirit of

Halloween. The one night of the year when everyone wears a mask."

"Do you often wear masks?" I asked. I was trying to tease, but I also wanted an answer.

"We all do," he said. I couldn't read his expression, and I wondered what he kept hidden beneath that handsome exterior. Darkness? Danger? Loss?

I realized I was staring when those lips curved up into a smile. "You're studying me like a book, Victoria Lindsey."

"Sorry." I dropped my gaze, my cheeks suddenly burning.

"Don't apologize. I've been warned you're an academic. An inquisitive mind is nothing to be ashamed of. Just remember what they say about curiosity and the cat."

Every word out of his mouth sounded erotic. I trained my eyes on his feet and the swish of my dress against the floor, taking several breaths to cool off before I spoke again.

"Please call me Tori. Nobody calls me Victoria unless I'm in trouble."

"Maybe you are in trouble."

He smiled, and I had to look away again. His flirting was over the top, but it had its intended effect on me. Was he doing this on purpose, to sway me? And if so, did I really mind?

His hand was firm on the small of my back as we passed close by the orchestra. With the tiniest pressure, he directed me where to go. Dancing with him was like a dream.

This whole thing was like a dream.

Still, this was *marriage* we were talking about. I was standing in front of the man I might spend the rest of my life with, and he was practically a stranger.

Not practically: literally. I didn't know anything about him.

"How old are you?" I asked.

"Twenty-six," he offered with a small quirk of his mouth.

He didn't ask my age. It seemed he'd been given plenty of information about me already. I bet he'd even been fore-warned about my tendency to spout awkward, unexpected facts about the history of certain words and languages. But even if he'd been given tips or advice on how to talk to me, how to flirt with me, we seemed to have a chemistry that couldn't be faked.

"You mentioned you had a sister?" I prompted. "Emzee?"

"Yes. She's a photographer—Mara Zoric. She works closely with our agency."

"Oh, of course! I've seen her stuff before. Not just in fashion. I think it was National Geographic—the mosaic tombs in Marrakech?"

He looks surprised. "Yes. She was so proud of that assignment."

I grin. "You're all so accomplished. Are you the oldest of your siblings?"

Stefan nodded, and told me about his younger brother Luka, who was living the dream of all 25-year-olds by draining his trust fund and getting a little too close to KZM's models. But, I was assured, he was a smart boy who had an MBA and a good heart. He just had some growing up to do.

As we both warmed to the conversation, my nerves eased, and little tidbits of information started coming back to me.

KZ Modeling was in the news enough that I could recall some of the articles that had been written about the company, its models, and Stefan's family. Their names were just as likely to appear in the headlines of *Buzzfeed* as they were in *The Wall Street Journal*.

"And what does your mother do?" I asked, but the moment I did, I remembered what I had read. I also remembered how I'd felt reading it. As if we shared a sort of kinship.

"She died," Stefan said. "When I was six."

"I'm sorry," I told him. "Mine too. I was two."

"She was beautiful," he mused. "She used to paint."

I smiled. "All I have are photographs. I wish I could remember her."

He didn't say anything. He didn't need to. At least, in this, we understood each other.

"I noticed your surname has Slavic roots," I finally said, trying to steer the conversation toward something easier. "Where is your family from, originally?"

"Serbia. But I was born and raised here," he said. "My grandmother always made the best paštete, but that's the extent of my ancestral knowledge. Are you a fan of pastries?"

"I adore them," I admitted. "I've always wanted to travel to the Balkans. Mainly to hear the spoken languages. The Cyrillic alphabet is so cool."

"I'm sure a trip could be arranged," he said. He slid his hand upward, coming to rest on my spine just below my shoulder blades. "Perhaps in the near future."

"I'd be amenable to that," I told him.

He tilted his head. "Amenable." He smiled. "Not a word I hear often."

"It's a great word," I said. "From the 1590s. A combination of the French word *mener*, to lead, and the Latin *minare*, which meant to drive cattle with shouts. Funny how specific some words are, isn't it? Who would have imagined that someone would need a word to describe getting cows out of the way?"

Stefan went silent. I couldn't blame him.

My father was right. Men weren't interested in smart women—especially ones who babble on about the historic roots of words when they should be flirting and waltzing.

"Ah, there I go again." I could feel my cheeks burning. "Not to worry though. I don't always go off on these tangents about words and their meanings..."

Except I did. *Shut up, Tori,* I told myself. *Men like mystery. Be mysterious.*

"I didn't know about the root of the word," Stefan said slowly. "But I do know some of its modern synonyms. Flexible," he spun me under his arm gracefully. "Pliant." He pulled me back into his arms. "Responsive."

He said the last in a husky whisper.

Oh.

I had always considered language to hold a sensuality of its own. But I had never imagined the power it could have coming from the mouth of a man like Stefan.

Responsive.

I felt responsive in his arms. Very responsive.

His hand was like a brand on my back, radiating heat down my body. For the first time since my father had announced that I would be marrying this man, I allowed myself to imagine what that would be like. What it would entail, to be man and wife in all regards.

Another shiver spread through me.

No doubt a man like Stefan, who handled himself with confidence and control on the dance floor, would be just as skilled in the bedroom. The hot, taut pull between my legs tightened even further. Unable to help myself, I moved a little closer, my eyes darting up to meet his. He was staring at me. Intensely.

"Why don't we get some air?" he asked, his voice low.

"Yes," I agreed breathlessly. "It's much too warm in here."

I let him lead me out onto the balcony. It was quiet out there except for the muffled sounds of the party, shut away behind closed doors. We were alone.

Without his arms around me, the chill air hit me full force, and I rubbed my arms to warm myself. Suddenly, a jacket—Stefan's jacket—was draped over my shoulders, enveloping me in his residual body heat and his rich, masculine scent.

As the jacket's silky lining slid against my bare skin, I felt that familiar twist in my lower belly. It made no sense. I barely knew this man, but there was no denying that he did something to me.

How much of this was an act, though? If we were just two people meeting at a party, would he have looked at me twice?

God, but his jacket smelled good. Like expensive, woodsy cologne and a hint of sweet cigar smoke. I wanted to take a deep breath, but I had to pull myself together. Be direct.

"So what are your thoughts on the arrangement our fathers have orchestrated?" I asked.

"The deal was no surprise to me. I'm sure for someone your age it seems strange."

"Strange is an understatement," I responded. "You're the last thing I expected as a birthday present."

He gave me a crooked half smile.

"Not that I'm disappointed," I rushed on, feeling my cheeks flush. "I mean, you're actually a very nice birthday present." I was rambling, but I couldn't stop myself. "Wow. I am *not* trying to say that you are an object—though I mean, you are kind of a gift because you're so nice to look at, but it's more appreciation than objectification and this whole thing is just kind of weird on the whole because who does arranged marriages anymore, you know?"

I was out of breath. He quirked an eyebrow.

"You think I'm good looking?" he asked, with the confidence of someone who knew exactly how handsome they were.

I nodded. This time I was pretty sure I was bright red. Not a flattering blush at all.

"I'm surprised you don't have a boyfriend already," he said. "Your father told me you don't even date."

I held my tongue, not wanting to get on the subject of my lack of experience when it came to men. "I've been trying to focus on my education," I said, which was at least half of the truth. "And honestly, I've discovered that most guys don't appreciate my nonstop word vomit."

Way to stop while you're ahead, I chided myself.

But Stefan only laughed. "You're funny."

He moved closer, adjusting the lapels of his jacket around my neck. My breath caught in my throat.

"And beautiful." He reached toward me and tucked a loose strand of hair behind my ear, gazing into my eyes. "And much more intelligent than anyone gives you credit for."

And that's when I knew I could have sex with this man. It would be good between us, I was sure of it. It would be really good.

"This whole thing is happening very fast," Stefan went on, stepping back. "But it doesn't have to be forever. All our fathers want is for us to marry. Once that's out of the way, we can do what we want. Make our own terms. What do you want out of this arrangement?"

"A degree," I blurted.

Stefan raised that eyebrow again.

"I've already been accepted to UChicago to study linguistics," I said. "I want to get my masters, maybe even a doctorate. But my scholarship won't cover the whole tuition. If we're married, maybe..." My voice trailed off hopefully. "I mean, I would pay you back. It might take awhile, but—"

"Your father isn't supporting you with this?" he interrupted.

"No." My smile was bitter. "I did try to talk him into letting me borrow the money...I even had his assistant put me on the calendar—*scheduled an appointment* with my own father—and went in with a loan agreement and a PowerPoint, totally thinking I had it in the bag."

"What happened?"

"He told me the program is a waste of my time and his money. And that men aren't interested in women with snobby degrees."

"Tori."

"God, I'm sorry. We just met. I shouldn't even be talking to you about this. I just—it's my dream." My voice got husky on the last word, and I had to look away.

He turned my face back toward him, searching my eyes. "There is nothing in this life," he finally said, his voice deep and measured, "that is more important than forging your own path. Making your own choices. You have to live for you, not for your father." His expression hardened. "Not everyone has the freedom or the privilege to do that."

"How can you say that?" I scoffed. "Are *you* living for you? Our fathers are the ones who arranged this...whole thing. A marriage that's going to dictate the rest of our lives. How can you call that your own path?"

He shrugged. "I'm getting exactly what I want out of this."

"And what is that?" I asked.

Something inside Stefan shifted. It was almost as if I could see a door shutting, keeping me out, and with that I realized there was more to him than just the charming, smiling, flirtatious charade. What was I getting myself into?

"You're going to that school," he said. "I'll call their finance office on Monday."

My heart soared, but I wasn't so easily distracted.

"Tell me why you're agreeing to this match. Please. I already shared my reasons," I pointed out. "Before we're in too deep, I just need to understand your side."

Stefan didn't say anything for a long moment, staring out into the cool, fragrant darkness surrounding the house. It seemed like he was warring with himself, unsure what to tell me. Or how much to reveal. Finally, he nodded.

"I want to take over KZM," he said. "I'm my father's right-hand, but he still runs the agency. He'll retire at some point, but he won't give me the company if I'm not married." He gave me a half-smile. "He's old school that way. Doesn't trust someone who isn't settled down."

I felt a kinship with Stefan in that moment. There had to be more to the story, things he wasn't willing to tell me yet. But it was enough for now. After all, we were both using this marriage to break free from our fathers' control, to get what we wanted. It made sense.

Stefan took my hands in his. They were warm, his grip strong and certain.

"Marry me," he said, and my heart dropped into my stomach. "We'll make our own lives. Our own choices."

It was tempting. So very tempting.

He reached into the pocket of the jacket wrapped around my shoulders and pulled out a turquoise ring box. I hadn't even realized it was there. When he opened it, a massive princess cut diamond ring sparkled in the light coming from inside.

This night just wouldn't stop leaving me speechless.

"Your father said you wouldn't wear anything over five carats," Stefan said. "But I can get you something different if you—"

"It's beautiful," I said, finally letting out the breath I'd been holding. I shook my head. "I just can't believe this is really happening."

"So—is it a deal?" Stefan asked.

I looked at the box, and then at him.

This wasn't what I'd wanted out of my life. I'd planned to get out from under my father's thumb, not let myself be trapped even tighter beneath it. I had dreamed of being rescued—but I wanted to rescue myself. Maybe I still could.

"It's a deal," I said.

With a smile, he took out the ring and slid it onto my finger. It was heavier than I expected, the stone spanning the width of my finger. But it felt good. It felt...secure.

"The first thing you should know if you're going to be my wife," he said, his voice dropping low as he leaned toward me, "is that I take what I want."

Before I could respond, he cupped my face in his hands and drew my mouth to his. The moment our lips touched, everything else seemed to fade away.

I gave myself up to him completely, following his lead as he deepened the kiss, coaxing my mouth open, stroking his tongue slowly against mine until I could barely stand.

His hands dropped to steady my waist, holding me tight

against him, and I moaned softly. The kiss was electric. I could practically feel sparks bursting between us, and my insides had gone loose and liquid. None of the furtive kisses I'd shared with boys over the years could hold a candle to this. Because Stefan was a man. A man who knew how to kiss.

I never wanted it to end, but finally it did.

My heart was pounding as he released me, stepping back, his defenses up again. I couldn't read the guarded expression in his eyes.

"We should return to the party," he said, taking my hand—the one now flashing an enormous diamond—and tucking it around his bicep. His firm, muscular bicep.

It wasn't the birthday present I had been wishing for, but maybe it was better.

As we turned to go back inside, I noticed my father. He was standing near the glass doors leading out onto the balcony, right within view of Stefan and me. And he wasn't alone. Standing next to him was the man I had seen Stefan speaking to earlier. The man I'd assumed was his father. Had they seen the whole thing?

My stomach knotted as I glanced over at my new fiancé. He was looking straight ahead. How much of that had really been for me?

And how much of it had been a performance?

TORI

CHAPTER 4

3 months later

THEY SAY you should never skimp on a professional wedding photographer, because the day speeds by so fast that you need to look at the pictures later to remember it. I'd never believed it before today, but as I sank onto a silk sofa in an empty room, white satin heels in my hand, I realized it was true. I'd hardly had a chance to take it all in, and now it was over.

Stefan and I were married. I was his *wife*.

I still couldn't believe it.

The last thing I really remembered in detail was peeking out into the packed event space, my heart in my throat, taking in the heady white scent of Stargazer lilies and the sea of faces. Everyone was whispering to each other excitedly, most of them either unknown or newly introduced to me. After that it was mostly a blur.

Our ceremony had been brief—the sooner to get to the lavish reception afterward—but to my surprise, Stefan had written his own vows. Or at least, someone had. I was so nervous that I only processed every few words, and they were all the usual ones about honor and support and facing new challenges together as we entered the next chapter of our lives.

But after the officiant had turned to me and said the last line—'As long as you both shall live?'—I froze. The entire room was holding its breath expectantly, awaiting my 'I do,' but I was completely paralyzed, my vision going dark at the edges.

Was this what they called cold feet? Was I going to faint at the altar?

And then Stefan leaned toward me to whisper something in my ear, something that only I could hear. Something I knew I would never forget.

Alis volat propriis, he said softly. Then he stepped back and smiled.

It was Latin. *She flies with her own wings.*

Realizing what he'd just said to me, everything came back into sharp focus. Suddenly my mind was completely clear.

I returned Stefan's smile. "I do, too," I said.

And then we kissed.

Later in the evening—I couldn't even say when—I'd been formally introduced to a large portion of the extended Zoric family. There was Stefan's father, of course, who I had spoken with only briefly on the night Stefan and I became engaged, but also tons of cousins, elderly relatives, and even a few young kids. The best moment, however, had been finally meeting Stefan's younger siblings, Luka and Mara.

Luka seemed to be quite the ladies' man, exactly as Stefan had described him, flashing his dimples at every female in sight—though he was nothing but sweet to me. Mara, the globetrotting photographer who had once loved Cinderella, threw her arms around me the second we met and insisted I call her Emzee like everyone else in the family did. With her dark, tumbling hair and kohl-lined grey eyes, she could have been one of KZ's models.

And then there were scores of other friends and relatives and my father's political acquaintances, so many names and faces I couldn't keep track. I wished someone had given me flashcards to help memorize all the names and pertinent information in advance, like I'd often gotten before my father's events. I could only hope I'd get to know everyone better later on, once Stefan and I had settled into married life. It was going to take some getting used to.

My dress rustled, echoing in the private room that had been set up for me just off the hotel's ballroom. It was the first moment since the day had begun that I was alone, and I just needed a second to let things sink in before I joined Stefan—*my husband*, I reminded myself—to say goodbye to our reception guests and then head upstairs to our room.

Our room.

The wedding suite.

I swallowed. Hard.

Everything had happened so fast that I hadn't had a chance to feel nervous about my wedding night yet. But it was finally sinking in.

"*You bitch.*"

My head snapped up and I turned to find my friend Grace poking her head in the door, a look of absolute glee on her face.

"Hey you," I said, smiling despite my exhaustion.

"This day was a-may-ziiing!" she sing-songed. "Everything was so perfect."

"It was all Michelle's doing. And thanks for coming. It was nice to see a familiar face." It wasn't a lie. "I don't even know half the people we invited. I think the paparazzi even snuck in."

"I wouldn't be surprised." She sashayed over in her flouncy dress, tugging her heels off and sinking to the floor beside me. "Stefan is fucking gorgeous, Tori. I danced with him twice during the money dance—not that you guys need it—and totally swooned. But don't worry. He didn't take his eyes off you the whole night." She grinned mischievously. "I think I finally understand why we need human cloning trials."

"You're horrible!" I shrieked.

"I know, I'm the worst. But you love me. God, where did you even find him? One minute you're stressing about tuition and course offerings and the next I'm getting this insane gold-leaf wedding invitation out of the blue. It's like this all happened overnight."

"He was a guest at my birthday party," I answered carefully. "The son of one of my father's friends. It happened so fast, I guess I just...haven't had time to catch you up."

There was no way I was going to tell Grace, or anyone, that it was an arranged marriage.

"I can't believe I was just laying around in Ibiza while you were pouncing on this guy! A Zoric! I'm never taking a vacation again. Tell me his brother is single. I couldn't get him alone."

"Luka? I'm pretty sure he is," I said. "Although I don't think he'd be into anything exclusive. But you never know. I'll put in a good word."

"You're the best!" Grace squealed, wrapping her arms

around my legs. "Listen, I'm gonna head back out to the party, but call me soon 'cause I wanna hear about all the deets. Especially after tonight." She winked.

"Let's not talk about that," I said, dropping my face into my hands.

"*Tori Lindsey*," Grace hissed. "Are you seriously telling me you still haven't given up your V card? To that man out there? The one you just freaking *married*?"

My silence was answer enough.

Confusion, and then understanding, dawned on her face.

"Ohhhh. It's all making sense now." She nodded slowly. "He has a virginity kink! God Tori, you lucked out. Not that it was luck. I can't believe all those years of chastity finally paid off. Go you! Wait. Does this mean you guys haven't even—"

"Oh wow. I am so tired," I cut in, humiliated beyond repair. "I think I should—

"Gah! Don't worry, I'm leaving. I know you need to save your strength," Grace teased, slipping back into her shoes. "Just remember, lube is your friend. That's the one piece of advice I wish someone had given me. And don't forget to call me. Love you!"

She scurried away, shutting the door behind her and leaving me in silence again.

I was anxious, but also felt like I could actually fall asleep right on that sofa. I was still decompressing from all the excitement. Maybe I'd better grab a coffee. I was going to be up all night with Stefan, wasn't I? My pulse raced just thinking about it.

Grace was right about one thing, though. Things had happened fast. Despite being crazy attracted to Stefan, we'd barely seen—or gotten to know—each other during the engagement. After my party he'd returned to Chicago for work, and I had stayed in Springfield, preparing to start at UChicago in the fall.

Michelle had planned everything within two months, which would've been impossible without the help of my father's contacts and the Zoric family connections. I had never seen her so thrilled, or so busy. Truthfully, I had been more excited about college than planning a wedding, so it was a relief to let other people take care of all the details.

I'd had no say in any of it, including my dress, which my stepmother had knocked out of the ballpark. It was a sophisticated column of silk with a plunging but tastefully narrow neckline and tiny pearl buttons down the back—the perfect mix of classic and modern. If I had felt like Cinderella on the night of my birthday party, well, I looked like a queen tonight.

It seemed like Stefan had thought so as well.

The wedding had been my first look at how much money and influence his family truly commanded. If they wanted it, money was no object. Michelle wanted my dress to be made by a Serbian designer in honor of my new husband's heritage? She had gotten it. She wanted the whole event catered by Chicago's hottest new chef? Check, check, double check. Every event, from the engagement party to the reception, had taken place at the most exclusive, upscale hotels in the city—all properties owned by Stefan's family. All I had needed to do was show up, put the dress on, smile for photos and kiss the groom.

Still, I remembered what Stefan had told me that first night, about living life for me.

I was excited for all the ways my life was about to change.

And nervous as well.

I had hoped that Stefan and I would have gotten a chance to get to know each other during the engagement. That we'd at least talk on the phone or send flirty texts once in a while. A part of me had even hoped that he might take some time out of his busy schedule to come visit and take me on a date.

It was terrifying to realize I had just married a man I'd never gone out to dinner with. Besides that one dance at my birthday party, we'd barely spoken to each other.

I knew I shouldn't be disappointed—in essence, this was going to be a marriage in name only—but still, I had allowed myself to get swept up in the romance of the evening we met. I had allowed myself to imagine a fairytale life with my husband, where we started out as strangers and ended up falling in love. Or, at least, falling into lust.

Because I knew what was expected of a wife. It was the hardest part of this deal to swallow, knowing I was about to give myself, body and soul, to a stranger.

At least I didn't have to worry about being attracted to him.

Stefan on our wedding day was a sight to behold, waiting for me down the aisle in a midnight black tux that accentuated his broad shoulders and narrow waist. He looked like a god.

We'd shared our second kiss at the end of the ceremony, and it was as electric as the kiss he'd given me on my birthday. I could only imagine how intense it would be when we were alone tonight.

I was ready.

Okay, that was a lie.

I'd thought about it a lot. Fantasized about what he'd be like with me. Would he be gentle and sweet? Or rough and demanding? I alternated my fantasies between both. But I knew reality wasn't the same thing as what I'd built up in my mind, and while I wanted to be ravaged in theory, the actuality of it was a little overwhelming.

The door to the anteroom opened again and I stood, my dress rustling with the movement. I was eager to get it off. I shivered at the idea of my husband helping me out of it.

But it wasn't Stefan at the door. It was Michelle, with a Louis Vuitton duffle in hand.

"Let's get you out of that dress," she said. "And into something you can wear for the goodbye, before you go up to the bridal suite."

The dress she had brought was a little more my style—a simple black sheath with a rounded neckline and cap sleeves. It was a gift from Stefan. Having clothes made for me by his personal tailors was a perk I was already becoming accustomed to. I loved it.

Michelle chattered on about how wonderful the day had been as she began the long process of unbuttoning the intricate fastenings down the back of my dress. I smoothed my hands down my skirt, the reality of the whole day finally sinking in.

I was married.

Legally and bodily bound.

To a virtual stranger.

My stepmother must have noticed my breathing getting faster and my hands trembling. She finished with the dress and turned me around, her gaze searching mine.

"I promise it's going to be okay," she said in her soothing Southern accent. "He'll tell you exactly what he wants. Nothing to be worried about. For most men it's...well, it's a boon."

I realized she was talking about my virginity.

My breath came faster.

"Oh, honey. I was in your shoes once." Michelle eased me back down onto the sofa and sat beside me. She smelled comfortingly of magnolias, her signature scent. "Your job is to please him. Just remember that."

I nodded. "Right. Got it. Except what if I can't?"

"All you have to do is follow his lead. You're getting a lot out of this deal, but remember what he gets—you. Your body. It's his now."

I tried to forget that her experience in the matter came from being with my father. I wasn't naïve. I knew what was expected of me. But there had been very little actual preparation in that department. Now, facing the moment, I was starting to have second thoughts.

"What if I can't go through with it?" I asked Michelle, my doubts getting the best of me.

She looked at me sternly. "This is not the time for talk like this. You can do this. You *are* doing this. You don't have any other options."

She was right. If I wanted the life I desired – if I wanted to get an education, if I wanted to escape my father's control —then I had to play this part. At least, for now.

"At least he's young and handsome," Michelle said. "And he approves of your academic pursuits. Some husbands don't want their wives working at all." She let out a sigh.

"I know," I agreed.

"Well, don't you worry. I got you a little something." Michelle pulled out a white glittery bag with an enormous bow on top. "It'll make tonight easier for both of you."

"Is it a double magnum of wine?" I joked. And then I pulled out the tiniest piece of lingerie I'd ever seen. "Oh. Wow."

The garment appeared to be a clever arrangement of

adjustable straps and bits of white lace. Completely see-through white lace. The top would barely cover my nipples, and though I understood the point wasn't to hide anything, I couldn't even figure out how it was supposed to go on. My brow creased in confusion. "What is—"

"The garter belt is removable, and that middle strap is a thong," Michelle said brightly.

I could feel my face go bright red. If it were possible to die of humiliation, I was on my deathbed.

If I couldn't even look at the underwear without total embarrassment, how was I going to ever wear it?

"You are his prize," my stepmother reminded me, standing again to help me step out of the wedding dress. "There's a reason they call us trophy wives, after all."

I squared my shoulders, looking down at the lingerie in my hands. I could do this. It was going to be fine.

Stefan was waiting outside in the hallway for me. He didn't say anything, but the way his eyes followed the curves of my body indicated that he liked the black dress on me. I could only hope that he liked what was underneath just as much.

I gripped the lingerie bag tightly and took the arm he offered me. My pulse jumped as he led me away from Michelle and back into the ballroom, where our guests were waiting with sparklers and confetti.

"Ready?" Stefan asked.

I wasn't sure, but I nodded anyway.

Together, we ran through the line of people as they cheered and shouted their congratulations. By the time we got into the private elevator that would take us up to the bridal suite, we were both covered in confetti.

"What a day," I said.

He only nodded.

I could feel tension between us, stretched tight. As scared as I was, I was eager to see him without his clothes on.

Apparently, I wouldn't have to wait long.

The moment the elevator door opened into our private suite, Stefan shrugged off his tux jacket and began unbuttoning his cuffs and shirt. My knees went weak, and I sank onto the bed.

I was mesmerized. Part of me just wanted to stay and watch the show, but I remembered the lingerie and Michelle's instructions.

"I'll just be a moment," I told him as I hurried into the bathroom.

Quickly, I undressed and maneuvered myself into the complicated outfit. Tugging out a mess of bobby pins and giving my hair a shake, I checked my appearance in the mirror.

The lingerie was...something.

It left nothing to the imagination, my pebbled nipples visible through the lace, every curve of my body accentuated by tight white straps. I was wrapped up like a present for Stefan to open.

My heartbeat sped up. This might be fun. It might be more than fun.

Feeling a little emboldened, I blew myself a kiss in the mirror.

Then I headed into the bedroom to seduce my husband.

He was already in bed, his bare chest and tight abs well-muscled and golden. A sheet tangled around his waist, obscuring the extent of his nudity.

He was also asleep.

Apparently he hadn't been anxious in the elevator. He was just tired.

I dropped down on the edge of the bed, hoping the movement might wake him. It didn't.

"Stefan?" I reached over and touched his shoulder, then slid my hand down to squeeze his bicep. "Stefan?" He was out cold.

All that build up, and for nothing. Didn't he want me?

Apparently not enough to stay awake. Then again, it wouldn't have been as exciting for him as for me. After all, he'd probably been with tons of women. And besides, it wasn't like we were actually in love.

I went back to the bathroom and changed into my usual pajamas, a cotton camisole and shorts. Then I crawled into the bed. It was large enough that I would've had to roll over several times just to get near him. I left a wide swath of space between us and curled into a ball on my side.

This was a marriage of convenience. There was no reason to be upset.

But I couldn't stop thinking I'd just made the worst mistake of my life.

TORI

CHAPTER 5

W hen I dragged my eyes open the next morning, Stefan was already dressed.

"I didn't want to wake you," he told me coolly. "But our private jet is waiting. They'll serve us breakfast on board. Hope you slept well."

"Yes. Thank you. I'll be quick," I said, stumbling to my feet.

We were leaving for our honeymoon, so I took a lightning-quick rinse in the shower, changed into leggings and a silk blouse, and then repacked the few belongings I'd used.

I hadn't actually slept much at all. Instead I'd tossed and turned all night, wondering if I had done something wrong, second guessing myself and worrying that I should have tried harder to wake Stefan up when I was wearing the lingerie.

The garment in question was currently shoved at the bottom of my carry-on bag. Surely I'd have another chance to wear it in Vienna. At this point, I was less scared about the experience and more eager to just have it over with.

The private jet was just as luxurious as the hotel had been, with spacious leather seats and fabric curtains in the windows, but Stefan barely seemed to notice as he handed the flight crew our bags and led me to the back of the plane where a meal was laid out for us.

There was actual silverware on the tablecloth and the food rivaled some of my father's favorite places in Springfield. We ate flaky croissants, honeydew melon and cantaloupe, herbed omelets and smoked salmon. There was even a full wine list.

I tried to make conversation a few times, but if I was hoping to engage him with my repartee, I was sorely disappointed. I could barely get a monosyllabic response to my questions.

I couldn't understand where I'd gone wrong. Was he angry about last night? He was the one who'd fallen asleep! Even now, as we finished eating and cleaned our hands with hot towels the flight attendant had brought, his gaze remained elsewhere—glued to his phone.

"Stefan?"

"Hmm."

"I know you've got a lot going on with your new job and everything, but I—did I do something wrong? I feel like we've barely said a word to each other since yesterday."

He looked up, but the usual warmth I felt under his gaze was nowhere to be found.

"You're fine," he said. "I have work to do." And then he got up and went back to his seat.

As I sat there by myself, I couldn't help feeling let down. This was our honeymoon. The first day of the rest of our lives together, and we were heading off on a tour of Europe to some of the most romantic places in the world. I understood that our marriage was more of a business deal than a love match, but why had Stefan even bothered taking this trip if he had zero interest in paying attention to me?

I had to remind myself that this was part of the gig. That all I had to do was be polite and smile at my husband when he took a moment to glance up from his work. I had seen Michelle do this exact thing for most of my life. That was just the price you paid when you married someone important.

And maybe he was just distracted with something big at KZM. Maybe he was even trying to get everything out of the way now, so he could focus on the honeymoon when we arrived.

It was a nine hour flight, non-stop, but since I hadn't slept the night before I took advantage of the fold-out bed that the crew had set up in the back of the plane. The sheets were nicer than the ones I had back home. I crawled under the covers, immediately exhausted. When a crew member woke me up, we were making our final descent into Vienna. Stefan's side of the bed had remained untouched.

As we stepped off the plane, we were greeted by a smiling woman in a navy skirt suit and a red and white striped neck scarf, to match the Austrian flag.

"Welcome to Vienna, Mr. and Mrs. Zoric. I have your itinerary all planned out."

We were going on a guided tour of the city, and I was thrilled. All the traveling I'd ever done had been with my father, accompanying him for work, mostly in the U.S. We'd been to Europe once, but most of the trip had been spent at a conference and I hadn't been allowed to explore by myself, so I mostly saw the inside of our hotel.

This was my chance to see the world.

"The ferris wheel you see is the Riesenrad, which means 'giant wheel.' It stands at just under sixty-five meters tall and was constructed in 1897..."

As I oohed and ahhed over each of the sights described by our host in her heavily-accented English, Stefan hunched over his laptop in the backseat of the private car. No doubt he had been to Vienna dozens of times and would rather be left alone to work, so I was touched that he was taking this tour with me. Luckily, he was even handsome when he scowled.

When we passed the Karlskirche church, a baroque confection of creamy pillars with a central dome the color of a robin's egg, I said, "The dome is incredible. I've never seen that shade of turquoise."

"It's verdigris on the copper," Stefan said, without even looking up.

"Well, I love it," I said. "It's so vivid."

No MATTER which way the car turned, we were surrounded by gorgeous historic architecture. There was so much to take in, but I found it all wonderfully overwhelming. With each attraction we passed, I couldn't help myself from exclaiming excitedly to Stefan.

"Isn't it beautiful?" I asked him as the tour guide drove us past the Hofberg, Vienna's most famous palace.

"Mmhmm," Stefan murmured, his focus directed on an email he'd been typing. "You can take a tour of it later on the trip, if you'd like."

"Would you like that?" I asked him, hoping to engage him in conversation.

"I've already seen it," he told me.

Of course. "Is there anything here you haven't seen? Maybe we could go there."

"I've seen everything here," he said, shrugging.

That thought made me sad. "Are you really so jaded that you can't see how amazing this place is? There's so much beauty all around us. What's your favorite spot in the city?"

"I don't have one." He finally looked up at me, but I couldn't read his expression. "Please, see the sights. Don't let me stop you."

I narrowed my eyes at him. No doubt he was purposely deflecting all attempts at conversation in the hope that I'd leave him alone to work. Unfortunately, he had married a Lindsey. We didn't know how to quit.

Our tour continued, the car continuing along the streets of Vienna while I did my best to take it all in. One particular building, however, took my breath away.

"What is that place?" I asked our tour guide.

It was warm-colored stone, in an opulent Neo-Renaissance style, with statues of men on winged horses at the roof's corners. A double row of open arches lined the front façade, and although the building was ornately detailed, it had a satisfying symmetry that spoke to me.

"Ah, the Vienna Staatsoper. The Opera House," she said with a reverence that matched mine. "It is *wunderschön*, yes?"

Beautiful didn't even begin to describe it. The Vienna Opera House was the grandest thing I'd seen all day. I could only imagine how it looked on the inside.

"Do they give tours?" I asked.

"Oh yes," our tour guide said. "Every day from ten until four pm. I can drop you off?"

Stefan stopped her with a hand. "We don't have time," he said.

I slumped in my seat.

"Besides, the best way to see the Opera House is to go to an opera," he said. "It's one of my favorite things to do in Vienna."

"So you do have favorites." He didn't smile. "Well, I'd love to see a Viennese opera. I've never even seen one at home."

"Maybe on our next trip," he said, his attention returning to his laptop. "We don't have room in the schedule this time."

"Do you have a favorite opera?" I asked.

"No," he said.

"What about a favorite movie?" I tried again.

He glanced up. "Haven't you ever heard the expression 'curiosity killed the cat'?"

I gave him a shrug, feeling passive aggressive. He started back up with the typing.

"Favorite band—come on. Everybody loves music. Is it Meat Loaf?"

He let out a long-suffering sigh, but I didn't miss the slight curve at the corner of his mouth. I knew I was annoying him, but he was also a little amused. I could get him to crack.

"Favorite color?"

"I don't have one."

"You must have a favorite color to wear, at least. What's your preferred color of underwear?" I asked.

He was still looking at his phone, but his thumb stilled. Just for a moment. I had his attention.

"On me or someone else?" he asked.

"Either." Thank god. We were getting somewhere.

"White," he said. "Lace."

My pulse kicked. Had he seen me last night?

"What about on you?" I asked, my mouth dry.

"I don't wear them," he said.

My gaze darted to his lap. When I looked up, he was watching me, his green eyes intense.

"Be careful, curious little cat," he said, his voice purring the warning.

He was making me hot, but I had to focus. I was finally getting information out of him, and I wasn't going to lose my momentum.

"Favorite song?" I prodded. "I know it's not really Meat Loaf. Is it?"

Stefan shot me a look, and I gave him an innocent smile.

"What will it take for you to stop asking questions?" he demanded.

"Answering them would help," I offered. "I'm just trying to get to know you."

"Give me thirty minutes of silence, okay?"

"Only if," I said, my brain whirling, "you take me for a ride on the ferris wheel."

He stared at me. "You want to ride the ferris wheel?"

"We're in Vienna." I gestured outside. "It's a famous landmark. Isn't that what people do here?"

"That's what tourists do here," he said. "And children."

"Well," I said, crossing my arms, "I'm a tourist and I'm excited to be here. I'll stop asking questions for half an hour if we can ride the ferris wheel. Is it a deal?"

I held out my hand.

Finally, he smiled. "It's a deal," he said. "You are extremely persistent, Tori Lindsey."

With amusement dancing in his eyes, we shook. Heat

spread through me, eclipsing any lingering fears I had about our connection. I wanted so much more from him than a ride on the ferris wheel, but this would have to be enough. For now.

TORI

CHAPTER 6

"Wow," I breathed, taking in the view.

"Impressive enough for you?" Stefan asked.

We'd reached the apex of the wheel, Prater Park and the whole city spread below. Everything in Vienna was a feast for the eyes, with so much lush greenery and incredible, castle-like architecture surrounding us that I felt as if I'd woken up in a fairytale.

I smiled, shaking my head. "I've never seen anything like this before. I mean I've been to the Skydeck at Willis Tower, but seeing Chicago from a skyscraper is nothing compared to this."

The ferris wheel cars, painted red with white trim, were huge—instead of small pods of single benches, they were spacious cabins with windows looking out on every side, big enough to hold several tables and chairs. Our car could have fit at least two dozen people, but Stefan had paid for us to take the ride alone. He'd even put his phone down to take in the sights with me.

The cabin gave a slight lurch, and I gasped in surprise,

the two of us rocking back and forth above the city. That's when his hand found mine and gave a reassuring squeeze.

My pulse leapt into my throat.

But before I could turn to him, he released my hand to pull out his phone, his focus back to his work life as if the tender moment had never occurred.

Even if he didn't want to acknowledge it, I knew that gesture would stay with me for the rest of the day. The five seconds he took to let his guard down was all the confirmation I needed that there was still something real between us. My fingers still tingled with the pressure of his hand. It boded well for the night we'd be spending together.

After a long day of sightseeing, during which I spent more time talking to our tour guide than with my husband, we returned to the hotel. The whole excursion had felt more like a business trip on wheels than a honeymoon, but I'd still loved every minute of Vienna.

Now that I was finally stepping out of the car and craning my neck to look up at our hotel, I was just as awed. It was like a palace—everything accented in gold.

"I feel like we're staying in a castle," I said.

Stefan nodded. "I thought you'd like this better than something stark and modern."

I smiled at him. "I love it. Thank you."

All the details inside were ornate and luxurious, from the lush patterned carpet to the heavy embroidered drapes that were pulled back from the windows with silken cords. The place felt historic and expensive. There was no doubt in my mind that it was both.

We got to the suite and I walked through each room with my jaw hanging open. There was a sitting room, a living room, a small office and of course a huge bedroom, complete with a carved four-poster bed and inlaid antique furniture.

"This room is straight out of a Jane Austen novel!" I yelled over my shoulder at Stefan.

Even from across the room, I could see that the bed was pure luxury, a high mattress draped in thick down bedding and piled with fluffy pillows. Unable to help myself, I ran over and jumped onto it, sinking down into the cool softness with a satisfied sigh.

I heard a throat clearing from the doorway and I sat up with a jolt.

"We're going out for dinner," Stefan told me.

"Come lie down for a minute," I said as I patted the mattress next to me. "You've been working all day."

It was the first time we had been truly alone since leaving the honeymoon suite in Chicago. My skin was tight with anticipation, but Stefan didn't move an inch.

"We leave in an hour," he said. "Wear something nice."

Then he disappeared to another section of our enormous suite, his ubiquitous laptop tucked under his arm. I was starting to really, really hate that laptop.

"Going out" probably meant a date, didn't it? Dates were for couples to connect. Dates led to sex. He'd take me out tonight and when we returned to our hotel, refreshed and completely finished with his workday, he'd have more energy for me. And more desire. Unless...

Was our chemistry completely one-sided? Our first kiss had felt so real, so intense. Had it only seemed that way to me because of my lack of experience?

I headed to the bathroom to take a shower.

True to form, I was surrounded by gold fixtures and gleaming marble floors. There was a clawfoot tub and a separate shower walled in by glass, stacks of fluffy towels and Turkish cotton robes waiting to be used. I took advantage of the well-stocked cabinet of luxury bath and shower items and then stepped under the spray, imagining the hot water washing away my insecurities.

Stefan *did* want me, I told myself. I'd seen the interest in his eyes when he'd watched me walk down the aisle in my wedding dress, especially when he had gotten a good look at the neckline. And our first kiss had been long and deep, his hands tight and needful around my waist.

The memory of that kiss sent a shiver through me. Despite the distance Stefan kept putting between us, I still wanted him. And wanted him to want me.

Closing my eyes, I tried to visualize what my first time would be like. I called up the sensation of his lips against mine, hard and hot, like the rest of his body. What would he do if he was standing here right now? He'd kiss me first, his tongue thrusting strong into my mouth, his hands gripping my hips firmly.

He'd be naked, of course. I'd gotten a look at his bare chest on our wedding night, and I knew it was broad and smooth and well-muscled. The rest of his body was no doubt just as gorgeous and I had no doubt that he was a man who knew what to do with it in bed.

The thought of Stefan pulling me against him, our naked, wet bodies steaming up the shower, made me tingle. All over.

With my eyes still closed, I slid my hands down my chest, imagining that it was Stefan touching me. I cupped my full breasts, pinched my nipples, rolled them between my fingers. Gently at first and then a little harder. I imagined he'd be a little rough. I liked imagining that.

Heat pooled between my thighs and my legs spread wider as I dragged my nails lightly down my stomach. I'd gotten completely waxed in anticipation of my wedding night so when my hand reached lower it met no resistance, just smooth, bare skin.

I gasped as I touched my swollen clit, imagining that my hand was Stefan's. He would be standing behind me, his body pressed against mine as he stroked me. I dipped my finger lower to trace my lips, fantasizing that Stefan was breathing close to my ear, letting out a groan as he finally pushed a thick finger inside. "You like that?" he'd say.

"Mmhmm," I murmured quietly, grinding against that finger. I probed in soft, slow strokes, my entire body starting to hum. This was what I'd needed. I'd been on edge ever since our first kiss but now I needed relief. I needed release.

Pressing my forehead against the glass wall of the shower, I fingered myself deeper, faster, my walls wet and hot, my breath coming fast as my hips pumped back and forth.

"Come for me," Stefan would say, commanding me. "I want to feel you come."

I pumped faster, one hand reaching up to squeeze my breast. I shut my eyes tight, pleasure spreading through my entire body as the orgasm built inside of me.

"Yes," I moaned softly.

Just before I climaxed, my skin prickled with the sensation of being watched. I opened my eyes and found Stefan standing in the doorway of the bathroom.

He was watching me, his jaw set, eating up the sight of me—his own desire visible, the front of his pants bulging. My body trembled as the shockwaves hit me, unable to prevent myself from coming right in front of him in breathless gasps.

When I looked back toward him, my spent body feeling loose and languid, I fully expected to see him shedding his clothes and throwing open the shower door to take me in his arms and continue what I had started.

Instead, I found an empty doorway. He was gone.

STEFAN WAS KEEPING to himself in the suite's office while I got ready. I chose a black evening gown that looked demure from the front, but when I turned around, revealed an almost completely open back. It was the kind of dress that I couldn't wear a bra with. I pulled my hair into a messy yet artful twist with some loose tendrils framing my face and finished off the outfit with a pair of heels and a small clutch. I was very dressed up, but I didn't know where we were going tonight, and I wanted to make sure people noticed me. Especially Stefan.

"Are you ready yet?" he asked, knocking on the door.

I flung it open but for a moment just stood there, taking in his dark suit, the scent of his cologne, his gold cufflinks. He was typing something on his phone, but when he glanced up his gaze zeroed on me and his hand dropped to his side.

"Is this okay?" I asked, turning in a slow circle, making sure he got a good look at the back.

His eyes blazed hot. Just like when he'd watched me in the shower. "You've done well."

"Where are we going?"

He pulled a cream envelope out of his pocket and handed it to me.

Opening the flap, I saw that there were tickets inside. Tickets to the Vienna Opera House. For tonight.

"I..."

"You're welcome." His voice was gruff, as if to quell my overpowering emotions.

"I never expected this," I finally managed.

He nodded. "I have something else for you."

Reaching into his jacket pocket, he pulled out a long, velvet box and handed it to me. I opened it to find the most gorgeous diamond necklace I had ever seen. It was composed of two strands of glittering stones with a large teardrop-shaped diamond suspended from it.

I was speechless at its extravagance, my fingers gently resting on the pear cut stone nestled in the velvet. Stefan came around behind me, reaching over my shoulder to take the box. His hand brushed mine, and I felt a spark.

He lifted the diamond necklace out and draped it around my neck. It was heavy, the teardrop nestling between my breasts. I touched the cool stone, holding it in place, as Stefan fastened the clasp. His fingers brushed the nape of my neck, then slid lower to caress my bare back. Once. Twice. Three times.

It couldn't have been an accident.

My skin tingled with each brief moment of contact.

I walked over to the closet mirror, gazing at the necklace, loving the way it sparkled against my skin.

"It's gorgeous," I breathed.

Stefan was stoic behind me, his expression giving nothing away.

"It is," he said.

I appraised our reflection. We were a handsome pair, in our matching black clothes. It looked like we belonged together. Did Stefan think so too? I glanced at him, but his eyes were on the necklace. My nipples went hard. I knew they would be visible through the dress.

"It looks like it was made for you," he added, his voice husky.

My eyes met his in the mirror. There was that intense, dark stare, and for a brief moment, I thought he might bend down to kiss me. But then he walked away.

TORI

CHAPTER 7

Looking more like a statement than an eatery, Restaurant Steirereck was housed in a façade of huge geometric blocks. The building's silver exterior reflected the streetlights back at us, and golden light spilled from wall-sized glass panels, revealing the diners within.

"Wait until you see the inside," Stefan said.

As he led me through the door, I felt like I was stepping into a contemporary art museum. The walls were paneled with pale wood and the décor was nothing but white linens and stark furniture, all simple, clean lines. The whole place oozed luxury and glamour.

"It reminds me of a Japanese zen garden," I said.

"Our garden is on the roof," the hostess said by way of greeting. "You have reservations, yes?"

Steirereck was our first stop of the evening, before we went to the opera. The restaurant was one of the best in Vienna, Stefan had promised.

We were led toward a private corner of the restaurant, but as we crossed the crowded floor, it felt like every person we passed was pausing to take us in. How could they not? We must have looked very important—Stefan in his expensive tux and me in my diamond necklace that kept catching the light and casting white flashes across the walls.

But when we reached our table, my heart sank. Because we weren't eating alone.

An older man was sitting at our table, sophisticated in that effortless, European way, his attention on his phone. Noticing our approach, he immediately put it down and rose to greet us.

"Marco," Stefan shook his hand. "This is Victoria. My wife."

The word gave me a thrill, despite my disappointment at having unexpected company.

"Delighted to meet you," Marco said, taking my hand and kissing my knuckles.

"You can call me Tori," I told him.

"You'll call her Victoria," Stefan corrected, shooting both of us a look that didn't allow room for argument.

I should have been annoyed at his controlling nature, but I liked it. I liked that he cared enough to be jealous. If that's what this was.

Marco didn't seem to mind the correction, giving me a wink as we were seated at the table. It soon became clear that this would not be a romantic dinner at all, and was actually more of a business meeting in an expensive setting with even more expensive food. Stefan even had an expensive wife, wearing an expensive necklace, at his side.

I fit right in.

Our food was good, though. In fact, it was incredible.

Unfortunately, it didn't seem like Stefan or Marco even noticed, they were so focused on discussing KZM's marketing platform. Was this who Stefan had been on the phone with all day?

I knew that business was important, but I couldn't believe he could so easily turn off his attraction to me after seeing how turned on he had been watching me in the shower.

I wished I could do the same, but I couldn't help reliving the electric brush of his fingers against my skin as he'd carefully fastened my necklace for me. It might have been wishful thinking, but I could have sworn he'd taken his time with it. The way he'd slid his thumbs softly up and down the nape of my neck until I had goosebumps.

I had to cross my legs and squeeze my thighs together to ease the ache building up.

"Did you know the word honeymoon was first used all the way back in the fifth century?" I interjected at a pause in the conversation. "It referred to the first month of marriage, the 'moon,' when newlyweds would drink mead."

I received two stares, one mildly amused (Thank you, Marco) and one blank (Stefan).

I cleared my throat. "You know, because mead is made from...honey."

Marco opened his mouth to respond, but Stefan cut him off. "So with Paris Fashion Week right on our heels I need you to send me stats and portfolios on..." he trailed off, drumming his fingers on the table, "at least twelve women and six men. Better to have options."

Marco nodded. "I have a few leads." He looked over and gave me an apologetic smile.

I smiled back and stood. "If you'll just excuse me for a few minutes," I said. "I'm just going to freshen up."

They were back to their conversation before I even left the table.

I took my time in the bathroom, touching up my lips and re-pinning my hair. I doubted that either of them would notice how long I was gone, and I wasn't in a hurry to hear more executive language. At least I had the opera to look forward to and, last I checked, we only had two tickets, not three.

But, threading my way across the room, I immediately noticed a change in Stefan's demeanor. Before, he was relaxed and confident, his hands resting on the table. Now he was leaning forward, his hands tightened into fists, his expression stormy.

"—all the funds and resources I've given you, you've still failed." His voice was sharp.

Marco held up his hands. "We've been all over the continent and into the Middle East, chased down any hint of a rumor," he was saying. "We've followed every lead, but—"

"*You will find her,*" Stefan said, his voice steely and dangerous.

Marco leaned back, and then noticed me. A fake smile immediately spread across his face.

"Victoria!" he said, like my name was his life raft. He jumped to his feet.

Stefan rose as well, a scowl still darkening his features.

"Grab your coat. The opera will be starting soon."

THE OPERA HOUSE was just as beautiful on the inside as it was on the outside. Although I'd spent the car ride trying to find out what had happened with Marco, Stefan had only blown me off. I wasn't going to just let it go, but for the moment I was able to forget how distant he was acting, my attention completely focused on the breathtaking architecture. It reminded me of a church with its ornate arches, elaborate balustrades, and a grand staircase carpeted in spring green.

Stefan had gotten us seats in a private balcony overlooking the stage. All of it was so breathtakingly romantic that when the lights went down and the music started, I reached for his hand.

He returned my grip and we held hands through the first aria before he gently released me. I didn't mind—by that point, I was so spellbound by the performance, I hardly noticed. Judging by Stefan's demeanor, he was just as riveted as I was. Gazing down at the stage, he was the embodiment of Prince Charming, and I allowed myself to imagine that he really was. When the opera finally ended, I couldn't believe it was already over. I'd been completely swept away.

We returned to the hotel late.

Between the day of sightseeing, the jetlag, the rich, multi-course dinner and the Opera House, I was exhausted. But not exhausted enough to forget what had happened in the shower earlier, or how Stefan's eyes had burned into me. I had a plan.

"Can you help me with this?" I asked when we were alone in our bedroom, turning my back to him and gesturing toward the clasp of the necklace.

I could have easily removed it myself, but I wanted his hands on me.

He did as I requested, his fingers brushing against the soft skin at the nape of my neck, just like they had earlier. I realized it had to be one of his hot spots, and I suppressed a smile. I was learning his tells.

I carefully put the necklace back in its box, enjoying the feel of the soft fabric against my fingertips.

"I'll be right back," I told him, dropping my voice to a more sultry register.

I had left my wedding night lingerie in the bathroom before we left, and I hurried to get it on, pulling the bobby pins out of my hair as I did. It tumbled down to my shoulders in pale waves and I stood in front of the mirror to adjust myself as much as I could within the confines of the ungodly array of tiny hooks and ribbon laces.

Taking a deep breath, I headed back to the bedroom, tilting my head and arching my back against the doorjamb in what I hoped was a seductive pose.

Stefan was on his phone.

"Are you ready?" I asked, my voice more wobbly than I would have liked, but at least I got the question out without stumbling over my words.

Stefan didn't even look up.

"I have to go out," he said, grabbing his jacket. "Don't wait up."

He left.

I climbed onto the bed, completely stunned, not believing what had just happened. Again. This was our honeymoon and he was going *out*? Was this a game? Did he get off on humiliating me? I knew I turned him on. So why was he avoiding me? Was it something to do with the person he and Marco had been arguing about at dinner? The "her" I wasn't supposed to have heard them discussing? He'd been more passionate during that small snippet of conversation than during any exchange he'd had with me.

Who was my husband looking for?

And what would happen to me when he found her?

STEFAN

CHAPTER 8

All I could think about was white lace. White lace, rosy pink nipples, those lush, supple curves begging to be touched. Dominated. *Owned*. In that lingerie she'd looked like a fine dessert. Gleaming behind glass, utterly tantalizing, and just out of reach. In a flash, my mind had been flooded with visions of laying her down on the bed and spreading her open to eat and eat and eat. The only thing holding me back had been my master self-control.

I was pretty sure Tori thought I hadn't been paying attention—that I didn't bother to look up when she came out of the bathroom. But I had. And I'd seen her. I'd seen everything.

My dick was still hard.

As I walked the streets in the cold, clear night air, I scolded myself to get it together before I reached my final destination. It was no easy task, though—and I was pretty sure I'd have that image of Tori, standing there radiating sex and innocence, burned into my memory forever. I'd been with plenty of drop-dead gorgeous women in my life, had scores of dirty sexy memories stored up—but for some reason, all I could think about was my new wife.

She was just so fucking irresistible with her guileless blue eyes and that ripe virgin body. I wanted to put my mouth over every inch of her. Wanted to bite and suck until she begged, until I left my mark. Until she couldn't go out in public without everyone seeing that she'd been branded. Claimed. Fucked into submission.

But it was an indulgence I was determined to deny myself.

It had been damn near impossible to walk away that afternoon when I'd caught her in the shower. I could see her again now, fingering herself under the steaming water with her head thrown back, squeezing her perfect tits together with the other hand.

I knew I'd left her confused and hurt when I had walked out the door. But that wasn't my problem. She knew what she'd been getting into with this marriage.

Though I had to admit, her determination to go to college had been unexpected. Most women would have been more than happy to get a lifetime of expensive clothes, luxury vacations and priceless jewels in exchange for agreeing to the deal.

Apparently, Tori wanted more.

She had focus and drive. I respected that. Hell, I admired it.

But I had to focus on KZM right now. Too many people were counting on me. I didn't have time for a real marriage. A real relationship. I wasn't going to let Tori distract me.

I was so lost in thought that I was startled to realize I'd arrived.

Every time I came to Vienna, I made sure to visit this pub. It had an otherworldly vibe I appreciated, the ceiling design like abstract origami and dim, recessed lighting that allowed its patrons relative privacy. It was the kind of place where no one would pay attention to you, where everyone just seemed to fade away into the shadows.

It suited me perfectly.

Marco was waiting on a stool at the bar, the report I had requested poking out of his bag.

"Is this everything?" I asked, grabbing the thick file.

"Everything from the last month," he said, taking a sip of the whiskey in his hand.

I gestured to the bartender for a glass of the same as I flipped through the pages, not exactly sure what I was looking for.

I'd been searching for months now. Years.

"She's not in Vienna," I stated.

Marco shook his head. "Nor in Bratislava, Graz, or Budapest. She's not in Brno, or Prague, or Krakow, or Katowice. And she's definitely not in Dresden. I wish it was better news."

The sheets of paper in my hand confirmed all he was saying, but in more detail.

"Fuck." I tossed the file onto the bar, frustration building inside of me.

Marco took another sip of his drink. Mine arrived and I ran a hand through my hair before downing nearly the entire thing. I stared at the file on the bar, debating what to do next. Marco said nothing but I knew he was waiting for my orders. For the next step.

That's when I realized my motives had changed. I had promised myself I'd never stop looking for her, but now I was more curious than anything. What had I said to Tori that very afternoon? About curiosity killing the cat?

Maybe it was time to take a break, focus on work. My

father would never retire unless he thought my full attention would be on KZ Modeling, and right now it obviously wasn't. Besides, work was something I could control. As much as I hated to admit it, I couldn't control this investigation.

"Shall we keep looking?" Marco asked.

I finished my whiskey and shook my head.

"Put the project on hold for now."

Marco's eyebrows rose but he said nothing. He knew better than to question my orders. That's why I put him in charge of things like this. Projects of a more personal disposition.

I gathered up the file. "I'll tell you when it's time to pick it back up again," I said.

It was a dismissal. Marco gave a short nod and got up from the bar, leaving me alone. I gestured for another whiskey, my fingers tapping the bar.

But it wasn't the report I was thinking about. It wasn't work, either.

Sitting in a hotel room all by herself was my innocent, nubile bride. Probably fuming about her distant, asshole husband.

The things I wanted to do to her...

I savored my drink, not caring that I was getting buzzed. Usually I didn't drink to excess, but tonight, well, tonight I was on my fucking honeymoon. Spending it alone in a bar, chasing ghosts and fantasizing about my hot, virgin wife. The wife I couldn't touch.

I leaned back and allowed myself a moment to imagine what I might do to Tori if she wasn't an innocent. If she wasn't so pure. So sweet. So inexperienced. I thought about her face during the opera, how captivated she had been—how her hand had reached for mine. I shouldn't have taken it. Shouldn't have encouraged her naïve romantic fantasies.

She wanted what I could never give her: Connection. Intimacy. Trust. That much was clear from the questions she'd been asking me, all her attempts to get to know me better.

If she knew who I really was—and what she'd married into—she'd stop asking. She'd stop trying to find romance in this arrangement. Because that's what it was. An arrangement. It wasn't a real marriage and it definitely wasn't a fucking romance. It was a contract.

Still, I couldn't help the fantasies whirling through my mind.

I imagined stalking back into the hotel room, finding her still wearing that lace lingerie. Waiting for me to give her a lesson on what it means to please a man.

Her body was perfect—supple and athletic, with just the right amount of curves. I'd start by ripping the lingerie off, leaving her naked and vulnerable while I stood there fully dressed, fully in command. I'd force her onto her knees, and when she looked up at me with those big blue eyes I'd whip my cock out, shoving it so deep down her throat that she'd choke on it. My wife would learn how to suck cock, and she'd love every second of it.

After I had my fill I'd push her up against the wall, my hand finding the smooth, soft skin between her legs. Her pussy would be wet for me. So fucking wet.

There'd be no resistance when I stroked her, her clit aching for my touch. I'd pump my fingers into her until she arched against my hand, begging for release, but I wouldn't let her come. Instead I'd spin her around, shove her against the wall before unzipping and slamming into her. It would be rough and fast and fucking hot as hell. She'd be moaning and clenching that tight cunt around me with each thrust.

Fuck.

If I knew what was good for me, I'd put those fantasies away. Permanently. I wouldn't keep torturing myself with thoughts of her on her knees, her pouting little mouth wrapped around my cock. Or her riding me, her virgin pussy squeezing me hard as she came, losing her mind over the first orgasm she'd ever had with a man inside her. Or taking her from behind, her hands fisting the blankets as I gripped her hips and jackhammered her into moaning submission.

I knew that I needed to stop thinking about her—and if I knew what was good for me, I'd ignore her completely.

But if there was one thing I'd learned by now, it was that I didn't give a damn what was good for me.

TORI

CHAPTER 9

I was the kind of girl who'd always dreamed of escape.

My Christmas lists all throughout elementary school had been filled with what I'd thought of as 'adventure supplies.' Flashlights, sleeping bags, hand warmers and canteens with built-in water filters—pretty weird for a nine-year-old. But even though the furthest I'd been allowed to wander with my compass and backpack had been the five acres of our backyard, that tiny taste of what I'd craved was enough to fuel years of suppressed wanderlust.

But here I was, waking up bright and early so I could *carpe diem* on my honeymoon—arguably the biggest adventure of my life—and my husband was nowhere to be found. His side of the bed wasn't even disturbed. Had he even come back last night? I had no idea.

I'd never felt so alone.

I remembered trying to wait up for him– though I'd changed out of the cursed lingerie the moment he left—but the day had worn me out so much that I'd fallen asleep pretty fast.

Wrapping myself in the plush hotel robe, I went searching for him in the rooms of our suite. Maybe he was making coffee or working in the office already, a willing slave to his laptop and smartphone.

On the plush sofa in the sitting room, I found a pillow on top of a neatly folded blanket. Well. At least he'd made it back last night. He'd just chosen to sleep on the couch.

I sank down onto the cushions, my head in my hands. I'd thought we had turned a corner. His hand had felt so good on mine during the opera, the sparks palpable. And then he wouldn't even share a bed with me. The sexual rejection had hurt, but this? It somehow felt worse.

"I'm heading out."

My head snapped up. Stefan was in a perfectly pressed Armani suit, looking like sex on a stick, and apparently gearing up to start his day. I glanced down guiltily at my robe.

"I must still be jetlagged," I said, smiling apologetically. "I can be ready in ten minutes."

"You're not going," he said, not even glancing up as he fastened his watch.

"Okay, I can meet you there—"

"You'll stay here."

I bristled at the command. But I wasn't so easily dismissed.

"Just tell me where you're going then," I demanded. "I want to know."

"You're on a need to know basis," he said. "And it's frankly nothing to do with you."

I bit my lip and recalled all the years of obedience training I'd undergone at the hands of Michelle and my father. Like I was no more than a dog, learning to sit and stay on command. Rage was boiling up inside me, but I reminded myself that I'd agreed to this marriage and all of its conditions. That this was temporary. That once we returned to Chicago, I'd be so busy with school that I wouldn't have time to worry about the status of my sham of a marriage.

But why had Stefan even bothered with a honeymoon or a visit to the opera? Why stare at me so hungrily while I was naked in the shower? I was getting so many mixed messages that my head was spinning.

Still, I couldn't go on like this. We couldn't go on like this.

"Where were you last night?" I asked, the question tumbling out before I could stop it.

He was fastening his cufflink and didn't even bother looking up.

"I was out," he said.

I stood up, fire in my chest. "Out where? I waited up for you. You ignored all my texts."

"It's not your concern," he said casually. "And in the future, don't bother waiting."

"In the future?"

He finally glanced over. "I'm a very busy man," he said. "You should understand that."

"I'd just like to know where you are, and when you plan on returning," I said, my hands on my hips. "As your wife, I think I'm entitled to that knowledge."

He looked at me, his expression impassive. "Remember what I said about the cat?" he asked. "And curiosity?"

"I'm not a cat." I held my ground.

"Oh, but I think you're acting like one," he said, his voice low. It shouldn't have been hot, but it was. "Careful with your curiosity, little cat," he said.

"This is supposed to be our honeymoon," I said, irritation getting the best of me. "But you're spending all your time glued to your work and keeping secrets from me—"

"Go to the spa," he said, glancing down at his phone as it vibrated with an incoming message. "Charge whatever you want to the room."

"You can't just leave me here alone, like some toy on a shelf that you get to play with whenever you feel like it!"

I was breathing hard, but before I could say anything else he was grabbing his wallet and his room key.

"I'm not going to the spa," I said, following him toward the door.

"Then go shopping at the boutique. Or take a swim. There's plenty to do in the hotel."

"But I want to be with you. I thought that was the point of this whole trip—to spend our time exploring together."

He turned to face me. "Then you're in for a disappointment."

My eyes were stinging with tears. "But when will I see you?"

"At seven. We have a dinner reservation at the hotel restaurant."

I was stunned at his coldness. He didn't even seem to notice that his words had hurt my feelings. Or maybe he noticed and just didn't care.

"This is ridiculous," I told him.

His hand was on the doorknob.

"Isn't this the exchange we agreed on, Tori? I get a wife, and a chance to take over my father's company. You get your college experience and a chance to get away from your father. You get an easy life of luxury and wealth, and you get to spend my money on whatever your little heart desires. What else could a woman like you want?"

A woman like me.

"Are you calling me a whore?" I said, my voice low with hurt and anger.

"Watch your mouth." He was finally meeting my hard gaze, his green eyes ablaze. "And don't talk about things you're too sheltered to understand."

He swung the door open and stepped into the hallway.

"Seven o'clock," he said. "Sharp." And then he walked away.

As the door closed behind him, I sank into the nearest chair, his words echoing in my mind. I couldn't believe this was the price of getting my degree.

Maybe things would be different when I started college, when I could have friends, and a life of my own outside of my marriage. But right now, it was just the two of us—and, obviously, Stefan's clients and business associates—in a foreign country.

I couldn't wait to get back home. I'd bury myself in school and studying and a full calendar of social events and more volunteer work—anything I could think of to keep away from Stefan. Away from the man I had been coerced into marrying.

Because if this honeymoon was any indication of what to expect out of our marriage, I was in for a hell of a rough ride.

TORI

CHAPTER 10

So he thought of me as a whore? Fine. I'd spend his money as if I'd earned it like one.

"Room service," a crisp, Austrian-accented voice answered.

"Good morning," I said sweetly. "Can you tell me what you have for breakfast, please? And is there champagne this early?"

I ordered recklessly, not even asking the prices. If I was going on this adventure by myself, I was determined to treat myself right.

Along with the champagne, I asked for an Italian espresso, a carafe of fresh-squeezed orange juice, and a pot of tea. I took the suggestions given to me and selected two different egg dishes and an artisanal bread basket, adding the roasted local asparagus and a platter of bacon and sliced ham.

"We...also have apple strudel and plum jam turnovers?" the voice said. "They're from a prominent local bakery. Though perhaps you won't have room for—"

"Why not? Give me two of each." And just to be extra

decadent, I ordered the Strawberries Romanoff—which came with three different flavors of cream.

Room service had to send up three carts to deliver my order. I tipped extravagantly.

There was no way I could finish it all, but I made sure to sample everything.

Full to bursting after my indulgent breakfast, I got dressed and headed downstairs to the luxury spa on the first floor of the hotel. I tried to be annoyed that I had essentially been banished here, but it was hard to keep up the sour attitude once I was presented with a pamphlet of spa options. I figured Stefan owed me the best massage that money could buy, to make up for all the hurt and anger and frustration he'd caused, but I couldn't even figure out where to start.

And then my eyes zeroed in on something with the right amount of dollar signs attached to it.

"What exactly is the 'Gold Package'?" I asked the young woman behind the granite counter. She was wearing a lab coat and a turtleneck, like a doctor, except she was all in black.

"It's a series of treatments using pure twenty-four karat gold, with a three-step full body massage, a gold leaf facial, and a gold dust mani-pedi. It also includes a gold flake martini and a selection of gold-dipped truffles." She smiled at my stunned look. "I realize it sounds a bit extreme."

I laughed. "It sounds perfect, actually. I'll take it."

Her eyes widened. "Of course, but...the appointment lasts approximately five hours."

I slid the suite's keycard toward her, and her gaze darted to my huge diamond ring.

"Charge it to my room," I told her breezily. "And I'd like to leave a generous tip as well. Including for yourself."

"We'll get you started right away." She was beaming ear to ear.

"Oh, and is there a cosmetologist on staff? Maybe a hair stylist? I have an event tonight. It would be amazing if I could get my hair and makeup done."

"We have a full salon," she answered. "And if you don't mind me saying so...your partner is going to be struck *dumb* when you show up to that event later."

"I'm counting on it," I said, flashing a wicked smile. "Believe me."

They started me off by leading me to a gorgeous, private changing room done up in wall-to-wall Italian marble, where I was given a robe so soft that it had to be cashmere, and then I was escorted into the spa to begin my experience.

But first, I was given my golden martini—delicious—and left alone to relax in a private steam room, lying there completely naked so my pores could open up. Soothing ocean sounds were piped in, and I felt my tense muscles start to loosen as the balmy temperature and the music coaxed me into a zen-like state. I was determined to enjoy this. I would not think about Stefan.

Before I knew it, I was back in my robe and being taken to another room, where a woman with a severe bun and a no-nonsense demeanor began scrubbing my body down with an exfoliating clay that shimmered with pure gold powder.

"That smells so good," I sighed. "Like lemon and licorice."

"It is anise and verbena," the woman told me. "Now turn onto your back."

Every time I felt a flash of hurt or anger toward Stefan, I reminded myself that I was here to indulge, to focus completely on myself. It mostly worked.

The aesthetician had come in to work on me, and I interrupted my gold leaf and collagen facial only long enough to ask, "Does the gold leaf actually do anything?"

"Of course. These treatments were used in Ancient China, and by Cleopatra. The gold lifts out toxins and stimulates cell reproduction. It's good for wrinkles too, not that you need it."

I smiled at the compliment and tried to imagine myself as Cleopatra, draped in pearls and oozing sex appeal. Stefan Zoric, eat your heart out.

After I was rinsed off, I was laid out on a table and a different woman came in and sprayed my body with gold infused massage oil. Then the masseuse went to work on my muscles. I felt like butter beneath her strong hands, all of my tension and stress melting away with each stroke of pressure.

After a while, I began to imagine it was Stefan touching me. Stroking me.

I closed my eyes, letting my mind wander as my body was taken care of. I imagined him leaning over me, his hands kneading into my neck and shoulders before moving lower, caressing my lower back. Then lower, massaging my gluteal muscles, his thumbs moving in deep, slow circles until the muscles relaxed under his hands.

He'd ease my thighs apart, fingers slipping between my legs, where I ached to be touched. I imagined him starting to stroke me, gliding back and forth with his thumb before thrusting a thick finger inside, his pacing timed to match my shallow, quickening breaths. His mouth would dip close to my ear, whispering naughty things to me as he touched me. Teased me.

"That's my curious little cat," he'd say, pumping deeper.

He'd be good with his hands. He was older, and experienced. He knew how to make a woman come. I bet he'd guess exactly what I wanted before I even figured it out myself.

As I lay there, the fantasy overwhelming me, I realized that I wasn't just mad at him for what had happened that morning...I was upset with myself. For believing that this could be something more. For *wanting* it to be something more. I had been naïve.

But I was attracted to him. Deeply. Regardless of the circumstances, I wanted to take our marriage to the next level, find out what our bodies were capable of. Unfortunately, I was beginning to realize that that had never been part of the deal.

"You're so tense," the masseuse told me, no doubt feeling all the tightness that was now building in my shoulders and back.

I did my best to relax again, but all I could think about was Stefan. Why couldn't I stay annoyed at him? Why did I want him to touch me, to kiss me, to caress me? He had made it clear that he wasn't interested, yet my body craved him.

Of all the people in the world, I had to be attracted to my arranged marriage husband. The one person who seemed to have literally no interest in me. Or if he did, he was more than happy to ignore that attraction. It definitely wasn't as important as his work.

Knowing I was playing with fire, I slipped back into my sexy daydream.

I imagined him standing above me, positioning me on all fours, pulling my knees wide. Exposing me to him fully. In my fantasy he spread my thighs with his hands and then licked my opening, already wet for him. He stroked me with his tongue, his fingers pushing into me at the same time, and I imagined my desperate moans, my orgasm coming fast.

He wouldn't even wait for my body to stop shaking before he'd position himself behind me. Then he'd slam himself deep inside, grabbing my hips for leverage as he thrusted hard, grunting with effort. Maybe he'd fist his hand in my hair to tug my head back, my pain and pleasure mixing in equal measure, pumping faster and faster until he came, groaning my name.

The intensity of the fantasy surprised me. I'd never thought of myself as the kind of girl who would want something like that—raw and rough—but my skin tingled with each new image that popped into my head. Because somehow, I knew how Stefan would be in bed.

He wouldn't be gentle, nor sweet. He'd be the way he was in real life. Brusque, intense, passionate.

Still, I knew it was pointless to even imagine having him, no matter how badly I wanted it. Maybe I was just desperate to lose my virginity and he was the most convenient person I could think of... No. That wasn't it at all. I wished it was, but I knew that my attraction to Stefan was unique. The way he looked at me, how fast the heat would build between us, the hum in my body whenever he was close by. I was positive there was something there, even if it was purely lust and nothing else. That's what made the whole thing so frustrating.

WHEN I FINALLY EMERGED FROM the salon, perfectly made up and expertly coiffed, I felt almost like a new person. Tugging my clothes back on in the changing room, I took a hard look in the mirror. There was no doubt about it

—I was glowing. From my professionally applied Chanel makeup to the shimmering polish on my toenails.

Stefan was probably going to freak when he saw the charges I'd been making to the room, but it would teach him a lesson not to taunt me about spending money and then leave me alone for a whole day in an expensive hotel.

Feeling a little better, I made my way to the lobby cafe for a late lunch. I couldn't believe I was hungry after the huge breakfast I'd eaten, but all that pampering had aroused my appetite.

It was a light meal, and I barely had room to try the city's world-famous Sacher torte, but I figured a celebration wasn't complete without dessert.

Afterward, I decided to explore the boutique that Stefan had mentioned. I had just stepped out of the café when I glimpsed a familiar figure out of the corner of my eye. It was Stefan, gliding across the lobby, his purposeful stride instantly recognizable.

Immediately my pulse raced, as all the fantasies I'd been entertaining during my massage came back to me at full force. Stefan's strong fingers between my legs, his grip tight on my hips, his body thrusting into mine. I felt very hot, my blood buzzing with anticipation.

I was so distracted that at first I didn't even notice that he wasn't alone. No, he had a leggy brunette with him, his hand resting on her lower back. I could only see them from behind, but he turned his head to whisper something to her and she pushed her hair behind her ear, giving me a look at her face.

She was gorgeous. Unbelievably, super-human gorgeous. With her impossibly long legs and wide-set Bambi eyes, she had to be a model.

No doubt she was exactly the kind of woman Stefan

was used to being around all day. Tall and angular, with high cheekbones and perfectly pouty lips. The little slip of a silk blouse made it obvious that she wasn't wearing a bra. As they got closer, I saw that she had winged eyeliner and a wet, pink mouth. She looked like a living doll.

She looked nothing like me.

Stefan led her toward the elevators, still whispering sweet nothings into her ear—or so I assumed. She was smiling and laughing, touching his arm and playing with her long, silky hair.

At least he wasn't playing with it.

I should have gone into the boutique. Should have turned tail and marched out of there and spent as much of Stefan's money as humanly possible. Instead, I followed them. I kept my distance across the expansive lobby, but there was no need. Neither of them noticed me standing there, off to the side. In fact, they were so caught up in each other that I could probably run screaming across the lobby and they wouldn't even bat an eye.

STEFAN, being Stefan, kept pulling out his phone. His date pouted a little and I bit back a smirk. Not even this gorgeous creature could keep him away from his true love—his cell-phone. But he still had his hand on her lower back. Already, he was touching her more than he had touched me during our entire honeymoon.

Jealousy tore through me.

The elevator dinged and the doors slid open. I watched as they got in—alone—and the doors closed. I rushed over to the bank of elevators and called my own down.

Were they going up to our room? Did Stefan actually

have the balls to think he was going to sleep with this woman in our honeymoon suite while I was still somewhere in the hotel? *In flagrante delicto* or not, I was going to rip them both to shreds when I got up there.

But when I arrived at our floor, the hall was empty. So was our room. I sat heavily on the sofa, where the pillow and blanket Stefan had left there last night were still perched. If he hadn't brought her here, they had to be somewhere else in the hotel. Together.

I swallowed, feeling a lump in my throat. Not only was Stefan doing everything he could to avoid being physical with me, but he was also spending our honeymoon fooling around with some other woman. A few hours ago, I had thought that things between us couldn't get any worse. That *I* couldn't feel any worse.

But now I realized I'd been wrong.

TORI

CHAPTER 11

"Have you ever been cheated on?" I asked the sales associate.

"Yes." She tilted her head, motioning me to turn in front of the mirror in the flounced skirt I was trying on. "I was still in *polytechnische schule,* how you say...high school. A dumb teenager. He was older. I thought he was so mature." She rolled her eyes.

After I had collected myself, I had marched down to the extremely expensive boutique in the hotel lobby, and found the store full of salesgirls more than happy to help me rejuvenate my wardrobe on Stefan's tab.

One of them, who was about my age, had introduced herself as Katharina. She had a shy smile, but she knew what she was doing when it came to my request for sexy and sophisticated. With her help, I picked out several brand-new outfits—things I would've never dreamed of buying for myself back in Springfield.

"So what did you do? After you found out he cheated, I mean?"

She allowed herself a little smirk. "I confronted him.

He was a waiter, so I went to his work at the busy shift and shouted at him in front of the entire restaurant. The girl he was shtupping worked there too. They both got fired."

"I can't believe you outed him in public like that!" This girl had balls.

She shrugged. "I didn't plan for it, I was just so angry. It felt good."

I stepped back into the dressing room to try on something else, and spoke to her through the door. "So...did he try to get you back?"

"No. After that night, I never saw him again."

That was a luxury I didn't have. I *would* see Stefan again, and as I glanced at my watch I realized that the hour of our reservation was drawing near.

Maybe confronting him would make me feel better, too. It probably wouldn't change anything, but I couldn't imagine playing along with our fake marriage for the next couple of years, going about my business as if I knew nothing and resenting him for his lies the whole time. Because I'd decided one thing: I wasn't going to ask for a divorce.

Not just because our fathers would be furious, but because I still wanted to have my college dream, and the security that Stefan's wealth offered. My degree was the one thing that would assure my future whenever this counterfeit marriage really did end.

I stepped out to look at myself in the mirror again, this time in a slinky black number as expensive as my iPhone. I did a quick turn, tugging the hem down when I saw how much of my thighs were visible. I felt so exposed.

"This one is so...*vavoom*. You must be very confident," Katharina said with a shy smile.

"I'd have to be, to walk around in something like this," I said, biting my lip as I studied my reflection.

"It looks like it was made for you," she offered. "It hugs you. But maybe too daring?"

Oh, but I dared. "Actually, you know what? I think I'll just wear it out of the store."

Katharina laughed, and it felt good to join in with her. Almost like I had a friend, though I knew this was just her job.

In the end, I had more clothes than I could carry. Beyond the dresses, blouses, and some practical slacks, I'd stocked up on totally impractical Jimmy Choo stilettos, some strappy Ferragamo heels, and an armload of cashmere wraps in rich, softly muted tones.

"I'll arrange to have everything sent up to your room," Katharina said.

"Wonderful."

I felt empowered somehow. Most of these clothes were tighter and sexier than anything I'd ever worn, yes, but it was the first time in my life I'd made all my own wardrobe decisions. My father never would have let me walk out the door dressed this way. And I doubted Stefan would have been happy with my choices, either.

But my father wasn't here. Neither was Stefan.

As Katharina rang up my purchases and wrapped each of them in layers of tissue paper, I spotted a purse that was displayed on a shelf just past the counter. It sat behind a thick pane of glass, and like a piece of fine jewelry, its own spotlight shone down on it. I couldn't help but notice how buttery soft the leather looked, the way the gold hardware gleamed.

"Excuse me, but what is that?" I asked, pointing.

She glanced over her shoulder and turned back with a

diabolical grin. "The lady has a discerning eye. It is a Birkin bag. It is made by Hermès." She pronounced it 'air mez.'

"I've heard of them," I said.

She told me the price. It was enough for half a year's tuition.

"Do you make commission here?" I asked.

She glanced around and then lowered her voice subtly. "I'm saving up for a semester abroad. University is free here, but not in other countries. I want to see the world."

I smiled. "In that case I'll take it."

"The lady dares again," she crowed. "It's stunning. Will you take it with you now?"

"I don't think it goes with the dress, but please send it up, and thank you for all your help."

I'd decided to take myself on a date at the hotel bar, after this. The last thing I'd need was to have too many drinks and forget where I'd set down my brand new, trazillion dollar purse.

Meanwhile, I sincerely hoped that when Stefan did return from whatever he was out doing with his leggy brunette, the sight of all the shopping bags would give him the kind of heart palpitations I had gotten when I'd spotted him with his mistress.

I felt a little guilty about the whole thing, but then I caught a glimpse of myself in the mirror again. The dress Katharina had called *vavoom* was sleek and slinky, hitting me mid-thigh. The whole thing was held up by tiny little strings criss-crossing my back that could barely be described as straps. I chose to finish off the look with a pair of sky-high stilettos in cherry red. I was ready to have some fun.

WITH ONE OF my new cashmere wraps in hand, I headed to the restaurant bar. I loved lots of things about Europe, but the drinking age was quickly becoming a favorite. I sat down on a stool and ordered the fruitiest, most ridiculous cocktail I could find on the menu.

Above the bar, the clock read 6:45.

I ignored it.

There was absolutely no way I was going to be meeting Stefan for dinner. I purposefully put my phone away so I wouldn't even see if he called or texted. He could sit and wait in the restaurant for hours for all I cared. Let him get a taste of how it felt to be someone's last priority.

I finished my too-sweet drink and ordered another one. I was starting to feel a little buzzed, but I liked it. Besides the occasional glass of champagne at one of my father's parties or a sip of wine at dinner, I hadn't done much drinking before this trip. I'd probably already had more alcohol today than I had in my past eighteen years. Europe was wonderful.

My next drink was as ridiculous as the first and tasted just as good. The bartender gave me a crystal dish of fancy olives as well, so I munched on those while sipping my drink through its pink curly straw. I had a feeling the bartender had added that just out of whimsy—nobody else in the place had been given a straw like mine, and I figured that since I wasn't partaking in the bar's famous wine list, he was probably just amused by my choice of drink.

I smiled at him as he refilled my pretzel dish. Everyone here was so nice. Nicer than my husband, that's for sure. At least the hotel staff seemed happy I was here. Probably because I was spending a ton of money and tipping them all so generously, but hey, I would take it. The bartender was definitely going to get a huge tip. I finished my drink and ordered a third.

"I like a woman who knows how to have a good time," said an accented male voice.

I spun on the stool to find a preppy hot guy on the next seat. He was blonde and compactly built, smiling at me in a crisp patterned shirt. He gave off a vibe of wealth and confidence—like Stefan did, but more relaxed. Way less intense than my husband ever acted.

He was very handsome, very polished and outwardly friendly, but my heart didn't leap at the sight of him. My pulse didn't race. My palms didn't sweat. Still, it was nice to have some company that I hadn't technically paid for.

"Your accent is different," I said. "Everyone speaks Austrian around here. But yours is more...French. Where are you from?"

I took another sip of my drink, awaiting his answer expectantly.

"You have a good ear," he said. "I'm from Rouen. It's the capital of Normandy, in the north of France. One hundred and thirty-five kilometers from Paris."

"I only know miles," I admitted, grinning. This wasn't so hard, this whole 'making friends' in a foreign country thing. Though obviously I was spoiled by his fluency in English.

"It's about two hours, by car," he elaborated. "And how about yourself? You are clearly American."

"I'm from Springfield," I said. "It's two hundred miles south of Chicago...that's three hours, by car. Maybe four if there's traffic. Actually, there's always traffic...I'm rambling."

"May I buy you a drink?" he asked, glancing at my wedding rings.

I gestured at the glass in front of me as if to say, 'I'm good.'

"Well, perhaps we can keep each other company."

"I'm okay with that," I said, taking a healthy swallow of my cocktail.

He leaned closer. "You're very beautiful, you know."

"I'm married," I said with a smile, flashing my ring pointedly. "This is my honeymoon, actually. But thanks for the compliment."

He held up his hands defensively. "Just a friendly observation. How are you finding the city? Have you had a chance to see much of it?"

"Vienna is amazing, but...my husband has been here before, and he's not into sightseeing." I shrugged. "I want to see *everything*, but he's been busy working. I've barely even left the hotel." My mood deflated. I nursed my beverage.

"Tsk, such a shame. There is so much here to discover. And you're a woman who likes to explore. I can tell by your eyes—they dance around the room. You hunger for experience."

"That's exactly right! I really do." I found myself smiling despite my reservations.

"Surely you've at least had Sacher torte? Visited the gardens at Schönbrunn, and the Belvedere Palace? What about the Danube Tower?"

"Just the dessert so far," I admitted. "It was great—"

He gaped at me dramatically. "Mais non! This is a catastrophe!" He checked his watch and downed the rest of his drink quickly. "We must go now. The gardens and the palace are closed, but the Tower is open until midnight."

"Ha ha, I don't know..."

"Yes. Come with me. If you want to see the best view of Vienna, there is no other way."

He tried to pull me off the stool and I couldn't help but giggle. Sure, I barely knew the guy, but by this point, the third drink had really begun to kick in...and I was starting to wonder what would be so bad about engaging in a little innocent sightseeing with my new friend. Sneaking out with him would be fun, romantic, adventurous. Essentially everything my honeymoon wasn't—but should have been.

"You said it's open 'til midnight?" I asked.

"You will love this tower. I swear it."

His hand rested lightly on my arm but I still held my cocktail. I lifted it, drinking it down slowly, stalling for time. Did I want to go with him? After all, it was clear that Stefan had absolutely no intention of staying true to me, so why shouldn't I do the same? Maybe this was exactly what I needed—to find a hot European guy I'd never see again, and just get the whole virginity thing out of the way.

There was no doubt this French guy fit the bill. He was hot, if a bit cartoonish, and clearly attracted to me. I would bet all the designer clothes I'd bought that day that if I asked to skip the sightseeing and go straight to his room, he'd be more than happy to oblige.

"Why don't we have another drink?" I said. "We have plenty of time before twelve."

"But of course." He motioned to the bartender for another round, and we were quickly served.

"You know the French invented the word affair," the Frenchman said meaningfully.

"That is not strictly true in the sense that you intend it," I informed him, raising my fresh drink for emphasis. "Though the term 'afaire' originated in Old French, the connotation of it being a 'to do' of an illicit nature didn't come into popular use until the 18th century, and that was the English."

My new friend looked perplexed. "I...see."

"Though of course the English were repurposing the meaning of the French phrase 'affaire de coeur,'" I plowed on, really hitting my stride, "which at the time referred to an episode of passion—but *not* in the sexual sense. So I guess you're technically right *and* wrong."

I smiled proudly, took a loud slurp of my drink, and plunked the glass down on the bar. Four drinks in, and I could still whip out my etymology knowledge with relative ease. Not bad.

"That was...very interesting," he managed after a moment.

We talked for a bit, and I learned all about Rouen and why Paris was the most romantic city in the world. I was surprised to find that I was enjoying myself. For the first time on this trip, I was getting some real social interaction. I hadn't realized how much I'd been missing it.

Of course, this guy may have been gorgeous—with a sexy accent and no trouble expressing his interest—but he couldn't hold a candle to Stefan's rugged, masculine intensity. Or those green eyes that burned straight through me. Just thinking his name had gotten me wet.

I took in the soft light reflecting off the curves of the amber bottles behind the bar, the murmur of voices around us, and I came to a decision. If I couldn't have sex with this guy, then I might as well get totally hammered. At least it would make the evening more fun. *C'est la vie.*

I swiveled on my bar stool toward the Frenchman, intending to tell him I was happy to hang out for a bit, but that I was in no way going to be leaving with him tonight. But as I did, I spotted a familiar figure striding into the bar. It was Stefan.

As he scanned the room his eyes narrowed, his jaw clenched. I knew he would see me.

I glanced at the clock and was shocked. How was it past eight already? He'd probably been waiting for me at the restaurant this whole time. I was tempted to check my phone to see if he'd called or texted, but didn't want to give any indication that I was hoping to hear from him.

Feeling bold, and a little vindictive, I twirled my hair around my finger and turned back to the Frenchman with a winning smile on my face. "Tell me again about the Danube Tower."

"It's located in Donau Park, and as the tallest building in Austria, it offers the best—"

I tilted my head back and laughed loudly, for no other reason than Stefan's benefit. The Frenchman was clearly surprised by the abrupt reaction on my part, but it didn't slow him down. Not for a moment. Instead, he leaned back and gave me a long, flirtatious smile.

"So I take it you're excited to see the...tower?"

"Oh, yes," I said, tossing my hair aggressively. "Very excited."

My current cocktail was still about half full, so I quickly downed the rest of it, prompting a raised eyebrow from my new companion. I was definitely feeling the warm, mind-hazing effects of all the alcohol at this point, but I didn't care. In fact, I felt great. I was wearing a new dress, my skin was glowing, and my hair and makeup looked fantastic.

And the way the Frenchman was looking at me—like he would be more than happy to help me slip out of that sexy dress of mine—made me feel pretty damn good. Especially since I knew Stefan was watching.

As the Frenchman waved the waiter down and ordered

me another fruity concoction, I peered surreptitiously through my hair around the bar, zeroing in on where Stefan was still standing. His face was stormy and his fists were clenched.

My heart skipped a beat at the sight of him and I was instantly annoyed at myself. Why couldn't I just be attracted to the guy sitting right next to me? The one who'd actually shown interest? Why was it that Stefan—and only Stefan—got me all hot and bothered?

I looked back at my new friend. Our next round had magically appeared in front of us.

"Cheers," he said, raising his glass.

I did the same. "Cheers," I said. "To new friends."

The Frenchman grinned at me, that grin full of sexy promises. Promises that would never be fulfilled. I'd already decided it wasn't going to go any further. I was flirting in full view of Stefan merely to give him a taste of his own medicine. I wasn't a cheater like he was, but he wouldn't know that I had no intention of following through with this stranger.

"To new friends," the Frenchman echoed.

I winked at him.

It was a mistake.

Out of the corner of my eye, I saw Stefan barreling toward us. His expression was one of fury. My heart raced—what was he going to do?

"Victoria," he said when he reached us, his voice hard. "It appears you've lost track of time."

I could hear the barely controlled rage in his voice, though it was doubtful anyone else would have any idea just how angry he was.

The Frenchman was still smiling, though his brow had creased in confusion.

"Victoria? You know this man?" he asked, looking at me.

For a moment, I didn't know what Stefan would do. Would he tear this poor guy to shreds or simply punch him in the face?

I definitely was not expecting Stefan to reach out his hand. The Frenchman shook it, the uncertainty still evident on his face.

"I'm Tori's husband," he said, politely. "And you're leaving. So get the fuck off that barstool and step away from my wife."

Immediately, the Frenchman grew somber. "Wonderful to meet you. I wish you both a pleasant time in the city." He withdrew his grasp and fled.

Before I even had a chance to glare at Stefan, he had his hand around my arm and was yanking me out of the bar. It was hard to tell what he was angrier about—that I had missed dinner or that I had been flirting with a stranger. Either way, he was furious. More furious than I'd ever seen him before.

He towed me across the lobby and practically shoved me into the elevator, and I almost stumbled on my high heels. Being drunk didn't help, though his anger was doing a lot to sober me up quick. We were alone in the elevator when the doors closed, but Stefan wasn't even looking at me. Wasn't even facing me.

He had his back to me, and I saw him take a deep breath, his hands clenching and unclenching. It was hard to tell if he wanted to throttle me...or kiss me. Because I had seen the blazing hot passion in his eyes when he had gotten a good look at my dress.

He was angry, but he wanted me too. I felt exactly the same way.

I could almost imagine him slowly counting to ten before he let out a string of harsh, angry curse words. He didn't look at me for the rest of the ride and by the time we got to our floor, I was fairly subdued by the tense experience.

The elevator doors opened and he stalked toward our room. I hurried after him as he swiped his keycard and walked inside.

"Aren't we having dinner?" I asked. "I need to eat something."

"Then you should have been on time for our reservation," he said as he whirled to face me. "Because I already ate. At seven."

"But—" I barely got the word out before he fixed me with a stare.

"Call room service," he said. "I don't have time for this. And you'd better ask for some aspirin while you're at it. You'll need it in the morning."

Then he turned on his heel and went to the bedroom, slamming the door behind him.

I sat down on the couch, my eyes wandering around the luxurious but cold, silent room, and in that moment I felt utterly alone. What had I done?

I had thought this marriage would be my escape.

Instead, I'd traded one gilded cage for another.

TORI

CHAPTER 12

As I sat in another private jet, this time en route to Budapest, I barely registered the luxury all around me. I had a pounding headache and a sour stomach, just as hungover as Stefan had warned, and it was all I could do to keep from getting sick. Besides the aspirin I'd taken this morning, he had ordered me a ginger ale and forced me to eat some crackers when we'd first taken off—all of which had helped, but I'd learned my lesson. I was never drinking again. At least, not like I had last night.

Our in-flight lunch was ash in my mouth as I kept reliving my argument with him from the night before.

I knew that I shouldn't have provoked him. Especially since I'd never truly entertained the possibility of cheating on him with that other man—Stefan might not wish to concern himself with honoring the marriage vows we'd taken, but I wasn't a cheater. However, I was sick of being treated like an annoyance or an afterthought. No one had told me that this whole vacation would be a business trip, or that my new husband would seem to have next to zero interest in getting to know me better. Or that he'd be sleeping around with other women before we'd even consummated our marriage. If that's really what I'd seen about to happen.

While I had been sitting on the couch last night, stifling my tears and picking at the food I'd ordered to be delivered to the suite, the only thing that had made me feel better was thinking about why I was doing this. *This* meaning the marriage to Stefan.

I was doing it for myself. For my future. For my love of language.

It had helped me in that moment to remember why I loved it so much in the first place.

Too dizzy from the alcohol to be able to close my eyes, I'd spent the next few hours going over the etymology of words in my head until the floor stopped tilting and I was finally able to drop off to sleep. The word game was a trick I'd learned when I was little. On nights I couldn't sleep because my father had been out of town for too long (and he'd missed too many goodnight phone calls), I'd hide under the covers with my flashlight and his massive old dictionary. Paging through the definitions and roots, inhaling the comforting, almost-vanilla musk of its paper-thin pages. With that dictionary, I was able to look up any word I could think of—or one I'd chosen at random—and completely lose myself in its meaning. Most of the time I'd wake up with the book still sprawled beside me, not even remembering when I'd drifted off.

"How's the work going?" I asked, finally giving up and setting my fork down.

"Hmmph," Stefan grunted.

He was taking up all the seats across the aisle from me, his laptop and phone and a thick file of model portfolios spread out on all the tray tables in his row.

"Let me know if you need anything?" I said. He nodded noncommittally.

My husband hadn't spoken any full sentences to me since our argument. Instead, he'd woken me up this morning and barked out brief orders for me to pack and be prepared to leave by a certain time. Since then, nothing.

I hoped his reticence would dissipate by the time we landed.

Despite this rough patch, I was looking forward to our time in Budapest. Vienna—regardless of all my frustrations with Stefan—had been absolutely beautiful, and though I'd only gotten a glimpse of all it had to offer, I couldn't wait to explore another historic city. Even if I had to do it without my husband. At least *one* of us was going to enjoy this honeymoon.

I was determined to take advantage of this once-in-a-lifetime trip. I would just have to find a way to reconcile myself to the fact that this truly was a marriage in name only, and that Stefan had no intentions of consummating it —or letting things go any further than the confines of a transactional relationship. I still wasn't sure if he had been more upset that I'd stood him up for dinner and more or less disappeared on him, or that he had caught me flirting with a stranger. Either way, he didn't strike me as the kind of man who would allow me to seek out a lover over the duration of our marriage...even though it seemed he was fine sleeping with other women himself. I guess I shouldn't have been surprised. Rules were different for men like Stefan. Men who were rich, powerful, and intense. Men who were used to getting what they want.

Not that it mattered what kind of rules Stefan set for me. I'd already realized that when it came down to it, I didn't actually want to sleep with anyone else.

It seemed I was destined to remain a virgin for the fore-seeable future.

Budapest came into view from the plane window, and I leaned closer to take it in. I saw a spire-topped building that resembled a wedding cake, a bridge spanning a winding river, and a sprawl of boxy buildings in pastel colors. Already I could see it was a beautiful city, full of history and gorgeous architecture. It would be an exciting place to explore and learn about.

I had prepared for this trip in my typical nerdy linguist way, spending the flight scrolling through an e-book I'd downloaded on Hungarian, the official language. I'd wanted to research Hungarian words, particularly ones that had no direct English synonyms. Those were some of my favorite words in any tongue. I loved the way the specificity of other languages revealed cultural quirks or preferences, or was a necessary means of ensuring survival. For instance, the Sami people who lived in northern Scandinavia had almost two hundred totally unique words to describe all the different types of snow and ice. How amazing was that?

Elmosolyodik was one such unique word in Hungarian, with no exact English equivalent. It was also a mouthful. It meant 'to smile,' but in a very particular way. It was the act of starting to smile, but in a manner that was subtle. Similar to a smirk, I supposed, but without the smugness or conceit.

I had thought of Stefan when I first found that word. He smiled sometimes, yes, and I'd seen him laugh enough times, but there were times when I would catch him looking at me—just before he'd turn away and pretend that he hadn't been—and the expression on his face would be something that I could have sworn was the first hint of a future smile.

For some reason, it only made me want to coax him into

smiling more, even though I knew he probably wouldn't appreciate my persistence. He seemed to put a lot of effort into coming off as gruff and unfeeling, but I knew he had feelings. I knew he had desires. No one worked as hard as he did, or was as driven to take over his family's business, if he didn't have some sort of emotional reason behind it.

It wasn't just *elmosolyodik* that reminded me of Stefan. There was another Hungarian term that described our situation so perfectly that it almost hurt. *Elvágyódás* wasn't any easier to pronounce, but of course I tended to love any term with an overabundance of syllables. The word was roughly defined as 'the feeling of wanting to get away.' Not specifically the desire to travel, per se, or go anywhere in particular...just knowing, innately, that you're missing something from your current reality and that you want to escape and go find it.

The word perfectly applied to my feelings about our marriage, which was definitely missing something (beyond emotional engagement and sex) that I couldn't quite put my finger on. Because it wasn't simply that Stefan was being distant or cold or cagey. I got the sense he was acting that way purposefully: holding himself back from me, putting things between us, and for a reason. I didn't understand why, but I wished we could leave behind all the struggles we'd been having and get away. Go out into the world afresh, find what we needed to make this relationship work. I didn't want to just flee this arrangement—I wanted to take Stefan with me.

I glanced over at Stefan, wondering if some part of him was feeling *elvágyódás* too. Maybe he'd always felt that way. Maybe that was why he buried himself so deeply in his work. To get away from his life. But what if we could both get away—together?

"*Elvágyódás*," I whispered, slowly sounding it out.

"Hmm?" Stefan said, turning my way.

I smiled. "Nothing. Just looking forward to this." He nodded and went back to his work.

That was the thing about words. They never let me down. There was always a word out there that I could use to explain the way I was feeling. I just had to find it.

We descended low over the Danube before landing at the local airport. As we got closer to the ground, I could even see a funicular climbing a hill toward what looked like a historical landmark. The whole place seemed magical in a way that was similar to, but also different from, Vienna. I loved these old cities, their history and culture. I wanted to immerse myself as much as I could, especially in the language. I was looking forward to meeting our translator and being able to pick their brain about Hungarian—maybe I'd even learn a few more interesting words.

But I was immediately disappointed. Instead of being met at the gate by a tour guide and translator, it was clear that the person meeting us worked for Stefan and had been instructed to speak only to him. I was summarily ignored by everyone, unless I asked a direct question. But even if I did, they looked at Stefan first, waiting for his nod of approval before answering.

Our luggage was loaded into the town car, including the new suitcases purchased in Vienna to store all the clothing I'd bought. Stefan hadn't said a word about my purchases. Was he so wealthy that it hadn't even phased him, or was the silent treatment just punishment for that as well as last night's attempt at flirtation and jealousy?

I thought we'd head to the hotel to drop our things off, but when we got there, instead of going up to our suite,

Stefan and I were led to a conference room. I was confused and the moment we were left alone, I turned to Stefan.

"Aren't we going out?" I asked. "Seeing the city? If you have a meeting, I can go myself."

"After the stunt you pulled with that French asshole?" he practically sneered at me. "I don't think so."

"Well...so when can we go?"

He cocked an eyebrow. "Given your behavior last night, I don't think you deserve a tour of the city. We're staying here. I have things to do."

My mouth dropped open.

"You're going to exile me to the hotel again?" Frustration was bubbling inside of me.

Another day of hotel shopping and using the spa would probably be some other girl's dream, but I'd had enough of it the day before. Even though I was feeling tense enough for a massage right now, what I really wanted was to explore. To see the city. To speak the language.

"Let's drop the charade, shall we?" Stefan crossed his arms as he faced me. "We both know what this is." He gestured between us. "I tried to be nice, give you a little taste of adventure and romance, but what did I get in return? You throwing yourself at a total stranger. How was that supposed to make me feel?"

I stared. *He* felt like the injured party? How was that even possible? He was the one sleeping with other women on our honeymoon. "How...did you feel?" I asked.

"I didn't feel anything," he said gruffly. He was clearly lying.

I shook my head. "It wasn't what it looked like. I just wanted to see the city, and we were talking about all the sights, and he offered to take me out."

Stefan's expression hardened. "He was going to take you somewhere."

"It doesn't matter, because I told him I wouldn't go!"

"I had already showed you the city," he countered.

"From the inside of a town car?" I shot back. "You know that's not the same."

He shrugged. "I'm a busy man. This trip wasn't just for you. It was for me and my work as well. I thought you understood my priorities when we entered into this agreement."

He made it sound so cold, and made me sound like a mercenary who just wanted to spend all his time and money. Is that how he truly thought of me? Was this why he was acting the way he was?

I couldn't help thinking back to our kiss. That first one, the night we became engaged—when we were still virtually strangers. He hadn't seemed so aloof then. He'd seemed interested. Attracted. Excited by the idea of marrying me. Like it was a pact we were making together, each of us getting something out of it. Was every bit of it a lie?

I could still remember his lips, hot and firm against mine. The way he had held me in his arms. The way he had touched me. I wanted *that* Stefan. Wanted to know how to get that version of him to come on this honeymoon with me, instead of this cold, distant man.

But I also understood what he was saying. This was his job, the whole reason he had agreed to marry me in the first place. To gain control over his father's company. To gain control over his life. That's what I had wanted as well, hadn't I? Control over my life.

I had thought Stefan and I were on the same page about that. I had thought he could see that we were the same. That we were both ambitious and driven, that I wasn't some gold digger who just wanted to max out his AmEx and go on extravagant vacations.

But it was clear after what had happened in Vienna that he didn't trust me. And I didn't trust him. Even though he was angry at me, that still didn't explain his mysterious brunette friend and why he had disappeared with her somewhere in the hotel while we were on our honeymoon. It also didn't explain why he had gotten mad at me for flirting with a stranger.

I was so confused.

"I understand about work," I said carefully, "but do you really want me to stay in the hotel all day?" My voice sounded small and tired, even to me. "Like in Vienna?"

"I think we both know that leaving you to your own devices is a bad idea," Stefan said, his arms still crossed.

I opened my mouth to apologize, but he continued before I could say anything.

"I've decided it's best for both of us—and my checkbook —if you just stay here."

I looked down at the long, polished table and rolling leather chairs. Where exactly did he expect me to be? Was I going to just be sitting in the corner during all of his meetings?

As if he could read my mind, he led me to the door and pointed to a sitting area down the hall from the conference room. There were chairs and a sofa, potted plants and a water cooler.

"I trust you'll find a way to make yourself comfortable," he said, before pushing me into the hall and shutting the door.

I stared at the closed door for a moment, awash in indignation at the way he'd treated me, but also trying to figure out a way I could turn this situation around. There had to be a way to get back on his good side. I wanted to explore Budapest. Wanted to see the city. Not just that, either. I wanted to see it with *him*. Sure, I could probably make a dramatic escape, book a ticket on a tour bus, and go see all the sights by myself. But it wouldn't be the same. It wasn't what I wanted, and it wouldn't make me feel better.

As I took a seat outside the conference room, my temper settled a bit and I realized that maybe this wasn't the worst thing in the world. I had wanted to get to know Stefan better. What better way to do that than to observe him in his element, working and pursuing his goals?

Maybe it would be the key to understanding him. To connecting with him.

Besides, I had an e-reader full of books. It wouldn't hurt to behave myself after everything that had happened in Vienna. Clearly, we were just having trouble communicating with each other. That had to be common in any new relationship. Maybe this would help and the rest of our honeymoon would be better. We'd find a way to mix business with pleasure. If not the kind of pleasure I had in mind, then maybe the kind of pleasure we'd experienced at the beginning of our Vienna trip.

I tried to get comfortable in my chair and pulled up another one of the academic texts I'd downloaded—it explored the historical roots of the Hungarian language and I hoped that reading it would help prepare me for the kinds of books I'd be studying in my upcoming college courses.

Every few minutes, someone would cross in front of me and I'd look up to see them heading toward the far end of the hall, turning a corner and disappearing from view. It kept happening, and after a while I started paying a little more attention to who was walking by me.

They were women. All of them. All as beautiful and

statuesque as the brunette in Vienna had been, wearing a variety of hair colors and figure-flattering (and revealing) outfits. It was almost comical, this parade of gorgeous women heading down the hall.

Unable to resist, I followed one of them around the corner.

There was another waiting area over there, but it was bigger—with a lot more chairs, almost all of them occupied by these gorgeous, leggy women—and had a huge window pouring light all over their perfect bodies. They all stared at me when I walked over, their gaze indicating that they weren't sure why I was there. I clearly didn't look like any of them, and they seemed confused that I was in their midst.

I spotted a reception desk and a bored-looking man sitting behind it. I walked over to him, flashing him my most charming 'senator's daughter' smile. He barely reacted, his eyes sweeping up and down my body. His expression grew wary. He also didn't think I belonged.

"What is this?" I asked.

He frowned at me, and then said something in Hungarian that I didn't understand.

"Do you speak English?" I asked.

"No English," he replied, his accent thick.

We both stared at each other for a moment, before he sighed and handed over a clipboard with a sheet of paper attached. The whole thing was also in Hungarian, but I recognized the logo at the top of the paper. KZ Modeling. From there, it wasn't hard to figure out what the rest of it said. It was a form covered with evenly spaced text and blank lines, asking for personal information—name, age, measurements, references—the kind of thing that would be necessary for a modeling casting call.

Was that what Stefan had been doing with that

brunette in the hotel in Vienna? Had he been meeting with her to discuss a modeling contract? The realization thundered down, reframing the context of his entire day. No wonder he'd been so pissed to find me flirting up some French guy in the hotel bar, totally drunk and having stood him up for dinner. He'd been working all day, just like he had told me, and I'd repaid him with my childish behavior. I'd have to make it up to him. I wasn't sure how, but I would.

Although I felt better that Stefan hadn't been cheating on me, I was still frustrated that our entire honeymoon was actually a business trip in disguise. Why hadn't Stefan just told me that? He had said we were dropping the pretenses, but he was the one who had made this seem like it could be a romantic trip with some occasional stops for business. In reality, it was the opposite. I didn't understand why he had even brought me along in the first place. I wasn't going to spend every day of this vacation sitting in a chair outside his meetings, staring at the wall like I was a child being punished. I wanted to see the sights, explore, take advantage of these beautiful new places. I was dying to experience all that my new life had to offer.

I looked back at the models, and then walked over to the window. The view was incredible—the river, the spires of the Parliament building overlooking it, huge red basilica domes and avenues of lush trees. It was calling to me with its siren song.

I had to get the hell out of there.

TORI

CHAPTER 13

W hy not just leave?

I could walk out of the hotel, grab a taxi and take my own tour of the city. That's what I was here for, wasn't it? But I knew that if I disappeared like that, Stefan's trust in me would be irreversibly shattered. And my ultimate goal wasn't to put a wedge even further between us, it was to figure this relationship out. If I knew what he wanted, what he needed...maybe I could figure out how I fit into all of it.

Another leggy model type walked past me. I felt something like panic and anxiety rise up inside of me. Even if he hadn't been cheating on me yesterday, who was to say he wouldn't do it now? Or in the future? Like my father had said, Stefan could have his pick of any woman wanted. We might have been married on paper, but it was clear that he considered it to go no further. If I couldn't convince him to take our relationship to the next level, did I really expect him to remain celibate, just to keep up appearances?

To calm myself, I let my brain drop into its usual defense mechanism. I thought about words. Words had meaning. They had history. You could break them down and understand them. I liked that.

Model. It was a wonderful word that could be applied to so many things. Not just models like the women walking back and forth, but in the more scientific sense—it represented an object or behavior or system that aided understanding. In that case, Stefan was my model. He was something I wanted to understand. Wanted to know.

Taking out my phone, I shot him a quick text with my request.

Still a little tired from the flight. Would it be okay to go up to our room and lie down?

Voila. It was honest, polite, and asked his permission to leave my post. Hopefully he would see it for what it was: an olive branch. A way to bridge the gap that was rapidly growing between us. A gap I didn't want growing any further.

My palms were sweating as I awaited a reply.

My phone vibrated in my hand as his response came through.

Go.

That was it. One word. Was he too caught up in there to say more? Or was he still pissed?

I headed up to our room, tired and confused.

As I pushed the heavy door open, I saw a feast for the eyes. The suite was just as gorgeous as the one we'd stayed at in Vienna, though it had a completely different feel. This hotel, though ornate and historic on the outside, had a sleek, contemporary vibe inside. I stepped into the room, soaking in the calm, minimal design.

Everything was sharp clean lines and white linens. An ivory comforter and snowy white pillows covered the massive bed in the center of the room, looking just like a cloud. The carpet was plush and I kicked off my shoes to wiggle my feet in the thick pile, so soft against my aching soles. Gold geometric patterns were embossed on the wallpaper, gleaming in the light that flooded from the floor-to-ceiling windows.

Peering through the gauzy curtains, I found a balcony with cushioned chairs and a wrought iron table. I stepped out, taking in the view of the city. It was incredible, even prettier from here than from the window up on the business floor. Being able to observe it like this from the private balcony of our hotel was more than I had ever imagined.

All of this, all the luxury and excess, was something I'd never really experienced before. I'd been lucky to never want for anything, but there was a difference between my comfortable life in Springfield and the extravagant world that Stefan inhabited. My father had a driver—but Stefan flew exclusively by private jet. It wasn't even the same ballpark.

And I wanted to be a part of his world. Not because I wanted his money or his connections, either. But I craved the experiences those things could provide. Adventure. Exploration. Excitement. *That* was something I could get used to.

I didn't want to feel like I was constantly battling Stefan to get those things, though. I wanted us to enjoy it together. To find adventure together. I wanted to be the wife he dreamed of and fantasized about. If only he'd let me.

A breeze teased my hair away from my face and I closed my eyes, wishing that things were better. That they were like they had been at the opera, with Stefan holding my hand. I craved his attention. His affection. Beyond wanting sex, I had emotional needs, and getting them met was vital to me. How could I get *him* to want that too?

I imagined us out here together. It was the perfect place to have coffee in the morning, or champagne in the evening. It would be such a dream to wake up and share a quiet morning with Stefan, taking in the gorgeous view of Budapest as we drank coffee and ate pastries before starting our day. Or unwinding in the evening, with chocolate covered strawberries and cocktails. The hotel was unbelievably romantic and it hurt to know that it was just a façade. That we weren't staying there because Stefan had hoped to spend a romantic honeymoon with me, but so he could work in the executive offices available on the upper floors. And keep a close eye on me. The whole thing felt even more depressing in the face of all this beauty and romance.

My suitcases were already stacked neatly on one side of the room. I felt a twinge of guilt when I noticed how much larger my pile was compared to Stefan's modest set of matched luggage. He'd brought a few custom-made suits and enough shirts to last a week, but thanks to hotel dry cleaning he hadn't had to bring much else.

Maybe I shouldn't have bought all those clothes in Vienna.

There was a settee at the foot of the bed, and I sat down there, wiggling my toes in the thick carpet. It soothed me a little bit.

The room was quiet and cool, exactly what I needed. I had a chance to gather my thoughts, to make a plan. But first, I needed to talk to someone who knew exactly what I was going through.

Michelle picked up on the second ring.

"Tori the explorer," she teased, an old nickname from my childhood. "How is Budapest?"

No doubt both she and my father had received copies of our travel itinerary. There was something comforting in that. Even though I was married and technically not their responsibility anymore, my parents were still looking out for me. I was still their daughter.

"It's beautiful," I said truthfully. "Mostly I've only had time to see it from the window of a taxi, but there are pretty old churches everywhere. I saw shop windows full of hand embroidered tablecloths and doilies, and this gorgeous cut crystal they make here in every color of the rainbow."

"How's the food?" she asked.

"We just got here, so I haven't had a chance to find out yet," I said, purposely leaving out the part about my epic hangover that was still lingering. "But I read about these rolled up meringue pastries filled with oranges that I'm dying to try. I know this city is going to be really special."

"Better than Vienna?"

I could hear the genuine eagerness in her voice. My father's work hadn't taken him out of the country often, and for all of Michelle's homegrown southern roots, I knew she had an adventurous spirit and longed to see the world.

"Vienna was magic," I sighed. "We went to the Opera House. It was like a palace. The singers had amazing voices. Every single person in the audience was enthralled. It was wonderful."

It was nice that I didn't have to lie about that. I held on to that memory, holding it up as an example of how things could be. Of how I wanted them to be.

"Lucky, lucky girl. How is...everything else?" Michelle asked, the real question obvious.

I was silent, struggling for the right words.

"Tori?" she prompted. "You still there? Everything okay?"

"Of course!" I lied cheerfully. "It's just...all the running around. You know how it is. It's just been exhausting. In fact, I should probably go take a nap."

She let out a slow breath, and then said, "Tori, I've known you since you were two years old. You put on a hell of a happy face, but I can tell when something's bothering you. Spill it."

I paused, not sure how to explain that I still hadn't consummated my marriage. I trusted her, but the last thing I wanted was detailed advice about how to seduce my husband, especially since I knew exactly who she'd used all her tips and tricks on. The mental images of her and my father were the absolute last thing I'd need while trying to lure Stefan into bed.

But the truth was, I did need help. And I didn't have anyone else to turn to.

"Stefan's not interested in sex," I blurted out. "I mean, he is. Definitely. But not with me."

This time the long pause came from her.

"Tell me what happened," she finally said, spacing out her words carefully.

I took a deep breath, humiliated but desperate for advice. "I dressed up for him in the lingerie, just like you said, and I was ready and everything." I was babbling, the words like a breaking dam. "Not just on our wedding night in Chicago, but again in Vienna too. But he was dead asleep by the time I came to bed the first night and I don't think he even noticed the second time. He's been totally ignoring me. He says he's 'working.' He's *always* working."

"Oh, honey. You've seen what it's like at home with your father and me."

"Yeah, but...I thought it would be different with us," I admitted. "At least at first. We're newlyweds." I could barely keep the hurt out of my voice on the last sentence.

I hated this. I hated feeling like a little kid in my own marriage. Hated feeling like I didn't have any control over what was happening.

"You knew what this was going to be," Michelle reminded me. "Stefan is like your father—his work is always going to come first. You understand how it goes. And you need to respect that."

"I do," I argued, absently tugging the ends of my hair with frustration. "And I'm not trying to keep him from his work..."

"You're not?" Michelle asked, her voice gentle.

I thought for a moment. "I'm not trying to."

"I believe you," Michelle's voice held no judgment. "But even if you're not intentionally distracting him, you're not helping either. That's our job. We're supposed to make our husbands' lives easier."

I knew she was right. I had done a variation of that for my father my entire life, always putting his needs first. Somehow, I had thought it would be different with Stefan. That he would want me to be more than just a warm smile and attentive ear at the end of the day. I thought we'd have something we could share.

"You need to rethink the way you approach him," Michelle said. "The way you communicate. You can't be one more thing he has to deal with—one more thing that requires his work and attention. You have to give him what he needs, when he needs it."

"How do I even know what that is?" I asked, feeling frustrated. "He won't tell me."

"He shouldn't have to," Michelle reprimanded me. "You need to take the initiative in your relationship. Figure out exactly what he needs, and be the person who gives it to him."

Initiative. I knew what she was implying.

"I tried that," I told her. "It doesn't seem like he wants me."

"Men never know what they want," Michelle said. "They *think* they do, but sometimes they don't really know until it's right in front of them."

"I *was* right in front of him!" I argued, feeling more and more frustrated. "I was ready!"

"It's more than just dressing up in lingerie and standing there waiting," Michelle chided. "You have to act like you want him. Tell Stefan point blank that you're there for him —that you're there to fulfill his needs. Then ask him what they are."

"I guess I could try that," I conceded, feeling embarrassed. Why hadn't I thought of that?

I sat there, twisting my wedding ring around my finger, processing her words.

"He's got a lot going on, Tori. He works so hard to support his family's business, and a lot of people depend on him," Michelle continued. "You need to prove to him that you're the person *he* can depend on. You need to provide him with an escape. When he's with you, he shouldn't be worried about business deals or bank accounts or anything else. *You* are the calm in the storm. You need to give him something that no one else does."

"But what about me?" The question slipped out before I could stop it.

There was a long pause.

"You should be grateful," Michelle said. Her voice was gentle but her tone was firm. "You're getting the opportunity of a lifetime. Not just this trip and all the luxuries that come with it, but you're getting your college paid for, remember? It's what you wanted, more than anything. So that's the trade-off."

"But..." My voice cracked. "He's so different than I expected. I don't know if I can love him."

"You'll learn to love him. But god, Tori. If you want this life, you need to understand the part you play and act accordingly. The relationship will grow with time. It won't just happen overnight, but it will happen. You just need to commit to the give and take, okay? Trust me."

When she put it like that, it made sense. Stefan was giving me the opportunity I'd been dreaming of. College had always been the goal. Here he was, handing it to me in good faith, and I'd given him nothing in return except a day of frivolous spending and drunken antics at a bar. I needed to prove that I was worthy of this gift.

"He barely even talks to me," I confessed, unable to tell Michelle any of the other things that had transpired between myself and Stefan. "How am I supposed to ask him what he wants?"

I knew she'd be horrified if I told her about the temper tantrum I'd thrown in Vienna—spending tons of my new husband's money and then standing him up for dinner out of spite. And if she knew I'd dressed myself up like I had, just to get drunk and flirt with a total stranger at the hotel bar, Michelle would probably fly all the way to Budapest and give me more than just a firm talking to. And I would deserve it.

I had been acting like a spoiled brat.

"Don't ask. Just point blank say to him, 'Tell me what you need.' It works every time," Michelle told me. "If he seems standoffish, it's probably because he's resentful that you haven't consummated your relationship yet, and the longer this goes on, the worse it will be for you. So get back in the game and seduce him."

"Are you sure? I mean...I just don't understand why he hasn't made a move first," I said. "Unless he doesn't want me."

Michelle laughed, not unkindly. "Think about it, Tori. He knows how inexperienced you are. He probably thinks you're afraid of him. That's why he hasn't made the first move! You have to show him that you want him."

Even though I knew she couldn't see me, I nodded, my mind whirling. Her practical, expert advice made perfect sense, as usual. And it had given me plenty of ideas.

We got off the phone and I composed a text to Stefan:

I'm ordering dinner in from room service. Is 7 good?

He responded after a lengthy pause. *That's fine. Thank you.*

I would do exactly what Michelle had told me to do. I'd seduce him.

And I'd do it so well that he'd never look at another woman again once we were done.

TORI

CHAPTER 14

I slid on a blue dress that I'd gotten at the boutique, knowing the cool shade would bring out my eyes. It dipped so far down in the back, you could see the dimples above my ass. Like the one I'd worn to the Vienna Opera House, I couldn't wear a bra with it. I was sure Stefan wouldn't mind. The silk skimmed my body, cool and luxurious against my skin, my nipples going instantly hard from the friction. The straps were halter style—one little tug and the whole thing would pool at my feet, leaving me standing there in nothing but a black lace thong.

I paired the dress with my new black stilettos. Grace would have called them 'fuck me heels.' I had to admit, they sent the right message. My calves were taut from the steep arch of my foot, and the added height visually elongated my legs, making them look a mile long. With the power of these shoes, I could give all those models a run for their money. Maybe Stefan wouldn't even bother taking them off before he took me to bed.

In the mirror I could see my cheeks flushing as I thought

about what it would be like to have my body spread out before him, naked except for my heels, ready and willing.

Tonight was going to be the turning point. From now on, I was going to show this man exactly the kind of wife I was.

As dinner time approached, my nerves skyrocketed. The room service staff came and went, arranging a series of domed silver trays amid a romantic table setting complete with candles, white roses, and soft classical music. The whole room felt like a private restaurant, a special hideaway just for us. I couldn't wait for Stefan to see it all.

I couldn't wait for Stefan to see me.

In addition to my sexy outfit, I had spent the last two hours making myself look as appealing as possible. I styled my hair to make him want to rake his fingers through it, leaving it down in soft, shining waves that fell across my shoulders and bare back. I kept my makeup minimal but sultry—thick, thick lashes, just a hint of a smoky eye, and wet, full lips that begged to be kissed. I had even dusted my cleavage with shimmering powder, to draw his eyes to the curves there. I gave myself a final once-over I looked good. I looked really, really good.

As the clock inched toward seven, I began to get nervous. And excited. My entire body seemed to vibrate with heady anticipation. It was like my wedding night all over again.

I sat at the table, watching the candles, my foot bouncing with impatience. I wanted Stefan to get here. I wanted him to come in the door, tense and spent from his long day, and then stop dead in his tracks at the sight of me.

His gaze would go hungry and primal then, and without a word he'd drop his bag to the floor and sweep me up in his arms, those strong hands roaming all over my body. I could almost feel the heat of his lips at my neck, my chest, my collarbone. A shudder went through me. And he wouldn't stop there. He'd draw my mouth toward his and with a low groan, he'd kiss me. Hard, deep, ravenous. Needing it the same way I did.

I'd kiss him back just as hard, plunge my tongue into his mouth as he tore the silk dress from my body. Gasping for breath, we'd knock over the room service trays that had been painstakingly arranged, too reckless to care about the crash of plates, and he would lift me onto the table, spread my legs wide open and slide into me like he'd been craving it this whole time and couldn't hold back anymore. I was ready to welcome his cock inside me. I wanted him to make me come. I wanted to make *him* come.

My skin tingled, my imagination running rampant as I pictured all the ways we could bring each other pleasure. Even though I wasn't very experienced, I fully intended to dedicate myself to learning exactly what Stefan liked. What made him hot and brought him to the edge.

I was certain he knew exactly what he liked.

But seven o'clock came and went. Under the silver domes, our food was probably getting cold. It had been sitting there for a while, untouched, but even though I was starving, I refrained from eating. Frustration began to bubble up inside of me, overpowering my anticipation and desire. If Stefan arrived and the food was cold, well, that was his fault, wasn't it? The candles began to burn precariously low, and I felt just as worn down. *Where was he?*

I took out my e-reader and figured I'd just dive into some Hungarian if he was running late. But it grew closer to eight and I started to worry. Was this more punishment for the other night in Vienna? It didn't seem fair—I'd already spent most of the day waiting outside a conference room in one of the most beautiful cities in the world. Wasn't that enough punishment for my transgression?

Finally, my phone buzzed. I grabbed for it, only to find a text from Stefan that said exactly the opposite of what I had been hoping for.

Something's come up. Go ahead and eat without me. Not sure when I'll be home.

Reading his text felt like getting a punch in the gut. I wanted to hurl my phone across the room. Wanted to shove all the food off the table, break all the dishes and make a huge mess.

Of course, I didn't. Because I wasn't that kind of girl. I might have been furious and ready to throttle Stefan, but I wasn't going to trash our room in an effort to get attention. I sat at the table, watching the candles finally burn out as I decided exactly what I wanted to do.

I was alone. In Budapest.

Stefan was out there, doing god knows what, expecting that I would just stay here in the room and wait for him like a good little wife.

Why was he so sure he could control me this way? I should be out on the town right now. Dancing and partying and having a good time.

Except I didn't want to. Not really.

The only thrill I had gotten from flirting with that stranger in Vienna was when I realized that Stefan was watching me. When I knew that I had made him jealous. That was the first time I felt like I had finally gotten his attention.

That's what I needed, maybe *all* I needed from Stefan. His attention.

He should know exactly how I felt. That if all he wanted from our marriage was to be two people with separate lives, then that was fine, but he couldn't treat me like this. Either we were strangers who rarely saw each other but kept up appearances for show, or we had a relationship similar to my father and stepmother's. One that still required a modicum of respect and consideration on his part.

I debated texting Grace, but I knew she had no expertise when it came to marriage. On the other hand, she probably had something to say about a man who acted so hot and cold all the time. She'd dated a guy senior year who acted just like that.

Picking up my phone, I started typing out a text to her, but then deleted it. I tried again, deleted it again. I couldn't do it. The issue of my virginity had been embarrassing enough, even with her enthusiastic support of it, and I wasn't confident that spilling my guts to her would actually help me come to a plan of action.

The idea of spending the duration of our honeymoon locked up in big, empty hotel suites, lavish as they were, was completely unacceptable. But so far I'd let Stefan call all the shots, mostly capitulating to all his demands. Maybe it was time to take a stand.

Instead of going out and looking for revenge somewhere else (or *with* someone else). I did exactly the opposite of what he had told me to do in his text. I waited up for hours. Even though the last thing I wanted to do was eat, I picked through our cold dinner, ate some, and left the rest. I refused to let the hotel staff come and clean it up. I stayed right there on the couch in my fancy dress, my hair and makeup still done, refusing to move a muscle until he returned.

He was going to know exactly how I felt about this situation, and he was going to know tonight.

I turned on the TV for background noise and dug deep into Hungarian on my e-reader. Technically, it was the following morning when he finally showed up, but I was still furious as hell when he came into the suite after three am.

He was wearing the same suit he'd been wearing that morning and it looked as annoyingly pristine as it had when he left. In fact, he still looked way too good for someone who had been out all night.

I hadn't looked in a mirror, but I wouldn't have been surprised if my hair was limp against my shoulders and my eyeliner had bled by the time he sauntered into the hotel room.

I tossed aside my reading, stood up, and lifted my chin.

"Did you have a good time?" I asked, keeping my voice even.

"What are you doing up?" he asked. "I told you not to wait up."

He walked right past me, not even sparing me, or my gorgeous dress and sexy heels, a second glance. Somehow, that made me even more furious. I might have been sitting around for the past several hours, my dress might have been wrinkled, my hair might have gone flat, but I still looked pretty fucking good and I'd put in all that effort solely for his benefit.

"We need to talk," I told him, following him into the bedroom.

"I'm tired," he said, shrugging off his coat. "It can wait."

I didn't want to stare, but I couldn't help it. Even in just his starched white button up, he was staggeringly attractive. His shoulders broad, his hips narrow, his body perfectly muscled. I forced my eyes away, hating that my attraction to him was waylaying my anger.

"It can't wait," I said, trying to focus as he began unbuttoning his shirt. "There are things we need to discuss."

"Not now," he said, turning his back to me. "I said I'm tired."

"Well, I'm *not*," I seethed, raising my voice.

Because I wasn't tired at all. I was amped up. Exhilarated. Ready for a fight.

"I've been waiting over seven hours for you to come home," I told him, my voice turning icy. "We had dinner plans."

"*You* had dinner plans," Stefan corrected me. "And I told you to go ahead without me."

"You agreed to those plans before you stepped out on me," I said. "And this is our *honeymoon*."

He turned to face me, revealing an expanse of his toned, perfect torso. I didn't want to, but I stared. His chest was just...so unbearably sexy. All that smooth skin, taut over pecs and abs so tight I could have bounced quarters off of them. I wanted to burn a trail of kisses down his chest, follow the trail of dark hair from just below his belly button to where it disappeared into the front his pants.

My attraction to him—throbbing palpably between my legs and burning me from the inside—just fueled my anger even further. I was furious that he could make me this hot even when I was so pissed off. I wanted him so bad that my body nearly vibrated from the intensity of it all.

"You know I have a lot going on right now," Stefan told me. "I was *working*."

We'd had this conversation before, but I wasn't going to let it end the same way.

"I understand that," I shot back, forcing myself to speak as calmly and rationally as possible, just like my father had taught me to do in an argument. "But you having a job to do isn't the point. It's not even that you're a workaholic—fine, I get that. It's that time and time again you've left me sitting around completely alone, with no consideration whatsoever, and that even if this marriage *was* arranged, I was led to believe—*you* led me to believe—that we'd at least treat each other with basic human decency."

I took a deep breath, searching his eyes. Had I gotten through to him?

"It sounds like you need to lower your expectations, then," he finally sneered. "It's not my fault your feelings got hurt because I have other things in my life that are more important than you."

I stepped back, his words like a slap. Why did he have to be so mean?

"I know my place," I told him, not bothering to keep the edge out of my voice any longer. "I know I'm not a priority to you. I also know that I deserve better than this."

"You deserve better than this?" Stefan waved his hand, gesturing at our beautiful room.

I flushed, angry that he kept twisting my words and throwing them back at me.

"Why can't you ever tell me what you're doing, or where you're going?" I cried. "You keep everything from me, running around god-knows-where with people I've never even met, and meanwhile I'm stuck in a hotel where you expect me to wait for you all day."

His eyes were cold, that impenetrable green, but something in them seemed to waver. Just as quickly as I noticed it, though, it was gone.

"I'll have my assistant forward you my itinerary, then," he said with a wave of his hand. "Are we done now?"

"That's not good enough."

"Victoria Lindsey, you are so much more work than I

anticipated. And I am fucking exhausted," Stefan said, shrugging off his shirt completely and tossing it onto a chair.

"I'm your wife," I reminded him.

"This is a marriage of convenience," he told me. "And none of this is convenient for me."

I couldn't believe his cruelty. His outright dismissal of me and my feelings.

"None of this is convenient for me either," I spat back at him.

"Why don't you just go out and buy something with my money?" he said, glaring at me. "That seems to be the best way to shut you up."

"Why don't *you* decide what you actually want?" I said. "Because I'm pretty sure you have no fucking idea what that is."

He stalked toward me, his eyes intense on mine. "I always know what I want."

He was so intimidating up close that my mind nearly went blank. Not only was he staring at me, his gaze unblinking, but his naked chest was inches from me, his entire body radiating heat and strength and power. It was hard to say if I was more angry at him or aroused.

"You never know what you want," I told him. "Not when it comes to me." Michelle's words came echoing back to me then, and I took a deep breath. "Tell me what you need."

He narrowed his eyes. "I need to live my life, and so do you. Getting in too deep won't benefit either of us. When this is all said and done and we go our separate ways, we can have a clean break—but only if we have boundaries. And this is one of them."

I shook my head. "You act like you know what you're doing, and you think you have it all figured out, but the truth is you're just as mixed up as I am. Neither of us knows what this marriage is supposed to be."

"I know *exactly* what this marriage is supposed to be," he said, but he didn't move. "You're the one who seems confused."

But I wasn't confused, or delusional. I saw his eyes rake down my body and back up again, right then and there, proving my point. This was infuriating.

I lifted my chin, ready to fight.

"Bullshit. You're hot and cold," I accused him. "One minute you're holding my hand on a ferris wheel in Vienna, the next you're parading some brunette across the lobby of our hotel. You take me to the opera one night, and lock me up in our room another. I think you want me, and I think you hate it. In fact, I *know* you do."

"And what makes you so sure?" he asked, his voice low and tense.

I closed my eyes, just for a moment.

"I saw you watching me," I answered. "When I was in the shower. And I could see that you..." For the first time I faltered. "I saw your..."

"My cock?" he asked, his voice cruel. He laughed. "Don't fool yourself, little kitty cat. I would have gotten hard watching any woman finger fuck herself."

He turned, as if to dismiss me, but I grabbed his arm, stopping him. His bare skin was hot beneath my palm.

"Don't," he warned.

"You want me," I taunted him. "You want to put your hands on me." I looked him straight in the eye. "Do it."

For a moment, I thought he would shake my hand off and walk away. Instead, his eyes flashed hot and before I could blink, his hands were hard and rough against my hips, his fingers gripping the flesh there. Holding me in place. My heart was hammering in my chest.

Immediately, I regretted pushing him. I opened my mouth—intending to apologize—but he kissed me before I could say a word.

He kissed me hard.

It was completely different from the few kisses we'd shared before. Those had been tentative, careful, measured. He had been assertive, yes, and I had been incredibly turned on, but this was nothing like those kisses. This was reckless and hot and intense.

As Stefan thrust his tongue into my mouth, one hand slid up to fist my hair, holding me in place. It hurt just enough to send a tingling shock from my head down to my toes. I opened my mouth wider and he fucked my mouth with his tongue, making me so wet I could feel it.

He was greedy with his kiss, taking everything he wanted.

I loved it. I loved every moment of it.

I kissed him back, meeting him thrust for thrust as our tongues parried, his free hand grabbing the curves of my body with a hungry roughness. I could feel the hard outline of his cock, and the slide of silk against my aching nipples made me dizzy as I arched against his chest.

I wanted more.

Instead, Stefan released me so abruptly that I stumbled back.

"There," he said, his chest heaving, his eyes angry. "You've been kissed. I hope you're satisfied."

Before I could respond, he turned and disappeared into the bedroom.

He may as well have slammed the door in my face.

TORI

CHAPTER 15

The one serious piece of dating advice that Grace had impressed upon me time and time again during high school was that the only way to know for sure that your feelings for someone were real—and not just a passing crush, or a fit of lust-at-first-sight—was to kiss them. The kiss would tell you everything.

If she was right, then I was in deep trouble.

Glancing in the mirror as I brushed my teeth the next morning, I could see how swollen my lips still were. My mouth felt like a bruise, still tender from the intense, unrelenting kiss I'd shared with Stefan. It was a kiss I had spent most of the night alternately cursing and craving.

He was the first thing I'd thought of when I had opened my eyes that morning. I hated myself for wanting him as badly as I did. I hated the way his touch, rough and self-assured and just barely under control, had gotten me so hot. I hated that even though I was furious at him, I still wanted him to carry me off to bed and torment my entire body, the same way he had tormented my mouth. But the worst part was, it wasn't just lust. That kiss had hit me like a lightning bolt. I realized I had developed real, undeniable, honest-to-god feelings for him.

It was time to send Grace an international cry for help.

We might have had a pretty surface-level friendship, but even though our hangouts had been solely for the purpose of studying, she'd always treated me the same as all her other friends—despite the fact that my father's rules and curfews kept me from joining them when they'd hang out. And come Monday morning at school, Grace would catch me up on all their antics: at the movies in the city, or with hot guys at the mall, or while joyriding around Springfield in Grace's cute little Bentley. She'd always acted like I was part of the group. She was the kind of girl who treated everyone like her best friend.

Budapest was seven hours ahead of Chicago, so that meant it was around 1:30 am for Grace. Knowing what her weekend schedule usually looked like, I would bet that she was still wide awake.

Even though Stefan was working in the next room, I glanced around the room just to be sure there was nobody around before I picked up my phone and started to type.

Hypothetical question: I texted. *Let's say there's this girl. Who really wants to sleep with this guy. And she knows it should have already happened by now, but it hasn't. And she doesn't have a lot of experience with that kind of thing yet.*

MM-HMMM, she texted back almost immediately, adding an emoji with a suggestive expression. *Do go on...*

So they've fooled around a few times, I wrote, trying to organize my thoughts. *But.*

I'd felt how hard his cock was through his pants last night. There was something about Stefan that made me feel desperate, hungry for him—but I clearly wasn't alone in this desire. He'd been just as turned on as I was.

Even though it's -obvious- that he wants her badly and chemistry isn't the problem, I concluded my text, *they still haven't gone all the way yet.*

Grace wrote back, *Yes yes, and your question is? Hypothetically speaking?*

I felt my face go hot as I typed, *Why does he keep stopping right as it starts to get good?*

I waited for her response, getting nothing, and was relieved when I could finally see the dots popping up that meant she was tapping out her reply.

Did this girl call him her ex's name by mistake? Bc if so, I've been there. Mega turn-off.

This girl has no exes, I replied.

Did this girl maybe start crying or otherwise get very emotional in the middle of things? Known to be a common killer of boners.

I'd been emotional, yes, but he'd kissed me despite my anger, not been turned off by it. And was I crying? Nope. I typed back, *That wasn't it.*

I watched Grace's ellipses appear and then stop and then come back again. Finally, a long text popped up on my screen. It was a whole paragraph.

To be honest, Tori, and this is just hypothetical of course, I'm guessing that this boy...who might have initially been attracted to this girl partly *because* of her inexperience...is having some cold feet when it comes down to actually doing the deed.

I nodded as I read along.

It continued, *BUT in my opinion, and experience, I have to honestly say— it will get better. I saw the way he looked at you at the wedding, and that man had eyes for no one else. If he's acting like he wants you it's because he DOES. And if the sex hasn't happened yet, it's probably*

*because he's all torn up about how virginal you are and is
afraid he'll ruin your first time. I know this all sounds crazy,
but don't be afraid to push his buttons. Sometimes men need
a little extra persuading to get the job done.*

Everything she was saying made perfect sense. Relief
was starting to wash over me.

PS! A fresh text had popped up. *Make sure he knows
how EXCITED you are for him to storm the castle*—here she
inserted a winking-faced emoji—*I mean, make sure this girl
knows to make sure that this boy knows that this girl is
waiting for him to...etc, you get the point.*

I sent back a *thank you!!!* and three emoji hearts, and
then put my phone down. I felt a lot better already.

I dialed down to room service and asked them to bring
me up a tray of coffee, fruit, and a selection of local pastries,
and then climbed back into the cloud-like bed to mull things
over.

Grace had to be right. Despite what Stefan had said
about setting boundaries so that neither of us got hurt when
we separated, I was willing to face those consequences and I
didn't see any reason why two consenting adults who were
crazily attracted to each other shouldn't take their relationship to the next level. Even if it was solely a marriage of
convenience, both of us walking around going mad with lust
for the next few years (years!) wasn't very convenient, was
it? In fact, I'd imagine that this kind of intense horniness
would make it very difficult for Stefan to concentrate on the
work that mattered so much to him. It was hard enough for
me to concentrate, and I was pretty much on vacation until
the fall semester.

I wondered what Michelle would have thought of
Stefan's behavior last night. Surely, she wouldn't chide me
for not trying hard enough to seduce him, though she prob-

ably wouldn't have approved of me yelling at him. At least, he had kissed me. Maybe that was the trick…getting him angry enough that he would lose control. My lips curved up in a wicked smile.

The thought was tempting.

Because Stefan, while extremely sexy all of the time, was unbearably hot when he was mad. The intensity in his eyes had practically caused my thong to burst into flames. He had approached me like a predator stalking its prey. And I had liked it.

I wanted more. I wanted to push him to the edge. Wanted to make him so mad that he wouldn't have any choice but to rip my clothes off and punish me.

Just the thought of it made me shiver.

This wasn't like me at all. Previously, when I had thought about sex and the men I wanted, I had always fantasized about someone who was sweet and kind. Someone who went slow—someone who took their time.

Now, all I wanted was Stefan. And whatever he'd expect in the bedroom, I'd be happy to give him. I had a pretty good idea of what I'd be getting, too. It would be hard, rough, and hot.

My phone buzzed.

I picked it up, expecting another text from Grace.

It was an email. From Stefan.

Sitting up, I opened it, my pulse quickening. He was literally in the next room—why was he sending an email? What could be so official, or so long-winded, that he couldn't write a text?

The subject was 'As requested,' but there was no text in the body of the email, just a document attached. I quickly downloaded it to find that he had sent me an itinerary. His itinerary for the entire day—*6:00 breakfast, 7:00 phone meeting with Cartier reps, 8:oo conference call with KZM associates in ...*

I skimmed down and my eyes caught on my own name: *Tori- sightseeing*. Blocked out between mid-morning and the afternoon, in black and white, was time set aside to go sightseeing. With me.

My heart gave a little flip.

It wasn't romantic by any traditional means, but I was touched nonetheless. Because while I had been ranting and upset last night, he had clearly been listening. And then he had done something about it.

Maybe the kiss had affected him in more ways than one.

I couldn't help smiling. I was going to get a chance to see Budapest and finally spend some quality time with my new husband. Maybe we'd actually get to know each other better, and in doing so, find a better way to communicate.

The door to the bedroom opened and I leapt to my feet, wishing I'd gotten dressed and wasn't still lying around in my pajamas. I did my best to smooth my hair down as Stefan came in, looking impeccable as usual in his suit. I tried not to drool at how good he looked, though I also wondered: Was he going to wear this sightseeing? If so, I could certainly take the Rock Church, which located inside an actual underground cave system, off my to-do list.

Just once, I wanted to see Stefan relaxed and casual. This whole 24/7 businessman thing was making it impossible for me to get to know him better. It wasn't just the perfectly tailored suit that made it difficult—it was the tense expression he always seemed to pair with it.

Did the man ever smile?

I offered my own as he came into the room, but he barely glanced at me—as if he hadn't sent the itinerary just moments ago, as if he hadn't made a point to add time for us to sightsee together.

I didn't understand. It was exactly what I had accused him of last night—he was hot and then he was cold. What did he want from me? Despite Grace's reassurances, I was getting nothing from Stefan but either sexy, soul-searing kisses, or a cold shoulder and total lack of interest. Was this normal behavior for new relationships?

"You look nice," I said, wanting to keep the peace.

He didn't say anything, his attention focused on his phone.

"A little formal though," I teased.

Nothing.

I was starting to feel that everything with Stefan was one step forward and two steps back. Would I ever know where I stood with my husband on a day to day basis? Would I ever know what he wanted from me?

"I just ordered up breakfast, but I'll get ready after that," I told him. "Are you going t—"

Before I could finish, there was a knock at the door. Stefan lifted his head lazily, as if he'd been expecting the intrusion. He headed toward the front of the suite, while I followed behind him, wrapping myself with a robe.

"Is that my room service?" I asked.

He opened the door, his body blocking whoever was on the other side.

"*Pree-vyet,*" a woman's voice rang out, her tone cheerful and warm.

"Pree-vyet," Stefan echoed, before stepping back enough for the woman to come into view. "Thank you for coming."

But before I could get a good look at her face, she was

kissing Stefan. First on one cheek and then on the other. All I could see was a thick curtain of shining black hair.

"Yak spravy?" she asked, stepping into the room.

Her face was still turned away from me, focused on Stefan, but I could see that her body was pretty spectacular. Much like the woman I'd seen with Stefan in Vienna, and all the girls at the casting call yesterday, she was tall and slim, with a narrow waist and full breasts. I tightened my grip on the robe, feeling self-conscious.

I had no idea what she and Stefan were saying. I was pretty sure she was speaking Ukrainian, but I didn't understand any of the rapid, guttural phrases. Meanwhile, Stefan seemed fairly fluent. The information both surprised and impressed me. It was pretty hot that he knew multiple languages.

I cleared my throat, unsure if she realized I was standing there.

Immediately, the woman swung around to face me. There was an enormous smile on her gorgeous face.

Before I could really react to her beauty, though, she had pulled me into her arms and was kissing me exactly as she had kissed Stefan, with a kiss on each cheek. To make matters even worse, she smelled just as good as she looked. Like some exotic, expensive perfume made of roses and sex appeal.

I wanted to hate her, but I couldn't help but smile back. It was the first time someone had really smiled at me since we arrived in Budapest. A real smile, that is, not the perfectly polite, slightly distant smiles I got from the hotel staff.

She was also vaguely familiar and as I stared at her, I realized that I'd seen her in the ads of magazines. She had to be a KZ model.

She started chattering to me, but I had no idea what she was saying.

"I'm sorry," I said. "I don't speak the language."

"Oh, of course!" she said, with a laugh and only a slight accent. "Stefan mentioned that you were a, how you to say it, a scholar of languages? I shouldn't have assumed."

I nodded. "Linguistics is all about languages, yes. But I've mostly studied the roots of words, and their histories. I'd love to speak more languages, but so far I've only taken Latin."

"But that is wonderful," she said, still smiling warmly. "Stefan has chosen a smart girl."

I didn't know how to feel. On one hand, I was extremely embarrassed that Stefan had told this beautiful creature that I was "a scholar of languages" only to have me stare blankly at her when she tried to converse with me. On the other hand, this meant that Stefan had told her about me. And not only that, but he clearly also knew exactly what I was planning on studying.

I shot him a look, but he was back to typing on his phone. Of course.

One step forward. Two steps back.

"You're Victoria, yes?" the beautiful woman asked me. "I am Oksana."

"Nice to meet you," I said, still confused as to why she was in our suite so early in the morning. I'd seen Stefan's schedule—there wasn't anything about a model meeting at this time.

My confusion must have shown on my face, because Oksana's smile slipped as she looked between me and Stefan.

"I am here for you," she told me, a wrinkle appearing between her perfect brows.

I turned to look at Stefan. "I don't understand."

"She's your babysitter for the day," Stefan told me, a little smirk appearing on his face.

I wanted to smack that smirk off his lips. Or kiss it off. I couldn't decide between the two at the moment.

"I don't need a babysitter," I told him.

"I'll be back late," he told Oksana, completely ignoring me.

Wait. He wasn't even coming sightseeing with me? Was that blocked-out section of his itinerary just for me?

But before I could say anything, he was heading out. I wanted to grab him, tug him back into our room, finish what we started last night—but I was barely dressed and in no state to go running after him. Instead, I had to watch him leave, the door slamming behind him.

When I turned back, Oksana was wearing that same big smile on her face, her hands clasped together.

"What should we do today?" she asked. "Stefan to take you wherever you'd like."

I studied her, the wheels in my head turning. "What is it that you said to Stefan when you first arrived?" I asked. "Pree-vyet?"

"Oh, you'd like to learn Ukrainian? *Duzhe dobrey.*" She winked at me. "That means 'very good.'"

"And pree-vyet—is that hello?" I prompted.

"Yes," she confirmed.

I was confused. That wasn't the first thing she'd said to me. "Then what does dobrey-dyen mean?"

There was a pause. "That also means hello," she said. "Just...more formal."

I understood. She had greeted Stefan with the more familiar form of 'hello,' which meant they were informal. Friendly.

I felt a twinge of jealousy. How friendly were they, exactly?

"The rest of it was just me asking how he was," Oksana said with a wave of her hand. "He told me he was doing well, just very busy."

I nodded, but I was only half paying attention.

"Why don't you get dressed?" Oksana said, clapping happily. "I will love to show you my beautiful city."

It was an offer I would have appreciated the day before, but now I was mostly just annoyed. With Stefan. Again.

"I don't need a babysitter, you know," I said, my tone more bitter than I intended.

Oksana's smile faltered, as if she didn't quite know how to respond.

"Stefan would like me to spend the day with you," she finally said. "He's a good man. He cares very much for you."

"I'm not so sure about that." It was hard to believe that Stefan cared about anyone other than himself. But clearly my derision wasn't acceptable, as Oksana shook her head passionately.

"No, no, no," she said. "He is a *very* good man. A very good boss. It is my great joy to give him...how do you say...favors?"

I stared at her, hoping that this was just another example of the language barrier. That when she said 'favors' she didn't mean the carnal kind.

Oksana put her hand on her chest, over her heart. "I owe him a debt," she said.

This surprised me. What exactly did she owe him? Money? Or something more intangible? How did a man like Stefan, so cold and distant, earn the devotion of someone as beautiful—and seemingly nice—as Oksana? It only made me want to understand Stefan better.

So even though I felt bitterly jealous over the idea of spending the day with a woman who felt great joy in giving my husband 'favors,' I also had a feeling that I would get more information about Stefan from her than from the man himself. Maybe I should just look at this day as a fact-finding mission.

Besides, Oksana was so friendly, surely it wouldn't be that hard to get information out of her. With that goal in mind, I pushed aside my frustration and discomfort. Quickly, I showered and got dressed, prepared to spend the rest of the day grilling her for details about my extremely private, extremely closed-off husband.

We took advantage of the room service breakfast I had already ordered and then headed out. At first, I was so in awe of the buildings and the charming, old-world vibe of the neighborhoods that I forgot my initial plan and just enjoyed myself as Oksana drove me around the city.

It wasn't that much different from my first round of sightseeing in Vienna. We drove past castles and museums, all ornate and exquisite. Oksana explained what each one was and gave me any information she could recall about their history or what they were currently used for, and then she showed me Castle Hill, where the famous Buda Castle sat, housing some of the city's most respected museums, like the National Gallery and the Budapest History Museum.

I wished we had more time and could visit all of the attractions we passed, but Oksana assured me that she was giving me a comprehensive overview of the best Budapest had to offer.

"Besides, we don't want to be stuck inside on a day like this," she pointed out.

She wasn't wrong. The weather was absolutely perfect, warm enough to roll up my sleeves but with enough clouds to offer intermittent shade, and after being cooped up in a hotel the past few days I had to admit it was nice to get out and drive around. We had the windows down and the whole city seemed to greet us as we passed.

After a while, we decided to park the car and began to explore. I was glad I had worn comfortable shoes as we trekked up and down the city's narrow, cobblestone streets. We walked past Parliament, where Oksana told me the crown jewels were kept. We passed the cupola that would take visitors up to St. Stephen's Basilica, a famous cathedral. My favorite, however, was the Fisherman's Bastion, a castle-like construction of white stone defense walls built by the fisherman's guild in the Middle Ages. With its turret and crenelated battlements, it looked like something from a fairytale.

"Do you like my city?" Oksana asked as we walked along the Danube. "It is called the Paris of the East, you know."

I could see why it was called that. I could've spent weeks there, just taking everything in.

Instead, as we stopped for lunch, I knew I had to focus on my other type of exploring. Exploring what made Stefan tick.

We sat down at a charming café, where Oksana switched to rapid Hungarian to speak to the staff, who took our menus before I even had a chance to look at them—not that I would have been able to read the names of the dishes anyway.

"I ordered for us," Oksana said. "I hope you don't mind."

I shook my head. "Not at all. I'm grateful to have you here to show me everything."

I might have been laying it on a little thick, but she seemed more than happy to receive the praise.

"So...have you been working for KZ Modeling for a long time?" I asked casually as we waited for our food to arrive.

"Yes. A very long time," she said.

So she was one of KZM's talents. That made sense. What didn't make sense was that this extremely beautiful and seemingly in-demand model was spending her day shuttling me around Budapest.

"Do you live here in Budapest?" I asked her.

"Not anymore," she said, looking down at the table. "I am mostly in New York or Los Angeles. But I was here for work. Very lucky for you, yes?"

I nodded. "Very lucky."

Even though she was still smiling, I noticed the more questions I asked, the less likely she was to make eye contact. I didn't like it. She was hiding something.

"Stefan tells me so little about his work," I said, adding a flippant little laugh at the end of my sentence. "It must be a very glamorous job to spend all day long with models."

Oksana shrugged. "Stefan is a good man," she said.

That was one thing she kept saying. Obviously, there was some sort of connection between her and Stefan. I just couldn't figure out what it was.

"He must be a very good boss as well," I tried.

Oksana nodded vigorously. "Very good," she said. "He always knows the best clubs and restaurants to go to. Last night we—"

"Last night?" I echoed, incredulous.

She immediately shut her mouth, looking anxious.

I was furious. Had Stefan been with Oksana last night? Is that why he had blown off the dinner I had arranged for us? To be with this model—his mistress?

I narrowed my eyes at her. Who was this woman? She'd been so nice to me all day...was it just out of guilt because she was sleeping with my husband? Or did I have it all wrong?

Before I could figure out how to best confront her, however, our food arrived. I'd never seen a model so happy to eat before. I did my best to eat as well, but I was too upset to enjoy it. We finished lunch in silence. As we were getting ready to go, my phone rang.

It was Stefan.

Annoyingly, my heart gave a little lurch. Even though I was pissed at him, I was still happy that he was calling. Not that I was going to let him know that.

I answered, fully prepared to say that I didn't appreciate him sending me out sightseeing with one of his mistresses and that I was done being treated this way. But before I even finished saying hello, Stefan's low, deep voice came over the line.

"Tori, I'm so sorry to tell you this. It's your father. He's had a heart attack."

TORI

CHAPTER 16

We pulled up in front of the hotel, but I just sat there, paralyzed. I barely remembered leaving the restaurant. The whole thing was a blur.

"Tori?"

I glanced up at Oksana. "I don't know what to do."

She gently unbuckled my seatbelt for me and helped me out of the car. I was only vaguely aware of her as we walked across the lobby and into the elevator.

Stefan's words still echoed in my ear. *Your father...he's had a heart attack.*

The words sounded so malevolent. And Stefan hadn't had any further information to give me yet. How bad was it? Was my dad dying right now?

He wasn't a young man, but he'd always been good about his health. He exercised, he ate mostly healthy meals (when he wasn't working through his lunches), and besides the high levels of stress inherent to his job, he took care of himself. A heart attack just...seemed impossible.

The door to our suite was open when we reached it. Hotel staff were moving around quickly, carrying things and speaking quietly to each other in rapid Hungarian. When I stepped inside, everyone stopped for a moment, their expressions frozen in sympathy.

I walked by them, my entire body numb.

Stefan was directing the staff but he, too, paused when he saw me. I didn't know what I'd expected, but it wasn't the gentleness in his eyes.

"Did they call again?" I asked. "Tell me what's going on. Is he—?"

"He's alive. He's still unstable, but they think he's going to be okay. They're keeping him in the hospital for monitoring over the next few days, just until he stabilizes."

All the air went out of my lungs. I sank onto the couch with relief, my legs gone to jelly. He was alive. He was going to be okay. I could have used a stiff drink, but it was obvious with the frenzy of activity in the room that Stefan was getting my things packed and ready to go.

"When am I flying back to Chicago?" I asked, hoping it was as soon as possible.

"We're scheduled to take off in an hour," he said.

"*We?*"

He looked at me, his expression softening just a little.

"I'm not letting you go through this alone," he said. "We'll leave for the airport as soon as this is done." He gestured at the packing going on around us.

I was shocked. The last thing I had expected was for Stefan to cut his business trip short to fly back to Illinois with me. This was a marriage in name only, after all.

"Thank you," I managed. I was still numb.

It wasn't until we were in the elevator that I realized Oksana was gone. I hadn't even gotten a chance to say goodbye.

Even though I didn't completely trust her and I was still

unsure about the nature of her relationship with Stefan, she had been kind to me. The thought of flying back to the United States with my husband—who was probably going to be working on his phone or laptop the whole time as I fretted about my father—was nearly unbearable.

I only felt worse when we arrived at the airport and I discovered that we weren't the only people on the private jet this time: Our return flight was full of KZ models.

IF I COULD HAVE PARACHUTED out of the hatch, I would have. With all the drinking, loud music, and high spirits, it was obvious that the models thought of the jet as more of their own personal party bus than a method of conveyance. Everyone was having a good time except for me. What a perfect ending to the honeymoon from hell.

I sat there, overwhelmed with worry for my father and, thanks to the women currently whooping it up, anger toward Stefan. To think, I had been grateful that he had dropped everything to come home with me. It seemed like he was just using the journey as an excuse to wine and dine his agency's most beautiful models as we headed back to the States.

It would have been better if he'd just stayed in Budapest and let me come home on my own. I would have gladly taken flying coach, in a middle seat, right by the bathroom, over watching a bunch of gorgeous women drink champagne and flirt with my husband.

In fact, I'd never seen Stefan so animated and charismatic—except for the first time I met him. When he had turned on the charm in order to get me to agree to the arranged marriage. I should have known it was a ruse.

Nobody is that dreamy in real life. As he teased and joked with the models, I could tell they were eating it up.

No wonder someone like Oksana was so enamored with him. It was hard not to be when he was like this. Even when he was being an asshole, I still found him charming and irresistible. Like now, for example. I had a hard time looking away as he smiled and refilled champagne glasses. The whole thing was surreal.

My chest felt tight. I didn't even bother to excuse myself. I unbuckled my seatbelt and headed to the back of the plane, where there was a private bedroom. Thankfully it was empty.

Curling up on the bed, I closed my eyes and let out a sob. The weight of everything I'd been through that day was crashing down around me as I thought about my father, weak and scared in his hospital bed, and Michelle, who was probably at his side, and how much I wanted to be there with them right now.

This flight couldn't go fast enough.

Just as I thought I had finally run out of tears, I heard the door open. Immediately, I rolled onto my side and raised my hands to cover my face. Whoever had stumbled into the bedroom didn't need to know I was back here, crying by myself.

I waited for them to leave, but when I heard the door close, it was followed by the sound of footsteps coming toward the bed. And then I smelled Stefan's familiar cologne.

I didn't understand what he was doing until the bed shifted under his weight. I felt him lie down behind me, his arms coming around to spoon me. He was warm and strong, his body strong and reassuring as it pressed up against mine.

Unable to help myself, I let out another shuddering sob.

It felt so good to be held, and when I turned in Stefan's arms, he looked into my eyes and gently pulled the hair out of my face.

"It will be okay," he said. "We'll be there soon."

As I let the tears flow, he stroked my hair and my back, his voice soft and gentle, assuring me that everything was going to be fine.

"Your father is a strong man," he said. "He will recover."

I clutched his shirt, not caring that I might be wrinkling it. Stefan didn't seem to care either, gathering me tighter against his chest as he soothed me. For the first time since we had gotten married, I felt cared for. I felt supported. I felt *seen*.

I cried until I didn't have any more tears left, Stefan holding me the entire time. As I drifted off to sleep in his arms, completely drained but feeling somehow lighter, I wondered if my heartless husband was really as heartless as he seemed.

TORI

CHAPTER 17

I'd been back in Springfield for a month. My dad was out of the hospital now and adjusting to life with a pacemaker. He had been ordered to take things easy, but it had taken both me and Michelle working around the clock to keep him from overexerting himself. Finally, his doctor had relented and allowed him to go back to work.

It was a relief for all of us to see him back on his feet and raring to go. The last month had been hard on all of us—getting my father to cut back on his workload and his drinking had been the hardest—but we'd all settled into a new, more reasonable routine.

Now it was time for me to head back to Chicago. To start school. To join Stefan in what would be our new home.

It was strange. Even though Stefan and I had texted occasionally during my father's convalescence, our relationship felt more harmonious now that we were apart, much like it had been during our engagement. He was warm toward me, caring, solicitous about my father's health. But all along, I wondered what would happen when we were together in person again. I couldn't let go of the memory of him watching me touch myself in the shower and that searing kiss we'd shared in Budapest. Would things be different now?

I was eager to find out, but nervous to see him again.

I hoped he'd be the kind, caring Stefan who had held me during the flight back to the States, whispering calming words into my ear. But I knew he could just as easily revert back into the controlling workaholic who had made me stay in our hotel room, who sent me out with a babysitter during our honeymoon.

I knew I'd be distracted by school, and he'd be focused on work, but what would our marriage look like once we were in the same city again? Once we were living together? Would we even share a bedroom? Or would it be like living with a stranger? Someone who at times seemed hell bent on ignoring me?

I was eager to head to Chicago, though. Not just to see how things would change—or not change—in regard to my marriage, but because I would finally be starting school. It was the whole reason I had entered into this arrangement in the first place, and I was more than eager to meet my professors and fellow students.

It would also be nice to get out of my father's house. After all, that was the other main reason I'd agreed to this marriage—to gain my independence. After a month of essentially waiting on him hand and foot, I was ready to focus on myself, on my marriage and my education.

"Are you ready?" Michelle stood in the doorway of my bedroom as I finished packing the last of my stuff.

"I think so," I said, looking around my mostly empty room.

The majority of my belongings had been shipped to

Stefan's place in Chicago after the wedding. If everything had gone according to schedule, we would have returned there after the honeymoon, but my father's illness had thrown a wrench into all those plans.

"How are you getting there?" Michelle asked as we headed down the hallway. "Should I arrange something with your father's driver? Three hours is a long time to be in a taxi."

"Stefan is sending a private car," I told her. "It should be here any minute.

He had texted me that morning to tell me when to be ready, but beyond the logistics, that was it. The formality stung. I had almost convinced myself that once we returned from our trip, he'd drop the icy exterior and turn back into the man I'd met at my birthday party. Carefree, good-humored, and genuinely interested in me. But maybe that man had been a lie all along.

Before heading downstairs, though, I went to say goodbye to my father. It was still strange, getting used to his tired, more fragile appearance. He looked a thousand times better than he had when I first arrived at the hospital, when he was pale and drawn in the stark white bed, but it was hard to reconcile this man in recovery with the fighter I'd always known.

"How are you feeling?" I asked him, approaching the bed where he was working on a lap desk strewn with papers, a tablet in one hand and a pen in the other.

He scowled, and I bit my lip, trying not to laugh at him. I knew he hated the pacemaker—he said it made him feel old and infirm—but he had always acted like such a baby whenever he was sick.

Michelle had taken the brunt of his bad moods, but she didn't seem to mind. Then again, she had spent the last fifteen years practicing her wifely duties. While staying with them, I had tried to observe how she acted, how she treated my father. I took tons of mental notes, knowing that it would all come in handy when I was reunited with Stefan.

"Leaving for Chicago?" he asked, the scowl still fixed to his face.

"Yes." I held up my bag. "The car should be here soon."

A horn blared from outside. Perfect timing.

Michelle smoothed the blankets around my father, who looked both grateful and annoyed at the attention.

"I'll let you know when I arrive," I told them.

My father just grunted, while Michelle came over and gave me a tight hug.

"We'll see you soon. And remember what I said," she added in a low voice.

I nodded. She had been baffled upon learning that Stefan and I still hadn't consummated the marriage, and she'd spent the duration of the trip sneaking up on me and pulling me aside to give me hints on all the various ways I could seduce my husband. It was equally informative and deeply embarrassing.

"Don't focus too much on school," my father said from his bed. "Men don't want wives who care more about their education than their marriage."

"Don't be so old-fashioned, Daddy. Stefan supports my academic pursuits." I was bluffing, of course. I knew he was happy to pay for my schooling, but I had no idea what bearing that had on our relationship. Or if we were even going to have a proper relationship going forward.

I leaned over, gave my father a kiss on the cheek, and headed out to meet my car.

~

WE ARRIVED in Chicago hours later, pulling up to an extremely nice, extremely expensive building. It wasn't until the driver helped me out of the car that I realized I had never seen Stefan's place. I had no idea what to expect.

The driver took my bags and escorted me into the building. At least he knew where we were going. I couldn't have said which condo was his. I didn't even know if this was the same place he had lived in before we got married or if it was a completely new place, or maybe even a wedding gift from his father.

When we knocked on the door, a friendly-faced older woman opened it.

"Welcome home, Mrs. Zoric. I'm Gretna. Your personal chef. Please, come in." Her dark hair was pulled back into a bun, a few loose strands framing her ruddy cheeks, and she had deep-set eyes that seemed to twinkle in amusement as she took in the way my jaw dropped at the sight of the elaborate foyer beyond her, all black marble and dark blue walls with gold accents.

"Personal chef?" I echoed, feeling like Little Orphan Annie.

She nodded, motioning me inside again.

"My god. I—I'm so glad to meet you. Please, call me Tori." I stepped into the condo, and Gretna took my bags from the driver and sent him on his way with a tip. The first thing I registered, beyond the echo of my steps on the marble floor, was how good the place smelled.

"Dinner will be ready at seven," Gretna said when I commented on the heavenly aroma. "Mr. Zoric will join us then. Would you like a tour?"

I hid my disappointment that Stefan wasn't there,

mainly because I should have expected it. No doubt he was working. He was always working. Obviously it was necessary in order to maintain a residence, and a lifestyle, like Stefan's.

Gretna took me around the spacious condo. It was richly decorated but still masculine in its dark, soothing tones, and I couldn't help noticing that it was also extremely well-kept. The place was spotless, with gleaming, polished furniture, leather couches, and starkly dramatic artwork on the walls. It looked like the world's most expensive bachelor pad. Clearly this had been Stefan's place before we got married and he hadn't changed a thing.

I didn't mind. In fact, it gave me a little more insight into who he was. Almost like peering into his brain. A brain that was very masculine and very intense.

"And here is the master bedroom," Gretna said, pushing open a heavy door.

She followed me in and set my bags on top of the bed. For a moment, I thought that there might have been a mistake, that she hadn't been instructed to put me in the guest room—but then I glanced into the huge walk-in closet and found a number of my dresses from Vienna neatly arranged on one side. Someone had unpacked all of them for me and organized them. I was sure Stefan wouldn't have let someone else do that without his explicit instructions. He was a man who liked to be in control, and I assumed that especially applied in his own home.

That meant we'd be sharing a bedroom. Interesting.

I had half expected, after everything that had happened on our honeymoon, that he would have completely dropped the pretense of a real marriage and given me a room of my own somewhere else in the house.

Not that I was complaining. Sharing a bed with him

would make it even easier to implement some of the techniques Michelle had tried to impress upon me.

All I had to do was wait for him to come home.

"I need to go finish up," Gretna told me, looking at her watch. "The rest of the family will be arriving just after seven. Is there anything I can get you in the meantime?"

I blinked.

"The rest of the family?"

Gretna nodded. "Yes, ma'am. Stefan's family—his father and siblings will be joining you for dinner. A very special dinner."

A special dinner? I glanced at the clock. And less than an hour to prepare?

The cook hurried off with my warm thanks and I immediately went into prep mode. I had to shower, do my hair and makeup, and pick out something suitable to wear. I had barely spent any time with Stefan's family beyond our introduction at the wedding—it was important that I impress them now that we'd be having more focused, intimate face time.

As I rushed through my shower, I barely registered the luxurious bathroom other than a perfunctory appreciation of its gleaming gold faucets and more of that veined black marble that Stefan seemed to favor. I managed to blow dry and style my hair in record time, and then wrapped myself in a warm, fluffy robe that had been left out while I went to the closet to pick out my outfit and corresponding jewelry. I knew I had to look incredible for Stefan's family—every inch the trophy wife.

I was bent over, looking through my suitcase for a pair of earrings, when I heard something behind me. I glanced back over my shoulder and found Stefan standing in the doorway of the closet.

He was wearing one of his designer suits—as always—but his tie was undone, his collar unbuttoned as if he had been in the process of changing. He was incredibly sexy like that; half in business mode and half at home. A hint of bare skin was showing, begging to be explored with my fingers. With my tongue.

He didn't say anything, but his eyes were intense. Hungry.

I'd seen that look before. It was the same look he had worn when I caught him watching me in the shower. But this time, I wasn't going to let him walk away so easily.

Slowly, I turned around, keeping my eyes on him. I dropped my hands to the belt of my robe, languorously sliding them toward the knot. His gaze darted to my fingers, carefully tugging the bow apart. I could see that he was at war with himself. With his desire.

It was a war I wanted to win.

Without looking away, I finished untying the belt and slid the robe off my shoulders, letting it drop to the floor. I was naked—completely naked—in front of him.

Heat sparked in his gaze, and we stood there at an impasse, neither of us moving, until finally he swore under his breath.

"You're playing a dangerous game, kitty cat," he said.

My blood ran hot. The battle in his eyes raged on. I lifted my chin in a challenge.

Before I could blink, I was in his arms. I gasped as he took my mouth with his, the kiss brutal and intense and everything I wanted. He pulled me tight against him, his hands everywhere—my breasts, my ass, my hips, my hair.

His mouth on mine wasn't romantic or sweet or cautious, his hands groping me so roughly that I would probably have bruises in the morning. I wanted more.

I arched against him, grinding my hips into his, my entire body hot and aching for his touch. I didn't care that I was being needy, practically begging him to get me off. His tongue was hot against mine and he broke away just long enough to grab my hair in his hands, yanking my head backward so he could bite and suck my throat.

Wrapping my leg up around his hip, I tried to get closer. I was naked but he was still fully clothed, and it was shockingly erotic to rub myself against him that way, feeling the hard length of his cock behind layers of expensive wool. I was desperate for relief, the months of anticipation building inside of me until I could barely stand it.

His hands moved downward, gripping, squeezing, slapping as they went. One hand tightened around my hips, pushing me away from him. I nearly wilted in disappointment until with hardly any warning, he spun me to face the mirror. His hand came around my front and delved between my legs.

"I want you to watch," he growled. "I want you to look at yourself in that mirror while I fuck you with my fingers."

I was already hot and wet for him, and I gasped as his fingers glided into me hard and fast. His hand was still fisted in my hair, forcing my eyes forward, forcing me to look at myself, at the glaze of lust in my own eyes.

Stefan had perfect, long fingers, strong and sure in their movements. I was panting, grinding myself against him as he fingered me, out of my mind with pleasure. I couldn't hold back, his deft strokes bringing me to the edge almost immediately.

He tugged my head back, his tongue deep in my mouth, his fingers pumping inside of me—it was almost too much to bear, the sensations overwhelming. I could feel my release building inside of me, and I reached behind me to clutch

Stefan's shoulders, my groans pitching higher, my breasts heaving with my shuddering breaths.

His mouth broke from mine, his voice hoarse as he sucked my earlobe between his teeth.

"Take it," he growled into my ear. "Take all of it, kitty cat."

His hand moved faster, his fingers switching to shallow thrusts designed to tease my g-spot. My body felt like liquid fire. The orgasm started to surge through me, and I moaned Stefan's name, giving myself up to the ecstasy.

I came in his arms in a hot, helpless rush, crying out as my entire body shook with release. His grip went tight around me as my knees buckled, my muscles going slack with relief.

But still it wasn't enough. He had made me come but I wanted more. I wanted him inside of me. I wanted him to come with me. I unclenched my hands from his shoulders, his fingers still moving inside of me, milking the last gasps of my orgasm from my body.

As I turned around and reached for his belt, my hands brushed against his hard cock, straining against the fabric. He was ready. And I was hungry for him. I wanted him now.

But just as I managed to unbuckle his belt, the doorbell rang.

TORI

CHAPTER 18

"Wait," I begged as Stefan pushed me away. "Please."

"Get dressed," he said gruffly, re-buckling his belt and swearing under his breath.

I was completely naked, wilting and spent after the intense orgasm he had just given me. I was still coming out of my haze, struggling to comprehend what had just happened.

It was the single hottest moment I'd ever experienced. And now it was over.

Stefan grabbed a new tie and fixed his buttons, looking over at me.

"Pull yourself together," he growled. "And make sure you look presentable, not like a whore who just got fucked in a closet."

His words should have stung, but they just made me hotter. I liked it when he was rough. When he was intense. I wanted more.

I wanted to wrap my body around him, slide to the ground, and unbuckle his belt before taking him into my mouth. I wanted to drive him to the edge and push him over, just like he had done for me.

But now wasn't the time. His family was here.

Stefan finished adjusting his clothes and stormed out of the closet. He was upset, but I didn't think it was because his family was here. I was sure that he had been seconds away from giving me what I wanted. Tearing his own clothes off and fucking me right on the floor of our shared closet. He had been about to lose control.

I had learned by now that it didn't happen often. Maybe that's why he was so pissed off.

Was that why he had been avoiding me? He didn't want to give up his power?

Somehow, that made me feel better about everything that had happened. Maybe Stefan did want me, and desperately, but because of some fixation on maintaining complete dominance, he wasn't allowing himself to fuck me. It wasn't serving me, but I had to admit it was kinky.

I quickly put on one of the more modest dresses I had bought in Vienna, a lavender, knee-length sheath that covered me modestly while still showing off my shoulders. I'd find a way to break through Stefan's ironclad control. I'd done it once, I could do it again.

With a quick check in the mirror, making sure I looked neat and presentable, instead of freshly fucked, I headed out to the dining room to greet Stefan's family.

This would be the first significant time spent with them since the wedding, when our interactions had been brief and perfunctory. If the huge reception didn't count, we'd never all sat down and had a meal together. I was looking forward to getting to know them better.

Four pairs of eyes turned toward me as I entered the living room. Three pairs assessed me with appraising once-overs—Stefan, his brother, and his father—and all seemed to approve of my dress. I ignored Konstantin's overly familiar gaze, and turned a friendly smile toward Stefan's younger brother, Luka. Ignoring the way his eyes were still weighing me up, I slid past him to greet my sister-in-law, Emzee.

During the wedding, she had been the friendliest of the family, unabashedly eager to get to know me better. I didn't know much about her personally, except that she was the baby of the family at twenty-two, and that her photography career was mostly centered around the family business.

"It's so good to see you again! I love your dress," Emzee told me.

"It's good to see you all again, too. Now that we're all here, shall we move into the dining room?" I asked, wanting to appear as much of a proper trophy wife as possible.

I had a feeling it was important to put on that show for Stefan's family, especially his father. I didn't love it, but I had accepted it as part of the deal. I really didn't like how Konstantin seemed to always be standing just a little too close to me. He was unbearably creepy, his eyes dragging over my body as I walked across the room.

I didn't know where to look. I could barely look at Stefan; I knew if I did, I'd think of what had just happened in the closet and the last thing I wanted was to be blushing and flushed in front of his family. I had zero experience trying to act casual after a sexual encounter.

We all sat down to a beautifully set table, Konstantin on one end, Stefan on the other. I was seated at Stefan's right hand, with Emzee and Luka across from me. Wine was poured, the food was served, and immediately everyone began discussing work. I shouldn't have been surprised.

"How was casting in Budapest?" Konstantin asked Stefan. "Did you find the kind of girls we're looking for?"

Stefan nodded, not looking at me. "I think you'll be pleased with the options."

"Options are good," Luka added, clearly looking for some way to contribute to the conversation. Emzee caught my gaze and flashed me an eye-roll.

Out of all of Stefan's family, Luka was the one I'd had the least amount of contact with. Though he was polite enough toward me at the wedding, he'd seemed like a total party boy—and no stranger to women—which was why I hadn't given him Grace's number. Not yet, anyway.

Not that I could blame him. He was young, handsome and rich, with his own MBA freshly under his belt. Of course he wanted to have fun, wield all those gifts to his advantage—especially when he saw the toll that working at KZM took on someone like Stefan, who seemed incapable of having any fun that wasn't specifically sanctioned by the agency.

"We're going to need at least a dozen more girls in the next month," Konstantin said, ignoring his youngest son.

"I'm working on it," Stefan said. "You'll get what you need."

"It's not what *I* need," Konstantin said, and laughed. "It's what the clients need."

Something about the way he said 'the clients' made my gut twist, but I didn't know why. I had to admit, Konstantin made me feel ill at ease in general. It probably had to do with the way I'd seen him hovering outside the balcony doors at my birthday party, spying on my conversation with Stefan and the kiss we'd shared after the proposal.

"I'll send you a list of requirements," Konstantin said, spearing a piece of asparagus on his plate.

I wanted to ask questions about the business, show that I was interested in and capable of following the conversation, but it was clear by everyone's tone and body language that this discussion was for the Zoric family only. Is this what it felt like to be a mafia wife?

I ate quietly, listening passively, perking up only when I heard a familiar name.

"I'm surprised Oksana didn't return with you last month," Konstantin said. "We were expecting her in the States."

Stefan gave an overly casual shrug, and suddenly I felt his hand on my knee.

"We never met up with her in Budapest," he said. "She was a no show. I've been trying to chase her down, but she's been out of pocket."

His finger tap-tap-tapped against my knee, signaling me to keep quiet. Why was he lying to his father? I was full of questions. Questions I was sure I'd never get any straight answers to.

I was confused, and more than a little annoyed. Stefan had ignored me throughout the entire dinner and now he was expecting me to cover for him? I debated 'accidentally' exposing his lies to his father, asking if he meant the same Oksana who had taken me sightseeing.

But as upset as I was with Stefan, I disliked my father-in-law more. Whatever was going on with Oksana, it was clearly being kept a secret for a reason. And I didn't want Konstantin to find out. In fact, I would have been more comfortable if Konstantin knew literally nothing about my life with Stefan, including the people we'd met up with on our honeymoon.

Konstantin seemed to notice that something unspoken was happening between me and Stefan, because he turned his unwelcome attention toward me again, those greedy, overly familiar eyes lingering too long on my breasts as he took a bite of his bloody, rare steak.

"And how is the little wifey enjoying her new palace?" he asked, gesturing around the room with his knife.

"It's lovely," I said. And then I excused myself from the table.

When I came out of the bathroom, I found someone waiting for me. It wasn't Stefan, and thankfully it wasn't Konstantin. It was Luka.

He was leaning against the wall, but he straightened up when I started to walk back toward the dining room. He put his arm out, blocking my exit.

"Excuse me," I said, flashing a tight smile. He'd been drinking vodka cocktails heavily the whole night, and I could tell by his glassy eyes that he wasn't anywhere near sober.

"You look good tonight." He gave me a long, appraising look, but it was different from the leer I'd received from his father. Luka's look was more clinical. Like he was trying to figure me out.

"Thank you," I said, trying to be polite. "The restroom's all yours."

But he didn't budge, just flashed me the charming smile that I'd seen work so well on all the single women at my wedding. He needn't have bothered. Luka was cute and charming, but that didn't change the fact that I was married to his brother. And I also wasn't interested. Especially after what had happened between me and Stefan in the closet.

"You're beautiful enough to be one of our talents," he said as he leaned closer to me, and I could smell the alcohol on his breath. "Would you like to model for me?"

"No thank you," I told him firmly, but he didn't seem to listen.

173

He reached out, pushing my hair back from my shoulders, exposing my neck. I hoped there weren't visible marks, considering how hard Stefan had been sucking and biting me there.

"I think you would," he said. "I think you'd get off on it. You strike me as the kind of girl who likes to be the center of attention."

"I'm not interested," I said, inching backward. I would have run, but there was nowhere to go. He was blocking the only way out of the hallway.

"I'd show you a good time," he said, stepping closer again. "It doesn't seem like Stefan will care."

I didn't know what to do. He wasn't letting me through, he wasn't listening to anything I was saying, and his hands kept reaching out to graze my hair, my shoulders, my neck, as if I was nothing more than a bolt of fabric for him to fondle. I should have pushed him away, or yelled for help, but I was paralyzed.

"Please let me pass," I said, trying to keep my voice from shaking.

Luka put his hand on my upper arm, starting to squeeze. Suddenly he was yanked away from me, grunting in pain as Stefan pinned him against the wall, his feet off the ground.

"Don't. Touch. Her," Stefan growled.

"I didn't do shit," Luka snarled back, but his face was abashed. "Put me down."

Stefan got in his face. "If I find you alone with her again, I'll fucking kill you. Nod if you understand."

I believed him, and it was clear that Luka did as well. His skin went ashy, and he stopped fighting. They glared at each other in a standoff for a tense moment and then Luka finally nodded. Stefan released his brother, who then stalked down the hall, back toward the dining room.

I was practically shaking, adrenaline still rushing, and was about to thank Stefan when he turned to me with vile hatred in his eyes.

"I signed up to marry a virgin," he told me, as if it were a threat. "Make sure that's what I get." He walked away before I could say anything.

I sagged against the wall, torn between relief and disappointment. I was glad Stefan had saved me from his brother. But my husband had also confirmed, without any doubt, that I was nothing more than a trophy to him.

TORI

CHAPTER 19

I wanted to punch a wall.

If I knew how to do anything after spending a lifetime with a politician for a father, it was how to pretend that everything was fine even when it wasn't. So despite my altercation with Luka, my objectification by Stefan, and my persistent uneasiness around Konstantin, I'd spent the rest of the evening silently fuming behind polite engagement and a cheerful smile. Michelle would have been proud.

For their part, Stefan and Luka managed to finish dinner without looking at each other or saying anything directly to the other. If Konstantin or Emzee noticed, they said nothing. Everyone acted as if everything was fine and normal. At one point in the evening, Emzee had pulled me aside to help her find a bottle opener in the kitchen (as if I'd know, anyway) and she'd quietly apologized for how her father and brothers were behaving.

"They're always like this," she said with a sigh. "It's always work, work, work. As if the world revolves around the agency."

"Sounds familiar," I said with a smile, trying to make light of it as I rifled through utensil drawers.

"Well, if it ever gets to be too much, just call me," Emzee said. "I'll come kidnap you and we'll go have a night out on the town, or do the River Walk. Maybe get our nails done."

This time my smile was genuine. "I'd love that. Really."

I handed her the opener.

Her face lit up. "Ooh, and have you been to the Logan Theatre?"

"Is that in Logan Square?" I asked. "They play all the indie movies and foreign films, right?"

Emzee nodded. "It looks like nothing from the outside, but on the inside it's totally wall-to-wall Art Deco. It's *to die for*. Like going back in time. And they have a full bar!"

"That sounds amazing," I said. "Guess I'll have to break out my fake ID."

"Gah, I keep forgetting you're underage!" she said, squeezing my arm. "We'll both get Shirley Temples, then."

We exchanged cell numbers and she had promised to reach out soon.

Back at the table, I finally gave in and drank a glass of the wine Emzee had offered me, just to try and relax. I hated the way Stefan was treating me, like we were back to square one, but I didn't know what to do about it. I wanted the man who had finger fucked me in the closet, not the man who was treating me like an object, or the man who acted distant and unyielding about the terms of our marriage, who was so on-edge about work all the time that he barely acknowledged me.

I was angry at myself, too. I knew the kind of man he was, yet I kept setting myself up for disappointment. And I was in denial about where our relationship might be able to go.

Finally his family left, and we were alone. Stefan didn't even look at me, just undid his tie, unbuttoned the top button of his shirt and grabbed a last drink before heading into the bedroom. I followed him. I wasn't going to let him ignore me. Not tonight. Not after what had happened in the closet and then later, with Luka.

I was so angry I was practically shaking like the ice cubes in Stefan's whiskey glass.

"You know I have to say, for someone who's so obsessed with the fact that I'm a virgin, you're pretty fucking prudish yourself," I said. The wine had made me bold.

I wanted to push him to the edge. Wanted to make him break so I could get past his walls, the way that he had made me break into a million pieces in the closet.

He ignored me, but I could see his shoulders tense. It was working.

"In fact, I bet you couldn't close the deal if you tried," I went on. "If I waited for you, I'd still have my hymen intact for my fiftieth birthday. But maybe that's what you want. The big man's gotta have all the control, right? Are you a big man, Stefan? Keeping me locked up tight like jewels in a safe so nobody can ever touch me?"

He turned to face me, anger in his eyes. Good. I wanted him angry. I wanted him pissed.

"Maybe I should call Luka up," I taunted, knowing it would drive him over the top. "Because if you're not going to do anything about my virgin status, I know for a fact that he will."

Suddenly, Stefan was in front of me, grabbing my upper arms with a vice grip.

178

"While you're married to me, your body is mine. Nobody else touches you. Do you understand?"

He was breathing hard, his eyes intense.

It was incredibly hot.

"If you ever even *speak* about giving your body to someone else, I swear to god I'll—"

"You'll what?" I goaded him. The tension between us was so taut I could almost feel it, like a rubber band about to snap. And yet, I wanted it to break. I wanted to break through the barriers between us. I wanted to make him lose control, give in to me.

His face was so close to mine that I could feel his breath on my cheeks.

"I don't think you'll do a goddamn thing," I said, smirking.

His lips crashed down on mine

It was just like it had been earlier that day. Wild, frenzied, and totally, completely hot. This time, however, we were alone. No one else in our apartment. Nothing was going to stop us from finishing what we had started all those hours before.

Stefan's tongue was hot on mine. I was ready for more, ready to take what he had to offer. I fumbled for his shirt, wanting to get rid of everything that was between us.

But before I could undo a single button, Stefan's hands were around my wrists.

"Don't," he ordered, forcing my arms up and above my head.

He walked me backwards to the wall, pressing me up against it, green eyes blazing. I couldn't have slipped his grasp if I'd tried. It was so fucking hot to be pinned there, unable to move. With one hand holding my wrists together, he ran his other down the side of my neck, down over my cleavage until it reached the neckline of my dress.

"Did I pay for this?" he asked.

I nodded wordlessly, my entire body throbbing with need.

With a hard jerk, he ripped the fabric from my body. The dress tore at the seams and fell to the floor, the material crumpling at my feet. I gasped with the shock and pleasure of it all. I stood in front of him wearing nothing but my heels, lace panties, and matching strapless bra.

"You're mine," Stefan said, thrusting his knee between my legs, forcing them wide.

His thigh was hard as it pressed almost painfully against me, stimulating my clit, and the sensation was so intense that I almost came from the pressure. Stefan caught my little groan of pleasure with his mouth, his hand still pinning me to the wall. I rode his thigh as his other hand tore my bra away, grinding hungrily against him.

I was naked except for my underwear, and just like when we were in the closet before, he was still fully dressed. His hand went to my breast, grabbing my nipple and twisting it roughly. It hurt, but I liked it. I liked it a lot, and I moaned against his mouth.

"More," I begged.

"You're mine," he said, twisting the other nipple. "Say it. Tell me who you belong to."

"I belong to you," I gasped.

His hand left my breast and I let out a sigh of disappointment, one that was quickly silenced as my underwear was torn away and his finger slid down to stroke my clit.

"You're so wet for me," he rasped, and then shoved his finger deep inside me.

I cried out. The penetration felt even more intense this

time, even deeper now that I had already climaxed just hours ago, and it wasn't long before he added another finger and was fucking me hard with both of them, my pussy stretching to accommodate their thickness.

"You're so fucking tight," he growled against my throat. "Your soaking wet little pussy is going to feel so good on my cock."

My knees went weak as he whispered all these dirty, forceful things to me. I wanted all of it. And I wanted it now.

Apparently, he couldn't wait either, because he released his grip on my wrists.

"Go to the bed," he ordered, slapping my ass—hard— when I didn't move fast enough.

I nearly raced across the room, turning to find that he was taking his clothes off with quick, jerking movements.

"Get up on the bed and spread your legs," he told me. "Leave your shoes on."

I did as he said, straining my neck to watch him as he peeled off his clothes. Finally naked, he was even more gorgeous than I had imagined, his cock long and rigid and perfectly formed. Something about the sight of it made my mouth water.

He stalked toward the bed, and I spread my legs even wider for him, my heels digging into the down comforter. I wanted this so bad. I was ready to do whatever he wanted.

"Are you on the pill?" he asked, crawling onto the bed.

I nodded, my throat dry.

"Good," he growled. "Because I'm not going to fuck my wife with a condom."

He shoved my thighs open until my muscles burned with the stretch, settling himself in between them. I could feel his cock nudging against my sensitive labia, and I swallowed hard. This was it. This was the moment I would lose my virginity.

"Is your sweet little pussy ready for me?" he asked.

I managed a nod, even though I wasn't sure. He had fucked me with his fingers, but his cock was bigger—so much bigger. Was I ready? My heart was pounding so hard I could hear the blood rushing in my ears, my breaths rapid and shallow.

Clutching the bedsheets, I tried to prepare myself as he rubbed his cock against my wet opening. He was so hard and so big. I waited for him to shove straight into me, but he didn't. Instead, with a surprisingly soft touch, he dragged a finger down my seam. Then another one. He slipped his fingers inside—two again—but he moved them slowly, savoring my soft moans.

I could feel hot tension building in my core as he fingered me. My back arched as my walls start to relax, and I moved along with the motions of his hand, thrusting in time to his strokes. Then, before I knew what was happening, Stefan withdrew and replaced his hand with the head of his cock.

He slid in slowly, slowly, so slow that I could only squeeze my eyes shut and surrender to the sensation of being filled. I could feel it when he reached maximum penetration, shoving himself all the way in, so thick and hard, stretching me to fit him.

I gasped and opened my eyes, looking down at him, buried deep inside me.

He was big. So big. And it hurt. But it didn't just hurt. It felt hot and wet and good.

It felt really good.

"Your pussy was made for me," he murmured against my throat. "Only me."

"Yes," I gasped because I couldn't say anything else. "Yes."

"You're mine," he said, and he began to move, pumping slowly, back and forth. "Your body is mine. Your tight little pussy is mine."

"Yes," I groaned, clasping my hands at the back of his neck as he thrust even deeper inside me.

"You're going to come for me," he ordered, quickening his pace. "You're going to come on my cock. Your tight little pussy is going to come for my cock and my cock only."

"Yes," I gasped, my hips undulating to meet his every thrust.

Pleasure built inside of me, coiling like a spring. I was close. I was so fucking close.

"No one else will ever touch you like this," Stefan said, spearing into me, faster now. "No one else will ever make you come the way I will. Come for me, my little kitty cat. Come on my cock."

"I want to come," I panted, moaning jaggedly as pleasure spiraled even tighter and hotter at my center. He pumped faster, his tight abs flexing with the effort. "Make me come."

He was fucking me now, full stop, every stroke hard and deep, no longer going easy on me. As he found his rhythm his eyes went dark with raw, animal lust. I couldn't keep up, so I wrapped my legs around his waist, feeling his cock deeper inside me than ever before.

This was everything I'd been waiting for, everything I'd wanted. I could feel myself cresting the wave.

"Make me come, Stefan," I said. He was looking into my eyes as he fucked me, and I slid a hand down over his heart. "Please. Make me—"

I gasped as the orgasm hit in a sudden torrent, the

shockwave surging from my head to my curling toes. My entire body trembled, the deep contractions pulsing at my core. I threw my head back, whimpering, tears pricking at my eyes. I had never felt anything so intense before.

"That pussy is mine," Stefan asserted, still pounding into my clenching pussy, chasing his own release. "Your pussy is mine."

"It's yours," I moaned, savoring the lingering pulse of my orgasm. "I'm yours."

His thrusts became sharper, more erratic, his short breaths coming faster. He grabbed my hair and jerked my head back, hungrily kissing my taut throat, my collarbone, my shoulder. I could feel him losing control. It was exactly what I wanted.

"I own you," he growled.

"Every inch of me," I panted. "You own me."

As he shuddered his final thrust into me, I came again with him.

TORI

CHAPTER 20

The advice you hear most often about marriage is that you should never go to bed angry. I'd always been a little skeptical of something that sounded so trite. But after I gave myself completely to Stefan, and we started to choreograph a new, sexually charged routine, neither of us ever went to bed angry again. And compared to the rough patch we'd battled through over our honeymoon, our rebooted relationship was a dream. Going to bed sex-sated and worn-out every night had turned out to be the key to marital bliss.

As I trudged into the apartment after a long day at school, I could smell Gretna cooking up something amazing.

"Gretna?" I called out as I slipped off my shoes and set my bags down. "I'm home."

"Good evening, Victoria," she said, waving at me over her shoulder as I went into the kitchen to grab a glass of water.

I'd tried to convince her to call me Tori, but she'd insisted on 'Mrs. Zoric.' Victoria was our compromise.

"What is that? It smells like heaven."

"Oh, probably the truffle velouté," she answered, step-ping aside to show me the cream sauce simmering in the pan. "It's one of the five French mother sauces. I make it with butter and heavy cream, some mushrooms, shallots, a bit of garlic...pretty simple," she answered. "That's to go with the lobster ravioli."

Everything in the kitchen was 'simple' to Gretna. I would bet the sauce had taken her at least an hour. I couldn't imagine being able to whip up even one of her side dishes. I was already drooling.

"There are also haricots vert and a simple salad with arugula and lemon. Everything will be ready in about ten minutes."

"Mmm, I can't wait. You're a lifesaver."

Having her had turned out to be a total godsend. Espe-cially since I'd grown up in a house where takeout and meal delivery were the norm. As a result, my personal cooking skills didn't extend much further than toast and eggs (scram-bled), sandwiches, or boxed mac 'n cheese. Blessedly, I was able to box up Gretna's leftovers for Stefan each night, so I could focus on my schoolwork. I didn't even mind that I had to eat alone most of the time. Compared to the chaos of my long days on campus, it was nice to go home and relax, letting myself enjoy the quiet.

Stefan was still a total workaholic, just as tied up with his packed schedule as always. Five and six days a week he spent at the KZM offices vetting contracts, appeasing demanding clients, or auditioning potential talent. But things between us had improved so drastically that I no longer panicked if he had to work late, or if he was stuck in a meeting and it took him awhile to return a call or text. He kept me informed and I knew that I could trust him...

even when it came to wining and dining the models. I also knew he was hyper focused on that brand new account— the one that Konstantin had talked about at the family dinner—and that he'd been scrambling to assemble a port- folio of fresh faces for the client. I didn't push him for details, but I knew that he was stressed, and that it was his top priority.

Meanwhile, I was utterly absorbed by my program at UChicago. My professors were incredible—brilliant and passionate, and always willing to chat with me during office hours, of which I took full advantage. My fellow students were as nerdy as I was, and we would geek out (both in and out of class) about semiotics and language acquisition. Apparently I wasn't the only one who'd nursed a teenage crush on the semiotician Roland Barthes. He had been a pioneer in the field, and was like the sexy Jeff Goldblum of French philosophers. It felt like I had found my tribe for the first time in my life.

"Here is a plate, and there is French bread toasting in the oven that should be done in a few moments," Gretna was saying, holding out a steaming plate toward me.

I was perched on the couch with a few of my textbooks and a handful of remote controls, trying to figure out which one would allow me to watch *The Bachelor*. I'd already changed into sweatpants and a tank top, pulling my hair back into a messy ponytail.

"Thank you so much," I said, taking the plate. Without asking, Gretna picked up one of the remotes I'd tossed aside, clicked through a few menu screens, and got my show started.

"Don't forget the bread," she said. "Five minutes, then take it out. Don't let it burn."

"I won't," I said. "I promise. Now go, you're almost ten

minutes past the hour! Have a good vacation and see you in five days."

She left, locking the door behind her, and as I settled in to watch my show I could feel the tension of the day rolling off me in waves.

Although my husband and I had separate lives when the sun was out, the night was a completely different story.

Wiped out from my day, I was usually in bed before he came home. I'd crawl under the covers, turn off the lights, and wait. I never slept. It would have been impossible to sleep even if I wanted to, and I never did. Because when he came home, he'd strip off his clothes, climb into bed, and fuck me until I came. Over and over and over again.

It was always in the dark. It was always rough. And I always wanted more.

I didn't mind that I barely saw him otherwise. Didn't mind that he would sometimes whisper harsh, cruel things in my ear as his thrusts were slamming me into the headboard, or that he didn't hold me afterwards. The sex was so intense that I didn't have any complaints.

Stefan never commented on the lacy little negligees I wore, either. He probably didn't notice them beyond his initial touch and how easy they were to rip off my body. That was one of my favorite parts—the intensity with which he destroyed the expensive lingerie I had painstakingly picked out before bed. There was something so hot, so naughty, about picking up the torn fabric off the floor the next morning.

Then again, I was pretty sure I'd consider anything related to sex with Stefan hot and naughty. He brought out another side of me, one that I never even knew could be there.

I noticed the time on my phone and hit pause on *The*

Bachelor to go to the kitchen and get the bread. My food was still hot, but I hadn't even touched it yet. As I pulled the bread out of the oven, I could hear the front door open and then close, followed by the sound of keys jingling on the entryway table.

"I didn't forget the bread, Gretna! I can't believe you came back. Don't you know what the word vacation means?" I teased.

Footsteps echoed from the marble foyer to the hardwood in the living room, and when I turned around to nudge the oven door shut with my hip, I saw that it wasn't Gretna who had come back. It was Stefan.

"Hi," I said, a little startled and breathless.

We stared at each other for a moment. He was wearing his usual perfect black suit, his tie neatly knotted, looking every inch the successful businessman. Meanwhile I was standing there in my chill-out clothes, my hair unkempt and loose in its ponytail. We couldn't have looked more like polar opposites.

"I...I thought you were Gretna," I said.

"Sorry to disappoint," he said, the corner of his mouth twitching.

I smiled, but I didn't know what to say. We were perfectly suited to each other in bed, in the dark, but now? I was completely tongue-tied. Maybe I should have felt more uncomfortable about it, but the truth was, whatever we had going on seemed to work for us. For now, at least.

"Can I make you a plate?" I asked, gesturing to all the hot dishes on the stove. "Gretna made lobster ravioli."

"Sounds good," he said.

I was surprised. I'd expected him to say he'd only stopped by to change before going out to a business dinner or heading back to work for another late night call to Tokyo.

This was early for him to be home; usually he didn't get back until after midnight. It was barely seven.

I put together a plate for Stefan and carried it out to the couch where I'd left mine.

"Is this okay, or would you prefer to eat at the dining table?"

"This is fine."

He took off his jacket, hung it neatly on the back of a chair, and rolled up his sleeves. Then he settled onto the couch next to me.

"I was watching lady TV, but we can switch it to sports or CNN or something," I said, feeling slightly embarrassed about my guilty pleasure.

"You can leave it on," he said. "I don't watch much TV anyway."

I pressed play, and for the rest of the episode, we ate in companionable silence. The whole thing was so cozy and domestic, I found myself relaxing despite the novelty of the situation. It was the first meal we'd eaten together since the night his father and siblings had come over. The first night we'd slept together. If Stefan realized this, he made no indication of it.

When he gathered up our napkins and empty plates and headed toward the kitchen, I decided to take advantage of the fact that he wasn't glued to the work on his phone or laptop.

"So there's an event at school tomorrow," I said, leaning in the doorway.

My voice came out quieter than I'd intended. Stefan's back was to me as he loaded the dishwasher, so I cleared my throat and spoke again, a little louder this time.

"It's like the collegiate version of a debutante ball for all the new majors in my department. An opportunity for us to meet the other students and get some face time with the professors."

Stefan started washing his hands, and for a moment I thought he hadn't heard me—until he gave the smallest nod.

"You could go with me," I added. "It's at 8 o'clock."

I instantly regretted it. Did I expect him to drop everything he had going on just to attend some freshman social event with me? He was an extremely busy man, and he obviously didn't have much time to spare.

He turned around to look at me. "I'll see what my schedule looks like."

I'd heard that phrase a million times from my father growing up, and I knew it meant 'not gonna happen.'

I tried to laugh it off. "Yeah. Of course. I know you're swamped right now. It's really no big deal."

Besides, I was just inviting him to be polite.

He went back out to the living room, picked up his jacket and briefcase, and disappeared into his home office. I didn't see him until several hours later, when he finally came to bed.

It was dark, and I was wearing nothing but a garter belt and thigh high stockings. Stefan didn't say a word, just threw me face down on the bed and fucked me from behind until we both climaxed. I fell asleep that night, thinking of nothing but the pleasure he'd given me.

I'D ALMOST FORGOTTEN about the invitation until the following night, when I came home to get ready for the event and found the house empty. My gut sank, although I wasn't really surprised. Of course Stefan wasn't coming to the event. He was probably in the middle of a huge meeting even at that moment. And I was sure he'd only been half-listening when I mentioned it last night.

Instead of letting myself wallow, I focused my energy on getting ready. The novelty of a closet full of perfectly tailored designer clothes hadn't worn off yet. Since most days I was at school and opted for comfortable jeans and blouses, it was exciting to be able to play dress-up again, like I had in Europe. Tonight I wanted to look professional, but still feminine, so I settled on a Diane von Furstenberg wrap dress that flattered me without requiring a pair of Spanx in the process. I paired it with some gold earrings and a chunky gold bracelet that I had bought in Vienna.

Since I'd probably be getting home around the same time as Stefan later tonight, I also opted for a pair of skimpy white lace underwear underneath the dress, cut high enough in the back that I wouldn't have visible panty lines, and a matching bra. He seemed to like lace on me; easier to tear off, it seemed. This set would be mere shreds by the morning. As I applied a finishing touch of mascara and transparent pink lip gloss, I shivered with anticipation.

When I headed outside the building to dial up an Uber, I was surprised to find a car waiting for me. The driver was leaning against the hood, holding a small sign that displayed my name in bold letters.

"My husband arranged this?" I asked the driver as I approached.

"Mr. Zoric, of course," he said.

Apparently, Stefan *had* remembered the event—remembered it enough to send me a car—but couldn't make the time to go himself. I was touched.

I was also disappointed, even though I knew it was irrational. I was his wife in name (and apparently in bed) only. I should be content with our arrangement and grateful we had such good sexual chemistry, and not expect anything more. I still couldn't help wishing he was there, though.

Arriving at the event, I was immediately overwhelmed. The alumni hall was loud and packed. I was excited to spend the evening getting to know my professors and the other students, but amid the cacophony I found myself feeling shy. So I grabbed a glass of champagne, hoping I wouldn't get carded, and then sipped it as I walked the perimeter of the room. Despite getting along with my class-mates during school hours, I hadn't actually gotten to know anyone on a deeper level, so I had yet to find anyone I'd call a true friend.

Most of my free time outside the classroom was spent haunting the gorgeous, gothic Harper Memorial Library on campus. I'd head there straight after my last class ended and study to my heart's content under the buttressed ceilings, surrounded by medieval-looking stone walls. It was like something out of Harry Potter. Unfortunately, it was also the only library on campus that was strictly for reading, so when I wanted to pore over stacks of linguistics texts, I'd have to visit one of the other libraries. But Harper held my heart, and I felt lucky to be able to work in such a beautiful setting considering all the hours I had to devote to the mountains of homework my professors assigned. The semester was hitting me hard, but I loved every minute of it. Unfortunately, socializing wasn't one of my course requisites.

Luckily, a few minutes in, my favorite professor showed up and pulled me aside. Her surname was Dhawan, derived from the Sanskrit word *dhav*, which meant 'messenger'; when she'd explained this on our first day of class, I'd felt relieved to know she thought of herself as a messenger, bringing knowledge to all of us.

Relief flooded through me. "Professor! I'm so glad to see you. I mean, not in class." My nerves had me rambling. "Not that I don't love your class. Which I do, as you know—"

"Of course I do! You're my best student," she said, and laughed. "Have you met the dean of the school yet?"

I shook my head, feeling a little nervous. I wanted to make a good first impression.

"Come with me," she said, leading me across the room. But halfway there, another professor cut in and asked to borrow Professor Dhawan, and I was left to meet the dean alone.

Dean Hutton was an imposing older woman with severe brows, short, dark hair, and a suit cut so sharply it would have given Stefan a run for his money. She was addressing a cluster of people in front of a glass case that gleamed with a variety of alumni awards and trophies. This woman oversaw the entire program I'd worked so hard to get into. I was incredibly intimidated.

I was just about to introduce myself, battling a resurgence of awkward shyness, when I felt a hand on the small of my back and inhaled the scent of a familiar cologne. For a second I was convinced I was imagining things, but when I turned around Stefan was standing there.

He looked polished and confident, just like always, but it was a nice surprise to see how well he blended in with the collegiate crowd. His suit was more subdued than usual, grey instead of black, and he'd traded out the dark dress shoes for brown oxfords. Not that he could ever fade into the background—though he was dressed appropriately, he was still the most magnetic man in the room. But he looked like he belonged there. With me.

"Dean Hutton." I held out my hand. "I'm Victoria, one

of the first years. I wanted to say how excited I am to be a part of the linguistics program." I turned to gesture to Stefan. "And this is my husband, Stefan."

"A pleasure to meet you," Stefan said, shaking the dean's hand.

Was that a smile on his face? It was! Stefan was smiling warmly at the dean, who returned the favor.

"Lovely to meet you both," Dean Hutton said. "Always glad to meet our new students."

"Tori's been singing the praises of your program ever since she started the term," Stefan said, oozing charm. "I have no doubt she'll be one of your most dedicated students."

I blushed. How could I not? Stefan was buttering up the dean like a pro, and all I could do was watch as he talked me up.

"I've heard nothing but good things," the dean said before turning to me. "Your professors are very impressed with your work so far. A genuine thirst for knowledge is something that will serve you well over the next few years. It's refreshing to see."

"You'd be hard pressed to find someone who loves language as much as my wife does," Stefan agreed. "I can barely get her to talk about anything else, but you have to admire that kind of passion. When I was a year deep into my MBA program at U Penn, I found that the one thing..."

He admired my passion. Why did it sound so good when he said it like that?

Something swelled in my chest as Stefan and Dean Hutton talked some more—about me. It wasn't just the fact that it was flattering, but that Stefan was talking about me like he knew me. Really knew me. And like he was proud of the person I was. Could it be that I was more than just a warm body to him? More than just a contractual obligation?

But all the emotion building up inside me was dangerous—because I knew exactly what it meant.

And I knew that falling in love with Stefan was the last thing I should be doing.

STEFAN

CHAPTER 21

oming to this event had been a big mistake. I wasn't even sure what had driven me to make such an impulsive, spur-of-the-moment decision. With all the upheaval at work, the last thing I had time for was a student mixer at my wife's school. I had no reason to play the doting, supportive husband. That was the role Tori and I played for our parents—for my father and for hers. To support *their* brand, *their* image. That was the whole purpose of our marriage, after all.

So attending this event, where the only possible networking opportunities would be with Tori's fellow students or professors, would do nothing to further either of our fathers' goals. Nor our own.

And yet, for reasons I still wasn't sure of, I was here. I hadn't even planned to come, but I'd found myself wrapping up my projects early, changing into a less formal suit of clothes I kept at the office, and then getting in a car to go straight to UChicago's campus. To spend what would doubtlessly shape up to be a total waste of an evening drinking cheap wine, making small talk with a bunch of academics, and blowing countless hours of my time. Why had I agreed to this?

In a word, because I was a fucking idiot.

I'd made a huge mistake when it came to Tori. I was normally an excellent judge of character, yet I kept finding that she surprised me. I thought I'd be marrying someone who knew the game, but was well aware of her appointed role in it—and of exactly how to behave like a good girl. And those things were true enough. But lately it seemed like she had lost any interest in acting like a good girl. She was starting to spread her wings, rebel against her boundaries. And like it or not, I had to respect her for it.

Despite her guileless charm and her obsession with pursuing a higher education, I had ultimately expected her to be just like her father—self-absorbed and hyper-focused on her ambitions, to the point of being oblivious to half the people around her. But with Tori, her ambition was benign. And self-absorbed was the last word I'd use to describe her.

But even still, I'd come to realize that she was far more of an innocent than I had thought. She didn't have any idea of the dark, grotesque work that lay just below the surface of what our families did. She was hopelessly naïve about the ways of the world.

It should have disgusted me. Should have pushed me further away from her.

Instead, it just inflamed my desire.

And tonight, I couldn't take my eyes off her. That dress of hers was something else. It was modest—everything was covered—yet it only managed to accentuate her curves, clinging to her tits and ass like a second skin. I couldn't wait to get her home and rip it off. To discover what she was wearing underneath.

It hadn't escaped my notice that she wore nothing but

fragile wisps of lingerie when I came to bed every night. My animal desire, my rough destruction of those expensive items, the torn scraps of lace and silk on the floor the next morning; all of it only seemed to make her hotter. I spent all day thinking about what she'd be wearing and how fast I could get it off her.

In fact, I was thinking about that even now. Wondering what she'd put on for me, and only me, underneath that silky blue dress of hers.

It wasn't just desire revving me up tonight. That was the main thing driving me, but I felt a sense of pride for her as well. This was a room filled with intelligent, ardent academics, and I knew Tori could hold her own with the best of them. It was irrational, I guess. I probably didn't know her well enough to be proud of her. I barely knew her at all.

Yet I could see the fire in her eyes as she chatted with her co-eds and instructors, brimming with enthusiasm and passion for language. For *words*, for fuck's sake. It should have been merely precocious. It shouldn't have been impressive, or be affecting me in any way.

Somehow it was.

I watched her hold court, charming her professors and the Dean, and found myself smiling at how animated she seemed. I didn't like the way that most of the men in her department seemed to be undressing her with their eyes, but I couldn't blame them. She was gorgeous, but sometimes I fucking hated the fact.

Didn't they know she belonged to me?

I'd never been possessive before, but Tori made me that way. Made me want to blacken the eye of any man that looked in her direction. I wanted them to know that she was mine.

It was illogical. I knew that all of this was temporary.

That whatever was happening between us was going to be over as soon as I got what I wanted.

I never should have fucked her.

That was where everything had gone wrong. I prided myself on my self-control and I had been able to hold out up until the honeymoon with hardly a second thought. But by the time she'd been called home to care for her father, I had secretly thanked god, because I hadn't known how much longer I would have been able to resist.

Apparently not long at all. The moment we'd been alone, my control had shattered. First, when she'd stood in front of me naked, in the closet, begging for my touch. Then, afterwards, when she had pushed me past my limit. Pushed me past the point of my reasoning mind.

Now that the floodgates were open, there was no stopping me. She was like a drug I couldn't resist. I wanted her all the time. I couldn't think about anything else but her tight, inexperienced body and all the things I wanted to do to test her limits. She never stopped me. Never resisted. She wanted everything I gave her.

It was hotter than I could have imagined, and completely unexpected. And entirely, utterly perfect.

That was the problem. I was becoming too accustomed to our new routine. I was beginning to look forward to the end of the day, eager to get home and fuck her. Make her come, moaning my name. It was all I could think about, the way her body felt under my hands, the way her pussy felt around my cock. Everything was new to her, and everything I did made her wet.

I shouldn't have liked it as much as I did.

Almost two hours had gone by, and I was becoming impatient with the situation. I shouldn't have come in the first place, and I wasn't going to stay any longer. Tori would come home with me and I planned to punish her for dragging me out to this event in the first place. I'd remind her what this relationship was. Nothing more than a contract, a marriage of convenience. Sex and convenience.

I put my hand on her back, leaning in to whisper in her ear.

"We're leaving," I told her. "Now."

Her brow creased, but she nodded. Quickly, she said her goodbyes. We were out of there in less than five minutes.

I didn't say anything as we got into the car I'd ordered to take us home. I was angry. At Tori. At myself.

I was letting myself get affected by this woman—this naïve, needy girl. She was driving me to distraction, and I hated that. I hated that I couldn't resist her.

"Thank you for coming tonight," Tori said, her voice quiet as she smoothed out the skirt of her dress.

A dress that would be in shreds once we got back home. I would take all these confusing, unwelcome emotions and push them aside, allowing myself to revel in the anger and frustration and nothing else.

"It won't happen again," I said gruffly.

"Well, I appreciate the effort and I'd still like to thank you," she said. "Properly."

Her hand settled on my knee.

"Watch your hand, kitty cat," I warned her. "You don't want to play with fire."

"Maybe I do," she said, a little smile playing on her lips.

They were a glossy pink tonight, soft and wet-looking, and I had thought about them wrapped around my cock from the moment I saw her. I was still breaking her in, and I'd been waiting to make her suck my dick. But she was offering now. And she could use some lessons.

It was exactly the kind of mindless I needed.

I glanced at the driver through the dark tinted partition and pushed the button for the intercom.

"Take the long way home," I told the driver. "Stay off I-90."

"Yes sir," he replied, and I turned the intercom back off.

Then I looked at my wife, taking her hand and sliding it from my thigh to my cock, which was already swelling behind my zipper.

"Tonight I'm gonna teach you how to suck cock," I said. "You think you're ready?"

She would have to make the next move. And she did.

Her hands trembling slightly, she undid my belt first, then slowly dragged the zipper down. My cock sprang free into her waiting hands. She squeezed me tentatively and I shuddered.

What was wrong with me? I liked my women experienced and eager, not fumbling and innocent. Yet here Tori was, driving me wild with a single touch.

"What do I do?" she asked, a tinge of fear in her voice. It only made me hotter.

"Wrap your hands around me," I ordered. "Then use your mouth."

She nodded and bent over to taste me, darting her tongue around the head.

"Make it wet," I told her. "Lick it like it's a popsicle on the Fourth of July."

As she switched to long drags of her tongue, tracing me from base to tip, I let out a groan. At the sound, she increased the pace. I closed my eyes and leaned my head back. She was inexperienced and awkward, but it was incredibly hot knowing she'd never done this before. I could teach her what I wanted. I could mold her to be, and do, whatever I wanted.

"That's good," I told her. "You got it good and wet. Now take it into your mouth. That's a good little kitty cat."

Encouraged, she wrapped her mouth around me, sucking softly.

She popped it out of her mouth. "And then what?"

"Try to get the whole thing in your mouth," I instructed.

"The whole thing?" She looked nervous, and my arousal ticked up a notch.

"All of it. As deep as it'll go. All the way to the back of your throat."

She did as I said, taking me far deeper than I would have expected. Frissons of electricity were shooting into my toes, and I started to thrust back and forth, keeping it slow at first so she could get used to it. When she moaned, I could feel the vibrations in my cock.

"You like that?" I asked her, palming the back of her head. "You like feeling my cock against the back of your throat?"

"Mmm-hmm," she moaned again.

"Good. You're gonna get some more, then."

I tightened my grip on the back of her head, guiding her hot, wet mouth up and down my cock, plunging deeper into her throat. She did exactly as I directed, fucking me with her mouth, her hand following the movement.

Knowing I was her first blowjob, despite her inexperience, had me getting close much faster than I would have expected, but I didn't want to come in her mouth. Not yet.

"Stop," I ordered her.

She pulled back, gasping for breath, her lips wet and swollen, her blue eyes wide as she looked up at me. I nearly came from the sight alone.

Thankfully, we had pulled up in front of the condo. I quickly zipped up and tucked my shirt back in.

"Go inside," I said, and Tori nodded before scrambling out of the car.

I paid the driver and then followed her in, avoiding her eyes in the elevator. Once we were back in the apartment, the door closed and locked behind us, I grabbed her roughly and shoved her against the entry table.

"You like my cock in your mouth?" I demanded, my hand in her hair, forcing her head back.

"Yes," she gasped as I worked my other hand up her dress, finding the crotch of her panties were already soaking wet.

I hooked my finger around the lace between her legs and gave a sharp tug, letting them slide to the floor at her feet.

"Now go to the couch and bend over it," I ordered. "Ass up."

I watched her walk to the sofa and bend over one of the arms, her hands holding tight to the cushion as I shoved her dress up over that peach of an ass. Then I dropped my pants to the floor and slid hard into her, pumping back and forth like a piston in hot oil. There was nothing gentle about it.

She cried out breathlessly, from surprise or pleasure I didn't know—but I didn't care. I was furious that I had allowed myself to get so distracted by her. To feel things for her. I wanted to fuck that emotion out of the equation. Wanted to fuck her until I remembered myself.

Because all of this was her fault. I reminded myself of that with each thrust. This whole thing was her fault. Her. Fault. Her. Fault.

Tori's moans pitched higher with each brutal thrust, but

she pushed her ass back against me, spreading her legs wider, so I knew she was enjoying it. I knew she wanted it.

That only made me angrier. I wanted to punish her for making me feel this way.

I gripped her hips hard and moved faster, pounding into her over and over again. I hadn't even kissed her. I wasn't going to. I was going to fuck her until both of us remembered that this was nothing more than a marriage of convenience. That what we had between us was money and an arrangement and sex.

That was it.

If she expected anything more, that was her fault. Her. Fault. And she deserved to be punished for it.

"This pussy is mine," I told her as I fucked her harder, my skin buzzing, my adrenaline rushing. "Mine. All mine."

She let out a gasp and I felt her come, her pussy clenching tight as a glove around my cock. That was all it took, and I was coming right along with her, pulling her head back by her hair and reaching around to grab her breast.

"Oh my god," she panted, the contractions still squeezing inside her.

As soon as the aftershocks were gone, I pulled out and left the room, abandoning her while she was still bent over the couch.

I told myself it didn't matter. Her feelings didn't matter. I couldn't let her get under my skin. I had to stay focused. I wasn't going to let a hot piece of ass get in the way of what I had worked for years to achieve.

Letting Tori distract me was the last thing I should be doing.

CHAPTER 22

I was in big, big trouble. After last night, I knew without a doubt that I was really and truly falling for Stefan. I'd known that I had feelings for him, sure, but this was bigger. Stronger. Deeper. I was *falling in love*. And it wasn't just the blazing hot sex, or the fact that he had come to my event to support me, though that had been the impetus for everything I was feeling.

It was the way he'd spent the entire night at my side, charming and schmoozing with everyone I was going to be working with for the next several years. He impressed them, and impressed me with his knowledge about the classes I'd mentioned to him in passing or the professors I liked best. It was a side of him I'd never seen before—a side that was interested in me and cared about the path I was on.

I also knew people would be asking me questions later about my extremely handsome, charismatic husband. I wouldn't blame them; because of my unusual relationship with Stefan, I hadn't said much about him to anyone. Seeing him show up out of the blue at an event like that, and considering the way he'd made such an effort to chat everybody up, I expected I'd be fielding a whole slew of questions. And I wouldn't mind answering them. I was proud that he'd been by my side. Proud to call him my husband.

After we'd left the party, I had wanted to thank him, to show him how much his attendance had meant to me. And the only way I could think of doing that was with sex. It was the way we communicated best.

I could still remember the way his hand had felt on the back of my head as he guided my mouth up and down his cock. I'd never done anything like that before—had never even wanted to. But with Stefan things were different. Everything about him turned me on.

I'd loved that brief moment of control, when he was thrusting in my mouth with his eyes closed and his head tilted back. Completely at my mercy.

But I loved it even more when we got back to the condo and he had taken that control back. It had almost felt like Stefan had *needed* to fuck me. Needed *me*.

I thought about it all night, long after he fell asleep. Part of me had wanted to move across the bed and lean my body against his, get as close as we'd been on the plane from Budapest. But I knew that doing that would be too much. It would be rushing things.

It would be a bad idea.

Because even though I was falling for him, there was no way to know if he was feeling the same way. We had agreed that this marriage was temporary. If I wanted things to change, if I wanted him to see that I could be more than just a convenient trophy wife, I'd have to show him how much sense we made as a couple. Not just in the bedroom, since we seemed to be doing pretty good in that arena, but in our day-to-day lives.

I had to show him that I could be there for him, the

same way he had been there for me at the UChicago mixer. It would only draw us closer together.

That's why I was walking through the lobby of the KZM building during my lunch break with a takeout bag in my hand. I'd forgone my afternoon study session at Harper and instead had taken an Uber back to the condo to change into something sexy and short and black. I normally wouldn't wear something like this during the day, but the dress was for him. I wanted to tempt him into taking a long lunch. Wanted to tempt him into taking *me* during his long lunch. Maybe on his desk. Or against the door.

"Where're you going to today, miss?" asked the security guard at the front desk.

"KZ Modeling," I told him.

"Do you have an appointment?" he asked.

My face flushed. "I...don't. I'm just here to drop off lunch for my husband. Stefan Zoric?"

I held up the takeout bag.

"I'm sorry, ma'am, but I can't let you up without an appointment. If you like I can call up there and talk to—"

"Oh no, please don't do that," I interrupted. "It's a surprise. He just works so hard, all these long hours, and I thought it'd be nice to bring him a hot meal. I'll be so quick."

Then I broke out my secret weapon of a smile that I'd honed over the years.

His expression melted. "Of course. That's very sweet of you. He's up on the twenty-ninth floor. You can check in with the receptionist up there."

"You're my hero," I gushed. Worked every time.

As I stood waiting at the bank of elevators, my skin tightened with anticipation at the thought of having sex with him in his office. That would be all the proof I needed that I drove him to distraction—successfully seducing him at work. Because no one worked harder than Stefan. His entire life revolved around his job, and I wanted to change that. I wanted to be a part of his life. Wanted him to make space for me.

I knew I'd have to fight dirty to get that. So I hadn't bothered with underwear when I'd gotten dressed.

I gave my hips a little extra swing as I stepped out onto the twenty-ninth floor, my excitement growing at the thought of seeing him. Even the reception area full of beautiful women, clearly waiting for an audience with the casting executives at KZM, didn't faze me.

When I got to the receptionist's desk, I thanked my lucky stars that after the wedding, Michelle had taken charge of getting me a new ID with Stefan's last name on it.

"I'm Stefan's wife, Victoria Zoric," I said, sliding my ID across the desk.

The woman smiled broadly. "Hello, Mrs. Zoric," she said. "Nice to finally meet you."

Mrs. Zoric. I liked the sound of that.

"I'm just bringing him lunch and then I'll be on my way. Is he in his office?" I asked.

She handed me a clipboard so I could sign in and then looked at her computer. "I believe so," she said, pointing toward one end of the hallway.

I thanked her and headed in that direction.

The KZ Modeling offices were absolutely stunning. There were modern, black and chrome details everywhere, but the colorful, blown-up photographs on the walls kept everything from feeling too cold and stark. I wondered if Emzee had shot them.

As I passed offices with frosted glass doors, and conference rooms with more glass, I started to get nervous. What if I couldn't find his office? What if he was in a meeting?

Maybe this had been a mistake. I walked faster down the hall, reading name plaques, peeking into open doors, and letting my gaze skim the faces in the conference rooms.

Most of them were occupied by men in suits, though some of the smaller offices had models inside, chattering excitedly as they perched on chairs.

At the end of the hallway, I finally found Stefan's office. It was across from his father's and both of them looked like they had incredible corner office views. Konstantin's door was closed, and I wondered if the elder Zoric was inside. I hadn't seen him since the night of the Zoric family dinner, and I was hoping to keep it that way.

I ducked into Stefan's office, a huge smile on my face. He wasn't there.

Dismayed, I set the bag down on his desk. Maybe the receptionist had been mistaken. Maybe she'd read the schedule wrong. At least the food would be here for him when he returned, I reasoned.

As I came out of Stefan's office, the door to Konstantin's was opening. I immediately recognized Stefan, but he wasn't alone. He had his arm around a woman in her early 20s—a KZM model, by the looks of her—and he was saying something to her in a low, soothing tone.

It was the same tone he'd used with me after my father's heart attack, on the private plane back to the States. It was his comforting voice.

I felt a twinge of jealousy until I realized the woman was crying. Her eyes were red and puffy, and she looked distraught. Even so, she was striking. With her pale skin and red, curly hair that looked like a halo of flames, I pegged her for an Eastern European redhead, not Irish. She had a beauty mark at the corner of her mouth, almost giving her a redheaded Marilyn Monroe look.

Stefan's whispers stopped abruptly when he looked up and saw me standing there.

"Just go home, try to relax," he told the young woman, who was sniffling into a tissue. "We'll reach out soon."

He gestured for her to head down the hallway toward the elevators. She nodded and did as she was told. The moment she was out of sight, Stefan had his hand around my arm and was pulling me into his office.

It was exactly as I had imagined.

Only right now, he was angry, not turned on.

"What are you doing here?" he asked as soon as the office door was closed.

"I—I brought you lunch. I just came to see—"

"You shouldn't be here." His voice was so harsh, I stepped back involuntarily.

I couldn't believe he was talking to me like this. Especially after the way he'd behaved at my event. My feelings had changed, but it was clear that his hadn't.

I couldn't help but think it had something to do with the woman he'd been comforting. Had I walked in on something he didn't want me to see?

"Why was that woman crying?" I asked. "Did somebody—assault her?"

"That's none of your business," he snapped. "Stay out of it."

I flinched. It was clear he was hiding something. "Is she...do you have a relationship with her?"

His eyes softened, and I saw a hint of the man I'd seen the other night. A hint of the man who, only moments ago, had been comforting a woman in distress.

"Of course not," he said, some of the edge gone from his voice. "But she's pregnant, and it's...come as a surprise."

Relief flooded me.

Then I realized the situation. "I guess her career's going to be on hold for a while."

No wonder she was so upset. This industry was impossible to get into, and who knew if she'd even get a second chance after having a baby.

Stefan nodded, letting out a long breath. "That's right. She won't be able to model anymore." Then his expression hardened again. "You need to leave now," he ordered. "Don't ever stop in unless you're invited. Are we clear?"

I nodded, even though I still felt like there was something he was hiding. Did he just not want his private life tangled up with his work life?

It made sense, but it still hurt.

I shouldered my purse and was just about to leave when he spoke again.

"And Tori?"

"Yes?" I turned eagerly. Maybe he'd finally noticed what I was wearing. Maybe he was going to apologize for being so gruff. Maybe he was going to thank me for thinking of him and bringing him lunch, or come clean to me about whatever he was hiding.

"I'm working late tonight. Probably all this week. Don't wait up."

I slammed the door on my way out.

TORI

CHAPTER 23

uming, I stormed out of the building and back onto the street. After the event at my school, it had seemed like things between us had shifted, like they were going to be different going forward.

How had I read the situation so wrong?

I didn't want to play by Stefan's rules anymore. If he wasn't going to come home for dinner, why should I be there either? He had told me not to wait up—well, I wouldn't. I was going out. It was time I had some fun on my own.

Since I'd begun my program at UChicago, Grace and I had texted a few times, but beyond assuring her that 'things' with my new husband had finally smoothed out, we hadn't been able to schedule a date to catch up. I was always so busy with school, and she had just left to go on a buying trip to Italy. I debated calling Emzee and taking her up on her offer to hang out, but I was worried she'd mention it to Stefan and my plans would be thwarted. Because I didn't just want to grab a coffee or see a movie. I wanted to party.

And the fake ID I'd mentioned to Emzee at the family dinner hadn't been a joke.

Is the invitation to join you guys for drinks still open? I texted my classmate Lila.

Some of the older students in my program had been begging me to come out with them ever since the term had started. I was always invited, but I'd been focused on my schoolwork, and making sure I was home at night to be with Stefan. On top of that, I knew the girls were all actively seeking their Prince Charmings, and I'd already found mine.

Or so I had thought.

Always, Lila responded. A feisty but sweet senior from Atlanta, Lila was the first friend I'd made in the program, and I'd helped her out a lot with her Latin 4 homework this semester. She always took charge when it came to planning the group outings. *We're hitting a few bars. You up for it?*

None of them knew how young I was, and I didn't plan to tell them. *Hell yes.*

She texted back, *Woot! Gonna get those goody two shoes a little dirty tonight!*

I couldn't help grinning at her enthusiastic response, and I typed back a smiling devil horns emoji.

Lila responded with a flurry of excited gifs to express her approval. I laughed as they almost tripled when she looped me into the group text for the evening, and the rest of the girls expressed their excitement over me finally joining them.

We're going to have so much fun! Diane said. She was a junior from rural Vermont, kind of a hippie, and getting a late start with her college education after spending a few years with the Peace Corps.

Wear something sexy, Audrey, the sophisticated New Yorker, added. *The lower the top, the more free drinks we'll get, LOL.*

I figured that even if I went out and had some drinks with my friends, I'd still be home before Stefan. I could probably take a long shower, change into something sexy, and crawl into bed without him being the wiser—though I was annoyed that I still wanted to dress up for him after the way he had treated me. The thing was, I still wanted him. Sometimes his aggressiveness made me want him even more. Because the thought of him turning those intense, angry eyes in my direction and taking out his frustration on my body gave me all sorts of sexy chills.

I couldn't help smiling at the thought of how pissed Stefan would be if he knew what I had planned. Not that I was going out to meet men, but I definitely planned to have fun. It would be my first time ever going out to drink and dance and have a good time.

I hurried to my closet to get dressed.

Tonight, it was all about me. I wasn't dressing to excite or impress Stefan. I wasn't dressing for one of my father's events, or for Stefan's family. I didn't have to be proper or enticing or anything I didn't want to be.

At the same time I didn't want to look too expensive— my party companions were all older students on scholarships or taking out loans to get their degrees—so the last thing I wanted to do was throw my wealth (or Stefan's) in their faces

I settled on a pair of tight black jeans and flowy silk top, but couldn't resist pulling out the fancy red stilettos I'd gotten from the hotel boutique in Vienna. Once I added a pair of sparkly statement earrings and my Chanel purse—

the one that always got me compliments when I brought it to class—I was ready for a night out on the town with my friends.

I couldn't wait to let loose.

Back in high school, I had to be so careful with everyone in Springfield watching me and judging me. As a senator's daughter, I had to be so squeaky clean it was exhausting sometimes. I'd agreed to let Grace hook me up with the fake ID at the start of senior year, but never had the nerve to use it. If I got caught, I wouldn't have only been in trouble with my father; I'd be on the news. It would have damaged my father's campaign and his reputation, jeopardized his career.

But in Chicago, I could be anonymous.

It was also nice that my new friends didn't seem to care that I was Senator Lindsey's daughter. To them, I was just Tori—fellow student and linguistics nerd. Who had a super hot husband.

After the mixer at school, I'd gained slight notoriety within my department for being married to a 'grade A hottie.' At least, that was how Lila had put it. I had no doubt that once we were all out in a more casual setting, they'd be pumping me for information about him. I'd keep the details to a minimum; I didn't want them to know the true nature of my marriage, and I definitely didn't need to share the more intimate details of our relationship either.

With one last swipe of lipstick and a final fluff of my hair, I headed out and dialed an Uber. I didn't use the private car that Stefan kept on call, that way he couldn't get a heads up from the driver on where I'd asked to be dropped off.

I arrived at the address Lila had texted me to find it was

a swanky bar in the Loop. The girls were in the back at a table already loaded with drinks. There were four shots lined up when I walked up to the table.

"Oooooo girl," Lila greeted me with a hug, then leaned back to appraise my outfit. "The free drinks are gonna be rolling in tonight!"

"Endless free drinks all around," Audrey agreed.

"Only because I'm with you babes," I said modestly but truthfully.

"You look really nice," Diane said with a grin, raising her drink in a toast.

The three of them looked incredible. They were all a little older than me—no fake IDs necessary—and had an air of worldliness that I admired. Everyone was dressed to the nines: Lila in a body-hugging floral dress that flattered her warm skin, Diane in dark jeans and a low-cut tank top, sporting fire engine red lips, and Audrey with her signature heavy eye makeup, in a tight black skirt and matching top that showed off just a hint of midriff.

It was quite a change from their usual look, being a bunch of exhausted college students in jeans and t-shirts. This was the first time I'd seen them all dolled up and ready to party.

"You guys look amazing," I told them as a shot of tequila was pushed toward me.

"We might be all business during the day," Lila said. "But when it's nighttime..."

"We go all out!" Audrey said, raising her shot. "To a good time!"

"A good time," we all echoed before clinking our shot glasses together and tossing them back.

The tequila burned my throat and my lips began to

tingle almost immediately. I didn't drink much straight booze—most of my experience with alcohol had been tastes of champagne or wine, or those fruity cocktails I'd gotten sick off of in Vienna—but I wasn't going to be the one person in the group drinking chardonnay while the others were tossing back shots. I was one of them tonight. Time to cut loose.

"So," Lila said, leaning forward conspiratorially. "We decided to mix it up tonight."

"Mix it up?" I echoed.

Diane nodded, tucking one of her long braids behind her ear. "We usually bar hop for a few hours and then find our way to one of our favorite clubs to dance."

"But..." Audrey glanced around at the others before turning to me with a big smile. "In honor of you joining us tonight, we thought we should do something a little different."

I didn't know whether I should be excited or nervous and I told them as much.

"Oh, excited for sure," Lila said with a huge grin.

"Finish up your drinks, ladies," Audrey said, checking her watch. "We're going to be late if we don't leave soon."

There were two more shots for each of us at the table and I gamely followed suit and tossed them back. I was definitely feeling the effects as we headed out of the bar and into the cold November air.

I hadn't even thought to bring a jacket, something I regretted as I realized we were walking to our next destination.

"Here, take my scarf," Diane said sweetly, wrapping the huge, hand knitted thing around me. It smelled like patchouli and incense, but it helped a lot.

"Where are we going?" I asked, trying to keep up with my new friends, who were all walking at a pretty brisk pace.

"It's not far at all," Lila said. She slowed her pace and put her arm around me as we walked, warming me up a little. "And trust me, when we get there, you're gonna be so hot you'll be glad you didn't bring a jacket."

It must be one of those trendy, themed night clubs with a hundred people packed onto the floor. The thought of it both scared and excited me. I didn't know much about dancing outside of the ballroom, but I figured it'd be easier to blend in if I was surrounded by bodies.

Suddenly, Audrey let out a crow of delight.

"We're he-ere!" she said with obvious excitement.

My mouth dropped open when I looked up at the building and saw where we were.

It was a strip club.

A male strip club.

"Now, we know that none of the guys here are half as hot as the man you have at home," Lila said, giving my arm a squeeze.

"But we're all single ladies and we need some man meat tonight!" Audrey said with a lecherous grin. "And don't worry about tipping," she added, pulling a fat stack of ones and fives out of her purse. "We are totally prepared."

My eyes widened at the amount of money she was waving around. It was a lot of small bills, for a lot of g-strings. Or so I assumed. I had never been to a strip club in my life.

"Don't worry," Diane said quietly, pulling me to the side after seeing my face. "We'll be together the whole time. And it's mostly just screaming women throwing bachelorette parties, or groups of women who can't stop laughing. Try not to take it so seriously. It'll be fun."

I didn't know what to expect, but I was grateful for my fake ID when security checked them at the door. The last thing I wanted was to embarrass my new friends by not being able to get in. I was sure they didn't know I was eighteen.

"You know, in the 1580s, a stripper meant someone who stripped the bark off of trees," I babbled as we headed in. "In the 1830s, the meaning changed again and a stripper referenced a machine or appliance. It wasn't until the 1930s that the term striptease was finally introduced, and that's how stripper evolved into the word it is today."

All three of the girls turned and stared at me. For a moment, my stomach sank. This was going to be high school all over again—people thinking I was a total weirdo for knowing things like this and bringing them up at the most random times. I guess it was one thing to talk about this stuff in school, but another to bring it up in public.

I braced for the comments about what a loser I was.

Instead, Lila grinned broadly. "I read somewhere that *Time* magazine is actually the first place where the word 'striptease' was used."

"Really?" I asked, impressed and relieved.

"That's so cool," Audrey said.

Clearly, I had found my people.

Between Diane's reassurances in the line outside and the word-nerding I'd just engaged in with Lila and Audrey, I immediately felt better. Until we were shown to our seats. Right in the front row. My phone buzzed and I pulled to out to find several missed texts from Stefan.

Leaving work, the first one said. *Don't wait on me for dinner*.

It had been sent almost forty minutes ago.

I nearly laughed out loud. He'd probably lost his mind

when he got home and realized that not only did I have no intention of waiting on him to eat, but that I wasn't even home.

The next several texts revealed exactly that.

Where are you? he'd sent about twenty minutes ago.

Ten minutes later: *I need to know where you are.*

Did he? I was an adult, and I'd decided to go out for once. There was no good reason for him to keep me on such a short leash. And besides, I was safe with my friends.

I put my phone on silent and put it back in my purse. I'd spent enough of our marriage sitting alone somewhere, wondering where he was—he could see how it felt for once.

The lights dimmed and an announcer told us the show was about to start. Apparently, this wasn't just a strip club; tonight they were having an all-male revue.

"Like stripping, but with a theme," Lila explained as a bow-tied waiter brought us drinks.

We were seated in a little alcove with cushy chairs and a table. There were a few of them clustered around the stage, all full of screaming, drunk women. Most of the tables seemed to contain the bachelorette parties Diane had told me about—girls wearing 'Bride-to-Be' sashes or 'Feyoncé' shirts and penis necklaces. It *was* pretty hilarious, and I started to relax.

I hadn't had a bachelorette party, not that there would have been many people to invite. The weeks leading up to the wedding had zipped by so fast, they still felt like a blur. In a way, I figured this night was making up for what I'd missed out on.

The music was loud I could feel the bass vibrating through me. That, combined with the booze, made me feel tingly and excited. I liked the idea of watching the strippers and then going home to Stefan. Maybe even doing a little striptease for him. If I felt like it.

It was fun being out with the girls. I made a promise to myself to do it more often.

Then the show began. The lights went down and the crowd went insane. Women were screaming and shouting, glowsticks whirling all around us, and Lila, Audrey, and Diane all joined in, shouting their appreciation for the dancers who were about to come out. To calm my nerves, I grabbed my drink, downing it so fast that the girls all giggled and applauded me.

"Go, Tori, go!" cheered Lila.

But before a single man could step across that stage, I was yanked out of my chair. I turned to find Stefan standing there, hulking over our booth, his eyes ablaze with anger.

"What are you doing here?" I sputtered, the combined effects of the noise, his rough treatment, and all the alcohol I'd had making my head swim.

"You're supposed to be at home," he said.

I crossed my arms, not wanting to get into an argument with him in front of my friends, all of whom were now staring at us, their eyes wide, their mouths hanging open.

He turned to them. "She's only eighteen. Did you know that?"

Lila, Audrey, and Diane all shook their head in unison, looking like chastised children. Diane glanced toward the bouncers, probably checking to see if they were heading over.

"We're going," Stefan told me.

"I want to stay," I said, holding my ground, but when I looked back at my friends I could see they all had wide eyes.

"Maybe you should go," Lila said apologetically. "Especially if you're not twenty-one."

I was furious. Furious at Stefan for ruining my night and furious at the girls for letting him boss them around. Grabbing my bag, I stomped out of the club. Stefan followed behind me. Once we were outside, I turned to confront him.

It was cold, but I barely noticed. My anger and humiliation kept me warm.

"How did you get into that club?" he asked before I could say anything.

"How did you find me?" I demanded right back.

I hadn't told anyone where I was going, and hadn't used his driver for that exact reason. Was he having me followed?

"I asked first," he said, crossing his arms.

There was no arguing when he got like this.

"I have a fake ID," I told him. "Like most teenagers in America. My friend got it for me when I was seventeen, but I never used it before."

"And they let you in with that? Unbelievable," he said. "Let me see it."

I dug around in my bag and handed it over.

"Great," he said, pocketing it. "Tonight was also the last time you'll ever use it."

My mouth dropped open. "That's not yours," I told him.

"Report me to the police," he shot back. "I'm sure they'll be happy to help you get your illegal fake ID back from your husband."

I was furious but I knew he was right.

"How did you find me here?" I asked again, knowing that he owed me that at least.

"I put a tracking app on your phone," he said, turning and walking away from me.

"What?" I hurried to catch up.

"After your little stunt in Europe, I knew I couldn't trust you," he said. "So I had it added to your phone so I'd know where you are at all times."

"You have no right!" I nearly shouted at him.

He turned, stopping me in my tracks. "I have every right. I pay the phone bill," he said. "In fact, I pay for everything you have. Everything you want. *Anything* you want. And as your husband, I need to be able to know where you are and make sure you're safe."

"That's not fair," I said. "I never know where you are."

"We're going home," he told me, but I didn't budge. It was freezing, but I didn't care. I wasn't going anywhere with him.

Without pausing, Stefan grabbed my arm and nearly dragged me to the waiting Town Car. I could feel the anger radiating off of him. I didn't know what he would do when we were alone, but the moment the car door closed, he yanked me toward him.

And kissed me.

The kiss was harsh and unrelenting and undeniably hot. His tongue thrusted aggressively, as if he were claiming me with his mouth. His hands were everywhere, palming my ass, tugging my nipples, pulling my hair. I groaned into his mouth and kissed him back. But the moment I did, he pulled away from me. We were both breathing hard.

"I need to know where you are at all times," he said. "You're my responsibility. Don't ever disappear like that again." Then he turned away, facing his window.

We drove back to the condo in silence. When we got there, he went into the bathroom and slammed the door behind him. I undressed and crawled into bed, waiting, but when he joined me he didn't reach for me. Didn't try to finish what we had started in the car.

I was confused, lying there in the dark. What did this all mean? He had been worried about me. That much was clear.

Was it because he considered me his belonging?

Or because he actually cared?

TORI

CHAPTER 24

"—Leaving for New York in an hour," Stefan said, jarring me from my sleep.

"What?" I sat up and rubbed the sleep out of my eyes. As I blinked in the early morning light, I saw that he was moving around the room. Making trips to the closet. Packing a suitcase. So he could leave me. "Why?"

"I have work there."

Of course he did. "On a Saturday?"

"You know I don't get weekends off," he said.

It felt like he was running away. From our fight. From me. I didn't like it—it made me feel defeated in my efforts to take our relationship further. And after all the upheaval last night, we hadn't had a chance to mend things, or even talk about them at all.

"Well, how long is the trip?" I asked, knowing I sounded petulant. But that's how I felt.

"A few days," Stefan said, not even glancing my way.

As he packed, I got up to start my day. I took my time in the bathroom, mulling over my lingering anger that he'd barged in on me at the club and embarrassed me in front of my friends. I would definitely need to text them later to explain. I'd gotten a few texts from them around 2 am, apologizing for taking me out when I was underage. Hopefully they still wanted to hang out with me after everything that had happened.

I stood in the closet, trying to decide what to wear while Stefan came in and out, taking a suit from his side and gathering other things from his drawers. I did my best to ignore him, standing there in my robe while studying my wardrobe with laser focus.

Did he really think I was going to just sit at home and stay put while he traipsed off to New York for the weekend? There was plenty of mischief I could get up to while he was gone, fake ID or not. He might have been worried about where I was last night, but he wouldn't be able to check on me when he was gone. Maybe I'd even get another phone, just for my nights out. As far as he'd know, I would still be in the condo every time he checked my location.

But despite my excitement at all the fun I was dreaming of having, I was mostly overwhelmed with disappointment. Because despite how Stefan had acted, I was sure things between us had changed in a big way. And that we were finally on the path to something stronger, something deeper and more real than just an arranged marriage.

I knew that under all the swagger and the power trips, he was a good, decent person. He had shown me evidence that he was. The way he'd comforted me after my father's heart attack. The way he'd shown up at the mixer at my school. Even last night—I knew he'd dragged me out of that club because he was genuinely worried when I'd disappeared, not simply to assert his control. He obviously *cared*. That this wasn't just a marriage of convenience for him.

"Where's your bag?"

Stefan's voice startled me out of my thoughts. I turned around, finding him standing there with an impatient look on his face. God. Why was he so damn attractive?

"Your. Bag," he said slowly, as if I was a child.

"Why do I need a bag?" I asked.

"I told you. We're leaving for New York," he said. "Plane's waiting for us."

My heart leapt. "I'm going with you?"

He *did* want me with him! And I was going to New York with him because he didn't want to be apart from me for the weekend. My sour mood immediately dissipated.

"You're only coming because I couldn't find a babysitter," he said. "And last night proved that you can't be trusted to behave while I'm not here."

My heart sank a little. On the other hand, even if he wasn't taking me because he was going to miss me, he was still taking me. That was the most important thing. I would get to go to New York, and I'd get to be with him.

"I've always wanted to see New York," I said. "My father took me a few times, when he had work stuff, but we barely left the hotel. It seemed so busy and exciting, though. Maybe I'll have time to go to a museum or something."

He nodded. "It's possible."

Quickly, I packed a bag. It would be cold and beautiful this time of year, and I had no idea what we would be doing there, so I made sure to pack something for every possible occasion; a night out at the theater, a stroll in Central Park, a trip to the Met, ice skating at Rockefeller Center. My suitcase was bulging by the time I got everything in it.

Stefan gave it a look when I lugged it out of the closet but said nothing. Instead, he just gestured to the doorman who had come up to help with the luggage, and in the blink of an eye it was whisked out of the condo, presumably down to the car waiting to take us to the airport.

"Are you ready?" Stefan asked.

I shouldered my carry on, almost as heavy and over-packed as my suitcase, and gave him an eager nod. I was going to New York. I couldn't wait.

When we stepped into the cabin of the private jet, it became blatantly obvious that this was indeed a business trip. Konstantin, Luka, and Emzee were all waiting for us.

"Tori, you came!" Emzee squealed, jumping up to greet me with a hug.

She immediately pulled me to the back of the plane where she could update me on everything that had happened since I last saw her. Even if this was a work week-end, at least I'd get to spend some time with her. I liked Emzee a lot. She was funny and friendly and could go on and on for hours talking passionately about her photography. We chatted while the crew readied the plane, but then she was called up to the front by Luka, who gave me a long, leering smile.

I turned away without smiling back, still disturbed by the way he'd cornered me in the condo and basically asked me to sit on his dick. I knew he was young and used to getting his way with women, but even if he'd been drunk, it was completely unacceptable. I was his brother's wife. But in a way, I was grateful—because his actions were what had led to me and Stefan finally consummating our marriage. I could only hope that Luka would give up the drinking.

We took off and I curled up on the couch, watching Chicago out the window as it got smaller and smaller below us. Luka and Emzee had settled into their own seats on opposite ends of the plane, with Luka scrolling through Instagram on his phone and Emzee flipping through a folder of recent photos she had taken. Overall, it was shaping up to be a mellow two-hour flight.

Up toward the front, Stefan and Konstantin were talking, their heads close together, hands gesturing emphatically. They were discussing KZM business, no doubt. I had smiled at Konstantin when we got on the plane, but tried my best not to make eye contact. He still made me uneasy in his presence, and the less time I spent with him, the better.

I watched their conversation from the back of the plane. I couldn't hear what they were saying, but judging by the hand gestures and the look on Stefan's face, it didn't seem like a very friendly conversation. It looked like they were arguing.

Finally, Konstantin pointed his finger directly into Stefan's chest.

My pulse kicked. I had no idea what Stefan would do. I could see a muscle in his jaw tense, and his own hand curl into a fist, but he didn't say anything. Instead, he just stared at his father and gave a nod. Then he got up and came to the back of the plane.

I half expected him to take a seat behind Emzee or Luka, but instead he sat down next to me on the couch. It was obvious he was angry about whatever he'd just discussed with his father.

"Is everything okay?" I asked gently.

Stefan didn't look at me, just straight ahead at the back of his father's head.

"It's fine," he said flatly. "Just business stuff."

It had to be more than just that, but I didn't press him. I had a feeling he wanted to stew with his thoughts for a bit, so I figured the best thing I could do was keep quiet and let him.

"Psst! Tori," Emzee was hissing at me. "Girl talk!"

I looked up and she motioned me toward the empty seat next to her. With a grin, I got up and moved to sit beside her. I was sure Stefan would appreciate the space.

"Let's lean our chairs all the way back," she said with a grin.

We did, reclining almost fully flat. Then Emzee shook out a blanket and covered us with it. In the semi-dark, it was almost like we were in a tent. Emzee's grey eyes sparkled with mischief.

"I feel like we're having a sleepover," I told her.

She laughed. "Exactly! So now we have to tell each other secrets."

"What kind of secrets?" I asked.

"I'll go easy on you," Emzee said. "You can tell me anything you're comfortable with."

I thought about it for a moment, but it didn't take long to come up with something.

"I'm not sure if this counts," I whispered, "but I used my fake ID to get into a strip club last night."

Emzee gasped, grabbing my hands. "You bad girl! I'm impressed. You seemed better behaved than that, but it turns out you're a wild woman. Just like me."

I laughed. "It wasn't that exciting—your brother found me and took my ID and dragged me out before I saw even one oily buff guy in a thong."

We both giggled, Emzee kicking her feet a little with glee.

"Now you," I said. "Tell me something good. Anything I don't know about you."

"I've got something even better," she whispered. "About my brother. If you're interested."

I lowered my voice. "Tell me."

"You've seen all the paintings hanging up at Stefan's place, right?"

I nodded. They'd been one of the first things that stood out to me about the condo. "Yeah. They're great. A little dark, but gorgeous."

I remembered angular swaths of shadow and light, bent figures, light spilling from windows, hands and trees and churning skies in thick impasto, like Van Gogh.

Emzee smiled. "Those are all our mother's."

My heart felt like it was cracking. "Your mom painted all of those?"

She nodded. "Stefan's always surrounded himself with them. Even when he was away at college. I have a bunch too, but I keep them in storage. It makes sad to see them. I hate that I don't remember her."

"I'm sorry," I said. "I lost my mother when I was young, too."

"I know," Emzee said. "That's why I told you about Stefan. I thought you'd get it."

"I do."

Emzee smiled, but it was a little less mischievous this time. "Your turn. Tell me something you haven't told anybody else."

I chewed my lip for a moment. "Okay. I'm glad I got married, for a lot of reasons, but one of the biggest ones is that...I'm glad to be away from my dad. I mean he's great, don't get me wrong, but I've always been like a pet to him. And he had so many rules for me growing up, it's just... really nice to be out on my own, doing my own thing, without him running my life."

For a second Emzee was quiet, and I wondered if I'd said the wrong thing.

Then, in the ghost of a whisper, she said, "I know

exactly what you mean. Moving out on my own when I turned eighteen was the best thing I ever did. So liberating."

We shared a smile.

For the rest of the flight, I helped Emzee go over the proofs of her photos, but I couldn't stop thinking about Stefan and those paintings. Whether he could admit it or not, losing his mother at a young age had scarred him, had made him feel completely powerless. And he'd reacted in the only way that made sense—by trying to control everything else around him. Even me. So maybe the reason he'd acted so cruel all those times wasn't because he wanted to hurt me. But because somewhere, deep down, he couldn't stand the thought of losing me, too.

TORI

CHAPTER 25

N ew York City looked as picture-perfect as a postcard, and I couldn't stop staring at all the tall buildings and yellow taxis and colorful denizens as the car took us to our luxury hotel. We had arrived that afternoon and headed straight there, a fancy building on the Upper East Side owned by someone with whom Konstantin and his family had a relationship. Thanks to the connection, we were given the total VIP treatment, each of us getting a suite on a separate floor.

The view from our window was breathtaking. I could see Central Park from one angle—all the lush trees and winding paths—and the rest of the cityscape from another. If Stefan had told me I had to stay in the hotel while he worked, I wouldn't have even minded, the view was that magical.

But instead, I was going to be accompanying the Zorics to a fashion show featuring a handful of models from KZ Modeling's roster. The designer was up and coming, and the fashion world was going crazy over her work, so it was going to be a big event with lots of media there. We arrived at the hotel, and I immediately began getting ready for the night ahead.

Unlike my ill-fated night out with the girls from UChicago, tonight I needed to look like the expensive, well-dressed wife of a man who ran one of the most prestigious modeling agencies in the world. People would definitely be looking at me, and I might even be photographed by the media. I wanted to make sure I'd get attention for the right reasons.

I spent hours on my hair and makeup, until my hair cascaded down my back like a gleaming wave and my makeup was flawless; sultry but appropriately subtle. I wasn't trying to make a scene. I just wanted to look like I belonged.

Knowing that we would be surrounded by celebrities and other wealthy members of New York society, I was glad I had chosen to bring the diamond necklace that Stefan had given me in Vienna. I'd been waiting for an excuse to wear it again, and it would be the perfect accompaniment to my Zac Posen dress. The design itself was simple—a chiffon v-neck with flutter sleeves and tiers of ruffles from knee to ankle—but it hugged my curves and showed off the necklace perfectly. A pair of black stilettos gave me a few necessary inches, and my beaded, Art Deco style clutch gave the whole thing a pop of color and excitement.

Stefan was just finishing up with his tie when I walked out of the bedroom. He glanced up and his hands stilled mid-knot as he stared at me.

"Will this work?" I asked, spreading my arms and giving him a little twirl.

We hadn't had sex last night and my body was already feeling the effects. He looked so good in his suit that I was tempted to get on my knees and try to improve my oral sex technique. I craved him. I also knew the rest of the evening was going to be a long one, and with our early departure the following morning, I had a feeling we wouldn't be able to do much tonight either. I also knew I wouldn't be able to fully concentrate on anything else until he fucked me again.

I wanted him to rip off my expensive dress and carry me into the bedroom, taking me fast and rough as he pressed me against the floor-to-ceiling window, wearing only my shoes and the diamonds he had given me. I'd come hard, moaning against the glass with the city of New York spread out before me. The thought was so perverse and decadent that my skin grew hot and tight imagining it.

It was clear that Stefan's mind was going to equally dirty places. His eyes were intense, dark with lust. Did he miss touching me, too?

He let his eyes travel the length of my body but he didn't say anything. His hands were still tangled in his tie. Then, he lowered his hands and took a step toward me. I took a breath, knowing that in mere seconds he'd be in front of me.

But before he could take another step, there was a knock at the door.

"Come on, big brother!" Emzee's voice came through from the other side. "The car is waiting!"

Stefan turned away from me, returning his focus to the mirror and his tie.

"I'll get it," I told him, trying to ignore my sexual frustration.

"Agh! You look like a dream," Emzee told me when I greeted her.

"You do too," I said, because she did.

Her style was a little edgier than mine, her dark hair styled in an arrangement of almost-Viking type braids, her black dress sporting dramatic cutouts along the shoulders and down the back. With her neon eyeshadow and signature combat boots, she was definitely going to grab some attention tonight.

She looped her arm through mine.

"Let's go downstairs," she said. "The boys can catch up."

I cast one last look in Stefan's direction, but he didn't even glance over—he was too focused on his tie.

"See you in a minute," I called out, and then followed Emzee downstairs, where a limo was waiting for us.

"I love New York," she gushed as we got in.

There was a bottle of champagne and Emzee poured us both a glass. I hesitated for a moment, but then figured that this was all part of the deal; it would be weird if I didn't drink. Plus, it wasn't like I'd be throwing back shots like I'd done last night at the bar. This was champagne. Hardly alcoholic at all. And besides, we were celebrating.

By the time Stefan, Luka, and Konstantin joined us in the car, the champagne had lifted my spirits and taken the edge off my intense desire for my husband. The hungry look he shot my way when he got in didn't help, but I was determined to spend the evening playing the role of attentive, respectful trophy wife. I would show Stefan how much of an asset I could be, and that it was to his benefit to bring me along to events like this.

We made our way through traffic across the city, heading to the show at another fancy hotel across town. It was a new collection of couture dresses, and everyone big in the fashion industry was going to be in attendance. Because KZM had provided the majority of the models that were walking in the show, we'd been given front row seats.

Cameras flashed as we walked the red carpet for the

event. Celebrities of all stripes were there, and I did my best to keep from gaping at them. While I'd met plenty of famous people through my father, it was still hard to not get star struck.

I did my best to adopt the same disinterested, polite smile that Stefan was wearing, all the while trying to keep my distance from Luka and Konstantin. Luka was easy; he was currently distracted by one of the models who would be walking in the show. A model that I recognized.

It was the beautiful redhead I'd seen at Stefan's office the other day. The one he'd told me was pregnant.

I gave her a quick once over. She wasn't showing yet, her body stunning in a silky midnight blue jumpsuit. Luka had his hand on the small of her back and was holding her close, whispering something in her ear that made her laugh. If I had thought she was beautiful when her eyes were puffy and red, then she was absolutely gorgeous dressed so glamorously, her face made up perfectly. She put her hand on Luka's chest, and said something that made him grin.

Was he her baby's father?

Konstantin was also distracted by the models surrounding us, but not so distracted that he hadn't sent a few lewd glances my way. Thankfully, he seemed more focused on work than on the way my necklace was sparkling between my breasts. The only Zoric I wanted to appreciate that was Stefan.

Since we'd exited the limo, he'd kept his arm firmly around my waist. Part of me knew he was likely doing it because we needed to keep up appearances for the cameras. But the other part of me knew he didn't need to keep his hand curled quite so tightly around me. That his fingers didn't need to be flexing and unflexing, stroking the soft curve of my hip. That he didn't need to hold me so close.

He was doing all of that because he wanted to. And because he couldn't help himself.

I smiled up at him shyly, and he gave me a smile in return.

We finished with pictures and headed into the event. Because KZM had been so crucial to the event, we were given backstage passes so we could go backstage and mingle, get an insider view of what was happening before the show began.

It was a flurry of activity, with hair and makeup artists barking orders at assistants and frantic models in various stages of undress. Some of them had curlers in their hair, some were being sprayed with hairspray to help the clothes adhere more tightly to them. The vibe was overwhelming and loud and fun.

Luka had abandoned his redheaded model and was now chatting up another girl with black hair, naked from the waist up. She was giggling and tossing her hair back, her breasts jiggling with every movement. Luka wasn't even trying not to stare.

I saw the redhead sitting at a dressing table, examining the bags under her eyes. I quietly stepped away from Stefan, who was talking to the ebullient designer, and headed over to the redhead. If we were potentially going to be connected through a baby, I wanted to be friendly.

"Hi," I said, startling her a little.

She met my gaze in the mirror. "Hello," she responded.

I waited for her to recognize me from that day at the agency, but it seemed like she didn't. Instead she went back to focusing on her reflection.

"Are you excited for the show?" I asked.

"Yes," she said, still not looking at me.

Had I guessed wrong? Was Luka really not the father?

Or was there something else going on? She wasn't going to talk to me, obviously. I took the hint and moved away.

All around me were models getting ready, but any time our eyes would meet, they'd turn away. I was getting the cold shoulder from all of them—the same women who were happy to greet my husband and his family with smiles and cheek kisses. Something wasn't right.

Judging by their accents, most of them seemed to be Eastern European, which accounted for the constant cheek kissing. It wasn't that unusual, I supposed, considering that that was where the Zorics were from originally.

The show was going to begin shortly so we were shown to our seats, and I tried to set my anxiety aside. I'd never been to a fashion show before, but it didn't disappoint. The whole event was beyond thrilling, all of the clothes exquisite and sophisticated. It was a true honor to sit in the front row and watch these women (and a few men) walk the runway.

When the lights came back up I thought we were done, but we moved on from there to a lavish after-party, where the Veuve Clicquot was flowing and the models were mingling with guests. I stayed close to Stefan's side, smiling as he introduced me to people and making polite small talk. After a while, though, I noticed that Konstantin seemed to be talking with a different model every time I glanced over at him.

I began to pay more attention to what he was doing, and realized that not only was he talking to different models, he was also making sure to personally introduce them to certain guests at the party. Most of them seemed to be men.

No, that wasn't right.

All of them were men.

I watched a leggy young model with a platinum pixie cut get presented to a man that was probably her father's age. She smiled and laughed and seemed to be having a good time. After Konstantin left the two of them alone, they chatted for a little longer and then, to my astonishment, walked out of the party together.

Staying close to Stefan, I started observing Konstantin more purposefully. It seemed like almost all of the models he had introduced to men—most of them older men—ended up leaving the party with their new acquaintances. Red flags were going up, but I didn't want to judge. People came to these things to have a good time. It was none of my concern who went home with whom. In fact, I wondered if the men were simply photographers or managers or other designers. Maybe they were heading off to talk business.

Then I got a better look at the next girl Konstantin homed on—the beautiful redhead I'd tried to engage in conversation earlier that evening. The one who Luka had been flirting with.

"Where's Luka?" I asked Stefan, tugging his sleeve gently.

He shrugged. "Probably making the most of the party. What do you need?"

"I'm fine," I said with what I hoped was a reassuring smile. "Just haven't seen him for a bit. Thought maybe he'd stepped out."

"You know how my brother is. Always making new friends. I wouldn't be surprised if he ducked out early with one of them."

"Yeah." I forced a laugh, but my stomach was turning.

I scanned the room, finally spotting him at the other end, chatting up yet another of the models. He was giving her exactly the same type of attention he'd given the redhead—and the topless model backstage—flirting and touching her, turning on the charm full stop. This current woman, a brunette with diminutive, cat-like features, seemed more than thrilled with the attention. She was laughing and leaning closer to him, her hand on his arm.

If he was the father of the redhead's baby, it didn't seem like he was very committed to her. Maybe that's why she'd been so upset. Luka's appetite for women wasn't news to me, but I was shocked he would so blatantly—and publicly —snub a woman that he'd gotten pregnant.

I glanced back over at Konstantin and my eyes widened. He was introducing the beautiful redhead to a tough-looking older man dressed all in white, with long sideburns and a cruel sneer. I never liked to judge a book by its cover, but he looked mean. The redhead wore a smile, but her tense body language told me she was afraid. Her shoulders hunched a little, her arms crossed, and her body angled away from the man in white, almost as if she wanted to run.

Surely, this introduction would not go the way of the others.

But to my surprise, the redhead nodded at the sneering man and then he was pulling her through the crowd toward the exit, his fingers digging into her arm. Her smile looked strained, and it even slipped a couple of times before they disappeared from sight.

Luka couldn't possibly appreciate his father pawning off a woman who was the mother of his child. And he definitely wouldn't be happy seeing her leave with another man— especially not one like that; a thug who had treated her like a piece of cargo, dragging her across the room with a self-satisfied smirk on his lips. Maybe Luka wasn't the father after all.

Or maybe he hadn't seen what had just gone down.

I couldn't just ignore it. Tugging on Stefan's arm, I led him to a relatively quiet corner and quickly told him everything I'd witnessed—Luka's behavior toward the model who'd been crying at KZM, the introduction his father had made, the scary older man she had left with.

I expected him to be as surprised and suspicious as I was, but he barely mustered a shrug.

"It's not our business to police the actions of our talent," he said. "We're their agents. Anything beyond that isn't our call."

"But it's strange, don't you think? Especially since she's pregnant?" I asked. Especially if the baby was Luka's. "I can't believe she'd willingly leave with a man like that."

"Maybe she likes older men," Stefan said, smiling and waving at someone across the room, seeming like he was only half listening to what I had said.

"It didn't seem like she 'liked' him," I said, exasperated. "How are your alarm bells not going off? It's obvious she was having fun with *Luka* before. She didn't seem to be having fun with this guy at all." I emphasized Luka's name to see if that prompted a reaction from Stefan.

It didn't.

"You're getting too involved in other people's affairs," Stefan said, finally looking at me. "It's not for you to intervene, kitty cat."

I got a little thrill out of him using the nickname he gave me.

"But—"

"Let's get out of here," he said. "I've had enough work for one day. We'll go back to the hotel. We don't have to talk about anything at all."

The look in his eyes told me exactly what he wanted to do when we got back to our room. If he wasn't going to be concerned about any of this, I supposed I shouldn't either. Maybe this behavior was completely normal in the modeling world, and I just didn't understand how these things worked. I mean, I had to be wrong. The baby couldn't be Luka's. I was misreading the situation, and there were more important things to focus on than a single pregnancy scandal.

He leaned forward to whisper in my ear. "We leave now, and I'll take exactly one order from your lips before I tie your hands to the bedpost. Deal?" he asked.

My cheeks went hot, my knees already weak. How could I resist?

"Deal," I told him.

TORI

CHAPTER 26

I rolled over in bed, stretching my arms languorously, lifting one eyelid to check the time on the bedside clock. With a shock of adrenaline, I realized we were supposed to be back in Chicago by now. I'd stayed up so late with Stefan last night, I'd slept until almost eleven.

"Stefan?" I called out across the suite. Had he left without me?

"You can relax," he shushed me as he entered the bedroom. "I've decided we should stay in town for one more day. The others went back early this morning."

Another day in New York! I was so excited that I immediately got up, thinking of all the things we could do. Until I realized that Stefan probably wanted to stay for another reason.

"So you have a lot of work to do, I guess?" I asked.

"No," he said. "I thought we'd get out. See the city."

He didn't have to tell me twice. I got dressed in record time, wearing a pair of lace-up boots, comfortable jeans, and a blue cashmere sweater. Regardless of my laid-back style choices, I could tell Stefan appreciated my attire by the way his eyes raked down my body.

I practically skipped out of the suite, unbelievably excited to spend the entire day in New York with Stefan. It would be like our first day in Vienna, only better—because as we got into the cab, I noticed that Stefan's phone was absent from its permanent place in his hand.

As the city passed outside the window, I asked, "Where are we going?"

"I'm gonna show you New York," Stefan said. "You told me you always wanted to see it."

He had been listening to me. My heart soared.

We spent the whole day sightseeing. We went to Ess-a-Bagel first, to get coffee and real New York bagels. They were fresh and hot, slightly crisp on the outside and chewy on the inside, and I finally understood what the big deal about New York bagels was. Stefan ordered his with egg and pastrami, and mine was piled high with apple cinnamon cream cheese. Then we went to see Rockefeller Center and the New York Public Library, where they had an exhibit on Jazz culture in Harlem and another one on Walt Whitman. Stefan even bought me a bag of roasted almonds after I exclaimed about the smell of honey and sugar on the street.

We got to the Metropolitan Museum of Art in the late afternoon and stayed until dark, me drooling over the American Jewelry collection and the ancient marble statues; Stefan clearly appreciating the rooms full of armor and Egyptian artifacts. Finally, he stopped and spent awhile slowly circling a gallery hung with modern paintings that were reminiscent of his mother's.

As he stood there gazing at one particularly imposing piece, I walked up and took his hand. "They remind me of hers," I said, pointing. "The strong lines, and the shadowy figures. There's a lot of emotion here, don't you think?"

He looked over at me, mildly shocked, and I worried that I shouldn't have said anything.

"Emzee told me about the paintings at home," I explained. "I hadn't realized they were your mother's. They're really stunning. Intense. But so good."

Stefan nodded. "I think so too. I'm glad you like them."

And then he squeezed my hand, and I felt so warm just standing there with him.

Afterward, we had dinner in Tribeca at Atera, which I realized must have been practically impossible to get a reservation at, since every single table was full and there weren't many tables. The décor was very much Stefan's style—all black leather, brushed steel, and acacia wood—and the eighteen-course tasting menu allowed me to sample a little bit of everything without feeling too stuffed. Every dish looked like a work of art on par with what we'd seen at the Met. My favorites were the sweet snow crab and the dessert, which was pine syrup-drizzled ice cream cut into a spiral of thin, paper-like sheets and decorated with tiny purple flowers.

We ended the day in the most romantic way possible—taking a horse-drawn carriage ride through Central Park.

I had never been so happy.

Cuddled up under a blanket next to my husband, our breath making little clouds in the chilly New York air, I realized we'd just spent the perfect day together.

As we circled the park, Stefan's hand found its way to my knee under the blanket. I leaned against him, warmth spreading up my legs, wanting more. His hand moved higher, stroking the inside of my thigh. I could feel myself getting wet as I shifted helplessly in the seat. Suddenly, my jeans were too much of a barrier and the carriage ride was entirely too long.

I wanted to be back at the hotel, with the Do Not Disturb sign hung on our door. Instead, I had to wait while we rode through Central Park and Stefan's hand stroked up and down my leg, causing taut anticipation to build within me.

Finally, the ride was over, and Stefan helped me out of the carriage.

"Are you ready to go back to the hotel, kitty cat?" Stefan asked, his voice a throaty murmur in my ear.

I was so turned on I could barely say anything, so I just nodded. We got in a cab and made it back to the hotel within ten minutes and to our room in another five. Before the door was completely closed, Stefan had me pinned up against the wall, kissing me ravenously. Apparently, he hadn't been the only one turned on during our ride through Central Park.

His hands on me were rough, but I liked it. "Fuck me," I murmured into his mouth.

Abruptly, he pulled away. I sagged against the wall, immediately missing his touch. His taste.

"Take off your clothes," he ordered. "And get on the bed."

When I hesitated, he nearly growled at me.

"Now," he demanded.

I hurried into the bedroom, shedding clothes as I went. Leaving everything on the floor, I climbed onto the king-sized bed. I was about to roll over, when Stefan's voice stopped.

"No, stay there," he told me. "Just like that."

I was on my hands and knees, my ass in the air. It made me feel vulnerable and exposed, but I liked it. I wanted him to see me, see my body on display for him. I wanted him to touch me.

When he did, it was a gentle touch at my ankle, but still I jolted at the spark of his skin on mine. His hot palm slid up the back of my leg, coming up to rest on my ass. Then, without warning, he drew his hand back and slapped me hard, right there.

It stung, but it felt hot and tingling and good. I arched my back, wanting more.

Stefan slapped my ass again. I moaned.

"You like that?" he asked. "You like that, my filthy little kitty cat?"

I nodded, wanting him to do it again, wanting him to leave a mark. When he did, the sound of his hand against my ass echoed in our hotel room. I braced my hands on the bedspread, my fingers gripping the comforter.

His hand stroked my ass, soothing the sting, and then slipped down between my legs.

"You're already so wet," he said.

I was. I was wet for him. Aching for him. The way he touched me made me so hot. I looked back over my shoulder and saw that he was still fully dressed. That made me even hotter. I loved being naked while he was completely clothed, making him seem even more dominant. But I also loved feeling his body—his naked body—against mine.

I loved it all.

"Face forward," he commanded.

I did as he said, and heard him undressing: the rustling of fabric, the sound of a zipper, the metallic clink of his belt on the floor. My heart was beating faster and faster, awaiting his next move. Then his body weight shifted to the bed. I remained still, not knowing what to do.

His body heat was behind me, his cock suddenly

pressing against my lips. He traced the outline of my opening gently, and I rocked back against him, wanting more, but he pulled away.

"Please," I whimpered.

"I'm going to fuck you when I'm ready to," he told me. "And I'm going to fuck you until you can't hold yourself up anymore."

My mouth was dry, I wanted him so badly. I felt his hand move up my back, between my shoulder blades. He pushed down, forcing my face against the comforter, my ass shoved even higher in the air. Then I felt him notch his cock against my pussy again. I could feel my wetness starting to drip down my thigh.

Fisting my hair in one hand, he steadied my hip with the other.

"Are you ready for this cock?" he asked.

"Mmm hmm," I murmured.

"Tell me you want it," he said.

"I want it," I panted. "I want your cock. Fuck me, please. Stefan—"

My begging was cut off as he split me open, thrusting inside me so hard and deep that we both moaned. Then he started pumping, slow and steady and then faster, picking up speed as we found our rhythm, my cries of pleasure muffled against the bed.

"You want this?" he rasped as his hips smacked against my ass.

I could only moan louder as his hand slipped around to touch my clit. He squeezed it between his fingers, the sensation so intense and so perfect that I almost came, my whole body shuddering beneath him.

"Oh my god," I breathed, my hips bucking in time with his thrusts. "Oh my fucking god."

My cursing only encouraged him as he steadied me with both hands now, pounding into me more aggressively.

"So big," I said, gasping. "So hard. Give me more."

He lifted a hand and slapped my ass again. And again. And again. Each slap was accompanied by a deep thrust as I pressed my face against the bedspread, my hips high in the air. It had never been this way before; so wild, so intense, so forceful. I loved it, and I loved that he was letting himself go with me. He was completely in tune with what I wanted, giving me exactly what I needed to get off, and losing himself in the heat of the moment in the process.

It felt like my entire body was vibrating with white-hot bursts of pleasure as he alternated between slapping my ass and pinching my clit. I knew my cheeks would be red and sore tomorrow, but I didn't care. I wanted those marks on my body. I wanted the reminder that I was his. That my body was his.

His thrusting sped up, and I could sense that he was nearing his own release. I spread my knees as wide as I could, allowing him even deeper. My orgasm built inside of me, unstoppable, and I cried out as I came, hard and deep, moaning his name.

As my pussy clenched around him, I felt him lose control. His fingers dug into my hips, and he groaned as he came inside me.

With both of us still breathing heavily, he eased his body on top of mine, pinning me to the bed. We stayed there for a moment, just catching our breath, and I could feel his heart pounding against my back.

Despite everything we'd been through, I felt like our relationship was only growing stronger and deeper as each day passed. He was supportive of my dreams, he took care of me, and, recently, he was finally starting to open up, one small bit at a time. And the sex we had just kept getting hotter.

In that moment, I knew that I loved him. I could only hope it was a matter of time until he realized he felt the same.

TORI

CHAPTER 27

They say the way to a man's heart is through his stomach.

If that was true, then everything was going exactly according to plan.

Things had felt different after Stefan and I returned from New York. It was hard to pinpoint precisely what had shifted for him, but it was indisputable. He still worked late hours, but now he made an effort to be home early enough that we could have dinner together. We'd sit in the living room or on the couch, chatting about our days (I always talked more, but that was par for the course and neither of us seemed to mind the dynamic) while Gretna served us one of her gourmet meals. I paid attention to which dishes Stefan responded to most, planning to surprise him with my own home-cooked meal.

And now, the culmination of all my efforts was simmering deliciously right in front of me.

I'd pulled Gretna aside a week ago and asked her, "What's a fancy dinner you can make for someone, that's also not too hard to prepare?"

She looked me up and down. "Are you cooking for Mr. Zoric?"

I blushed. "I'd like to. And I'd give you the night off, of course. But I don't have a lot of experience, and I want him to be impressed. Really impressed. What can I do?"

Gretna tilted her head, glanced around the kitchen, and nodded. "Risotto. It tastes like a million bucks but it's just an elaborate preparation of rice. Everybody can make rice."

Smiling, I said, "That sounds perfect. I know he loves seafood—can I put something like that in there, too? Or will that make it too complicated?"

"It's not complicated," she said. "But which seafood are we talking?"

I thought about Stefan's preferences. "How about scallops? And shrimp? Maybe some clams or mussels?"

Grinning, Gretna nodded again. "Clams and mussels are easy—they open up their shells when they are ready. The scallops are a little more delicate, but we can practice."

"You'd do that for me?" I was overjoyed.

"Of course. I'd never forgive myself if I left you to over-cook a scallop. They get chewy. Tastes like rubber. A perfect scallop will melt in the mouth."

I decided I'd sear the scallops and serve them beside the risotto, and then chose asparagus with poached eggs as the side. Gretna gave me scallop-searing lessons for the whole week leading up to Stefan's surprise. I was shocked to find that it was easier than I'd expected—just a quick few minutes to cook each side—and that I was enjoying myself. Learning to poach eggs was a different story. I struggled time and time again, ruining countless eggs by turning them into disintegrating, inedible blobs.

"I just can't get it right," I'd told Gretna on Thursday

evening. "I'm following the directions exactly. But every time I pull them out of the water, they fall apart."

"It takes a lot of trial and error to poach an egg," she said sagely. "Some people never master it."

I frowned. "Is there anything else I can do? What if I fry them instead? I can fry eggs."

"Of course you can." Gretna brightened. "I should have thought of it myself. It will still be an elegant presentation. And he will love it."

I took her words to heart and tried to convince myself to relax.

And now here I was, standing in the kitchen in a cute apron I'd picked up from a boutique near campus, a gorgeous pan of buttery seared scallops sitting on the stove beside my bubbling risotto. The asparagus was in the broiler, almost finished, and my fried eggs and parmesan were waiting to become garnish. I was sweating, and high on adrenaline, but I couldn't wait for Stefan to get home.

I just hoped he wouldn't walk into the kitchen and see the disaster I'd wrought. The counters were covered in bits of parsley and lemon juice, spilled salt and pepper sprinkled left and right, grains of rice on the floor and shrimp shells in the sink. Not to mention the dirty measuring cups and spoons and pans everywhere. I'd clean it up later.

Untying my apron, I dashed upstairs to change. I hadn't wanted to risk setting a sleeve on fire or splashing oil or clam juice on my silk dress, but I realized when I got to the closet that I was still covered in a fine sheen of sweat. This would not do. I jumped in the shower to soap up and rinse off, then dried quickly and slipped the dress on.

But looking in the mirror, I saw that my mascara had run, my face was shiny, and my hair was a limp wreck. I touched up my makeup and tousled my hair under the hairdryer, then put on the teardrop diamond necklace from Stefan. Heels seemed like overkill for a dinner at home, but I still tried on a few pairs before finally settling on bare feet. I didn't want to scuff the floors.

Stefan was going to be so floored when he saw what I'd done for him—when he tasted what I'd done for him. He'd walk in, tired out from his long day at work, and come to find me in the kitchen in my sexy little dress, just about to put the finishing touches on the plates with sprigs of parsley and lemon wedges. One thing was certain: Gretna deserved a fat bonus for all her help and guidance. I couldn't believe I'd actually pulled this off.

I had just given myself a last look in the mirror when I heard a shrill beeping sound. That's when the smell hit me. Something was burning. *Fuck.*

I rushed to the kitchen amid the screeching of the smoke alarm and found smoke pouring from the oven. The asparagus! It had only needed three minutes to broil, and I'd left it for—at least twenty minutes, maybe thirty. I turned off the oven and flung the windows open to let the smoke out, breathing hard as the cold November air poured in all around me.

"What is this?" Stefan asked.

I whirled around. I hadn't even heard him walk through the door.

"Um," I stammered. "Hi. I made you dinner."

"Is that what this is?" He looked around at the mess, the haze of smoke, the pans on the stove. The alarm continued to beep. Stefan got a chair and climbed on it to disable the alarm. The beeping finally stopped.

The whole kitchen smelled like burnt asparagus. I knew when I opened the oven door, they'd look like sticks of charcoal. But at least the risotto was okay.

I rushed over to the pot and pulled the lid off, waving my hand over it with a flourish.

"It's seafood risotto," I told him proudly. "We can just skip the veggies tonight."

I dipped the serving spoon into the pot to show off, but it stuck fast into what had turned into a gluey brick of rice and bivalves. My heart sank as I realized I'd left the burner on the simmer setting for the last half hour. It was ruined. "Oh no."

I nearly deflated right there. In my efforts to do something nice, I had basically destroyed our entire kitchen and almost set the place on fire. Stefan was probably furious right now.

Why had I tried to make a big, fancy dinner when I could barely make myself toast?

"I'm sorry," I said. "I wanted to do something nice for you—I'll clean all of this up."

My eyes stung with tears. I was upset that I'd ruined dinner, but more than that I was humiliated that he'd come home to find me like this. I was a total failure.

I looked up and saw the slightest hint of a curve at the corner of his mouth. *Elmosolyodik.* "Are you laughing at me?" I croaked.

"Shh," he said, reaching out toward me. "Come here." He pulled me against his chest.

"This is so embarrassing," I moaned, covering my face with my hands.

"There's nothing to be embarrassed about. You know what you've made, Tori? The world's most perfect appetizer." He led me over to the scallops sitting on the stove, speared one out of the pan, and popped it into his mouth. As he chewed, I could see the gratification in his eyes. "This is flawless," he said after swallowing. "You're a pro."

He turned me to face him and traced the curve of my cheek with his palm.

"You look nice," he said. There was heat in his eyes, and that smile still teased his lips.

"Thank you," I murmured.

"I'm going to make a call right now and have someone come in to straighten up in here," he said, gesturing at the destroyed kitchen. "You, get your coat. I'm taking you out."

I bundled up and we got in the Town Car. I still felt bad that I'd botched what was supposed to be a romantic gift to Stefan, but at least he seemed charmed by my complete and utter lack of culinary skills. When I heard Stefan tell the driver where to go, I was pretty sure that I had heard him wrong.

I turned to him. "That restaurant has a waiting list six months long. We'll never get in."

He shrugged. "I know the Executive Chef."

I sat back, still worried. There was no way we'd get in on a Friday night during the dinner rush. I could only hope that Stefan had a back-up plan when we got turned away.

But when we arrived at the restaurant, there was a hostess waiting out at the curb for us. We were escorted inside and shown immediately to a table.

"Did you think we wouldn't get in, kitty cat?" Stefan teased as we sat down.

I could only nod, trying to take everything in. The restaurant itself was fairly unassuming for a place that people were clamoring to eat at. It had a quiet, rustic vibe, with live edge wood tables and industrial fixtures. There was no menu, either—everything was *prix fixe*, like our meal at Atera in New York had been. Based on that experience, I couldn't wait to see what kind of courses would be brought out for us.

While we waited, the waiter brought us a bottle of champagne.

"Are we celebrating something?" I asked Stefan.

"Just a night out," he said. "You can have a small glass."

I nodded, sipping at the drink and trying not to feel too dejected about the dinner I'd ruined. As excited as I was to be here, we'd only gone out because I'd made something inedible.

"What is it?" he asked, noticing my silence.

"I wanted dinner to be a gift to you," I confessed to him. "I wanted to impress you. And now you're taking *me* out."

Stefan's glass of champagne stilled just before it reached his mouth. He paused, took a sip and then lowered it.

"You do impress me," he said. "And you don't have to be the perfect housewife to do it. My mother couldn't cook either. She loved food, she appreciated food—but there were other things that mattered more to her than spending hours in the kitchen each day. Sounds like someone else I know." He grinned. "Don't knock yourself if your talents lie elsewhere. And I'm not just talking about your schoolwork."

I felt my cheeks heat, my heart leaping in my chest. When I looked back up at him, his gaze was intense, as always, but there was something else there too. Something softer.

He had just finished telling me a story about the time his mother set their kitchen on fire with a pan of frying bacon when the waiter brought out our first course. We were still laughing together as the plates were set before us.

I couldn't believe this was my life. That I was married to this man.

Stefan raised his glass in my direction.

"Enjoy," he said.

I fully intended to.

CHAPTER 28

Dinner was absolutely incredible. The food, the champagne, the company; everything had been just perfect. I was a little buzzed by the time we got into the Town Car heading home, but it was a good, nice buzz. I wasn't drunk, I was just happy. Comfortable. In love.

I looked over at Stefan and found that he was gazing at me. His expression was half in shadow, but I had a feeling that even if I'd been able to see his face completely, I still wouldn't have known exactly what he was thinking or feeling. He was still so often a mystery to me. One that I desperately wanted to uncover.

"Thank you for dinner," I said. "For everything."

He nodded. "It's my pleasure. All of it."

And then he took my hand.

We arrived back at the condo and headed upstairs. While we were out, the kitchen had been returned to its usual pristine state, almost like magic. I couldn't even smell the slightest hint of smoke, and the counters were sparkling, the dishes cleaned and put away.

I felt Stefan's hands on my shoulders and was surprised to find him helping me take my coat off. He removed it and carefully hung it over a chair, beside his own. Turning toward him, I waited for him to sweep me into his arms, to devour my mouth hungrily, the way he always did.

Instead, he picked me up and carried me to the bedroom.

As I nuzzled against his neck, I realized how drastically things *had* changed between us. It wasn't just my imagination, or something I had been hoping for. Things were different. The way he touched me was different, and now as he bent to kiss me, his mouth pressing firmly but gently against mine, it became clear that this was different too.

He took his time kissing me, as if he was savoring a meal. As if we were still at dinner, and I was the chocolate soufflé at the end of the evening—he was licking and tasting and enjoying me. I nearly melted into his arms.

In the bedroom, Stefan laid me down on top of the blankets. He climbed over me, pressing his weight against my body as he continued to kiss me, slowly and languidly. His fingers were in my hair, tightening just a little bit as his tongue stroked against mine, hot and hungry. I could tell he wanted to go faster and harder, but something was holding him back. Something inside of him was demanding he go slow. That he take his time.

He wanted to enjoy me. To ravish me. And I wanted to be ravished.

"Turn over," he ordered.

My entire body heated at his words. The last time he'd taken me from behind, I'd had a red mark on my ass the following day from all the spankings I'd gotten—a mark I kept surreptitiously touching as I remembered how hot it had been.

But instead of pulling me up onto my hands and knees like before, I felt his hands at the back of my neck, where the zipper for my dress was. I felt him slowly, slowly, slowly slide the zipper down until the cool air in the room brushed my bare skin. I wasn't wearing a bra, and I felt Stefan's hand on my back, tracing a line along my spine all the way down to my lower back.

I waited for the slap. Waited for him to pull me into the position he wanted me in. Waited for him to grab me roughly and fuck me hard the way he always had.

Instead, he kept his motions agonizingly slow. I was nearly dying with anticipation as he slipped the dress off my shoulders, exposing more of my bare back.

"Sit up," he ordered. "Face me."

I followed his orders. He pulled me to my feet and then slid the dress off my shoulders, letting it drop to the ground and pool at my feet. I stood in front of him, in nothing but my lacy panties and a pair of Jimmy Choo heels.

He removed my underwear next, hooking his fingers into the waist band and tugging them down until they dropped onto the pile of fabric on the floor. He gestured for me to step out of the dress and the panties, and when I did, he kicked them away.

Then Stefan swept my hair aside, exposing my neck and my bare breasts. He placed a palm on my chest and with a gentle push, forced me to sit down on the bed.

Then, to my shock—and extreme arousal—he knelt in front of me.

His hands were on my knees, and he pushed them apart, spreading my pussy wide open, exposing me completely. I could feel the air against my wetness, every nerve ending charged. He looked at me and his lips quirked. It was a devilish smile, wicked and self-assured.

"What are you doing?" I asked, my heart racing.

"Lay back. You're going to like this," he said. "Trust me."

I settled back and waited, my breaths already turning shallow and fast with heady anticipation. He was still fully dressed, kneeling between my legs. I didn't know what to expect, but I was ready for him to tug his clothes off and take me like this, my body ready for him.

But he didn't.

Instead, he bit the inside of my knee. I gasped at the sensation, almost pain, almost a tickle. My skin broke out into goosebumps, and I shivered. Then he pulled away, his breath warming the soft skin of my inner thigh. Unable to help myself, I let out a helpless little moan. Then he bit the sensitive skin there, applying gentle pressure with his teeth, and my moan pitched higher. He licked me at a leisurely pace, gradually dragging his tongue higher. I was panting for air. Finally, I felt his tongue trace a line up my wet seam, stopping to rest on my swollen clit.

I cried out, the intensity too much to bear.

All I could feel was burning need, a deep ache, my desperation for him. No one had ever put their mouth on me before, lapped at me like that before. Not even close. And now, he was spreading my thighs even further apart, making room for himself as his tongue drew maddeningly slow circles around my clit. The sensation was overwhelming, and I arched my hips toward his mouth, not knowing exactly what I was asking for, only knowing I wanted more.

He gave me more.

Stefan pinned my knees to the bed, my thighs burning as he stretched them wide apart to dip his head and thrust his tongue inside me. I groaned, pleasure spreading through my body like wildfire. I bucked under his strong hands and wet mouth, his tongue fucking me hard and fast.

He licked me up and down, breaking to tease my clit with his tongue before thrusting inside of me again. He would bring me right to the edge and then back away just as I was getting close. It was the most delicious form of torture I'd ever experienced, and my head thrashed from side to side as I cursed and moaned, begging him to bring me release.

I felt him smile against me, and I knew he was enjoying tormenting me. My hands fisted in the blankets and I thought I might go insane from what he was doing to me. Nothing we'd done before felt as intimate as this, and I lost myself in it completely.

Just as I started to feel tears of frustration gathering in the corners of my eyes, Stefan's hand moved from my knee, all the way up my leg. He slid a finger inside of me, and then another one, his hand fucking me while his tongue lapped at my clit.

It put me over the edge.

I came hard, my voice jagged with moans, hips jerking as my pussy contracted around Stefan's fingers. I was pretty sure I screamed his name out loud.

I'd never felt anything like it before. My entire body was limp, and I lay on the bed, feeling completely worn out. Completely satiated.

But we had just begun.

Stefan rose from the floor, pulling his clothes off with impatient jerks. Once he was naked, he crawled up on the bed, making room for himself between my legs. He was gorgeous and ready to fuck and I couldn't stop staring at him. Because he was mine. He was all mine.

Holding his perfect cock in his hand, he rubbed the

head against my already sensitized pussy. I jerked at the sensation and he smiled. He knew exactly what he was doing to me. He rubbed against me again, and this time I let out a little moan. God, it was good.

"Are you ready, kitty cat?" he said, positioning himself against my soaking wetness.

I was so turned on, I could only nod, my bottom lip caught between my teeth. Gripping my hips, Stefan thrust deep inside of me. Both of us let out a moan of pleasure as his cock went deeper than it had ever gone before. I could feel his entire length filling me up.

He stayed there for a moment, not moving, his body throbbing inside of me, his arm muscles taut and straining as he held himself above me. Our eyes locked. It was intense and intimate and perfect. It almost felt like we were having sex for the first time. Like we were making love for the first time. My heart seemed to swell in my chest.

Then he began to move and all I could focus on was the pleasure he was giving me. Each thrust was long and deep and languid. He took his time, savoring me the way I was savoring him. There was no rush, only the electric connection between our bodies, and I lost myself in the feel of his cock. He paused to kiss me, slow and deep, and then resumed his agonizing pace. I wrapped my legs around his waist, drawing him even deeper inside me.

Already, I could feel another orgasm building, shocks of heat twisting and tightening with each of Stefan's powerful strokes. This time, though, I wanted him to come with me. I wanted to watch him lose control. Wanted to watch Stefan lose himself in me.

I slid my hands up his back and down again, pulling him even deeper. Lifting my hips, I locked my ankles behind his back.

"Come with me," I begged. "I want you to come inside me."

I was grinding in rhythm with him, urging him to move faster, harder. He heeded my silent urgings, thrusting so roughly that my head started knocking against the head-board. I pressed my hands back against it, using it as lever-age, meeting each of his thrusts with my own.

I felt it when he began to break, his thrusts turning less smooth, more frantic. Looking up, I watched the muscle in his jaw tense as he clenched his teeth, searching for control. I didn't want him to find it.

But he was more experienced than I was. And he had a hold on his control that I couldn't even compare with.

Sliding his hand between us, he pinched my clit and gave it an agonizing squeeze.

"Oh my—*fuck*," I panted. "Stefan."

He squeezed again, and I heard myself moaning help-lessly, my pitch desperate. The spot where he was touching me was white hot, the alternating pressure and release shooting through my whole body like lightning. I was losing my mind.

"*You're mine*," he told me, and I felt myself start to slip over the edge. "Your body is mine and your orgasm is mine. Now give it to me. Give me everything."

I exploded beneath him, crying out and shaking as my body clenched around his. I gave him everything. Even my heart.

Somewhere in the middle of my own orgasm, I felt Stefan's control finally break as he slammed his hips against mine, riding out his pleasure as he jerked deep inside of me.

As we fought to catch our breath, he rolled onto his back, chest heaving, running a hand through his hair.

My body was languid with pleasure and my heart was full. I shifted onto my side.

"I...I love you," I whispered, the words slipping from me before I could second guess them. He'd asked for all of me. This was part of it.

An emotion I couldn't identify seemed to flash across his face. I hadn't expected a response, but without warning, he turned to pin me on my back. His skin was hot, his weight heavy and perfect against me. I slid my hands down his back, relishing the way his body enveloped me. Our eyes met. I let myself drown in that intense green, and then he kissed me. Taking his time, long and slow.

He hadn't said the words—but it felt like his kiss had said everything.

TORI

CHAPTER 29

I had always imagined that sex could bond two people, but I never realized it could feel like a drug. I spent the next few days on cloud nine, slowly coming down from the emotional ecstasy I'd felt in bed with Stefan the night of my ruined dinner. Things between us had never been better. We had dinner together almost every night, and he was beginning to open up to me—talking more and more about work and his day, or what he'd seen on the news—and at night we would burn up the sheets together. Sometimes I came home from school and he was tearing my clothes off before I'd even put my bags down, dragging me off for the same kind of hot, intense fucking as in the early days of our relationship. But other times it was sweet, so slow and satisfying that it made my heart ache.

I was completely, head-over-heels in love with my husband, and I was convinced that he felt the same way—or at least, was starting to. The thought made me so happy. This wouldn't just be an arranged marriage that we were both anxious to get through. It would be a love match. The kind of marriage I'd always dreamed of having. The kind I'd secretly hoped for.

That morning I got a call from my father, who was making a last-minute trip to Chicago. It was the first time I'd seen him since helping him with his recovery over the summer.

"I'm going to be in town taking care of some business at my Chicago office. Does my favorite daughter have time to meet up for lunch?"

I laughed at his lame dad joke. "She might. Depends on where we're going."

"Playing hard ball, eh? I've taught you well. I'm thinking Russell's on Bellevue."

"In that case, I think she can pencil you in," I teased. "Meet you around one, one-thirty?"

"Perfect. See you soon."

We met at his favorite place, an upscale steakhouse with an old-world, Prohibition-era vibe and a view of Lake Michigan that was unparalleled.

I felt my anxiety kicking in as the hostess led me toward the plush leather booth where my father was sitting. It was the first time I'd seen my father since the night Stefan and I had consummated our relationship, and I couldn't believe how much had changed since then.

As my father stood to greet me with a kiss on the cheek, I noticed how good he looked—a lot healthier than when I'd seen him last. A little thin still, but the color was back in his cheeks. It seemed his old appetite had returned as well.

"Does Michelle know you're eating steak and drinking whiskey again?" I asked him after he'd ordered his usual.

"No," he said. "And you're not going to tell her. Or my doctor. It's been nothing but plain oatmeal, boiled chicken, and broccoli for weeks. I can't even use salt! You know what she brought me for dessert last night? A quarter cup of *raw almonds*." He shuddered melodramatically.

"She's a monster," I agreed, stifling a smirk.

"You don't need to tell me that," he said, but when his food arrived, I noticed that he pushed half of it to the far side of the plate.

I'd dressed to emphasize that I was a professional now, that I wasn't a little girl anymore. I was wearing a neutral sheath dress and a matching jacket that would have impressed even Michelle, my ears glinting with modest diamond studs. My hair was pulled back in a simple twist and even my makeup was subdued.

I had hoped my father would comment on my appearance in some way; say that he'd noticed my effort, or that I looked more grown up. But if he realized that I looked different, that I was carrying myself differently, he certainly hadn't said anything.

A lot had changed for me, even if it wasn't visible on the outside. I wondered what my father would say if I told him how I felt about Stefan. He'd probably think I was being naïve.

He'd always seemed to think that of me, just because I was curious by nature and tried to approach things with an open heart. But I was an adult now, making my own decisions, doing the work involved in building a mature, committed relationship, while also pursuing my education. My father had no say over my life anymore. My chest felt lighter just thinking about it.

I loved my father, but knowing that my life was mine alone made our lunch even more enjoyable. I didn't worry about impressing him or pleasing him or saying the wrong thing.

"How's school?" my father asked halfway through our meal.

"So amazing," I said. "The program is a challenge, but I expected that. Just been hitting the books extra hard and camping out in the library. But I really love it. My psycholinguistics professor said—"

"I'm glad you're having fun, Tori, but you need to make sure to prioritize your marriage," he told me, stabbing his baked potato with his fork. "I can only imagine what Stefan's going through with you gone all the time. I hope you two have help around the place. A man needs a clean house and a hot meal to come home to at night."

My annoyance flared, and I silently reminded myself that my father came from a different generation.

I shrugged, forcing a casual tone. "He's so busy at the office, he's hardly ever around anyway. To be honest, I think it's actually a good thing that we're both working so hard."

My father let out an amused chuckle. "Oh, you think so? You have no idea what it's like to be in his shoes, having to listen to his wife babbling relentlessly about her own concerns after putting in ten, twelve hours on the job. Take it from me, it gets exhausting."

"Stefan doesn't seem to mind when I talk about school," I said. In fact, he seemed to enjoy it when I got so excited I couldn't stop myself from rattling on and on...probably because it meant I wasn't asking him a lot of questions. And frankly, he seemed much more at ease when I was guiding the conversation instead of trying to persuade him to tell me about his work.

"He's humoring you, I'm sure. You need to give him a chance to talk. It's important that you keep the man happy," my father reminded me.

"I'm aware," I responded with a tight smile, though

when it came to keeping Stefan happy, the last thing I needed was my father's advice. I was figuring things out on my own.

"How's the campaign effort going?" I asked, changing the subject. "I'm excited to see your ads on TV soon."

He warmed up the second I brought up his reelection campaign, so we spent the rest of our lunch talking about how that was going. He seemed in high spirits, which made me happy.

While we were waiting for the check, I got a text from Emzee, who was also in Chicago for the week to shoot some brand new talent for KZM.

Editing photos this afternoon—wanna come see? I also have some of you and Stefan from NY that I had printed up. They're kinda genius, if I do say so myself ;)

I had been so focused on the fashion show, and Konstantin's perplexing behavior with the models, that I barely remembered Emzee taking pictures that night. But I was intrigued. The only photos I had of us together were from the wedding, and although they were beautifully composed, they were so overly formal and posed that I hadn't wanted to hang any up in the apartment. But these would be candid. Maybe I'd find some that would look good on our walls.

I'd love to see them. You're amazing, I texted back.

She replied, *I'm in the Loop all afternoon. Come over whenever*!

So she was at the KZM offices...where Stefan had explicitly told me not to go. I chewed on my bottom lip as I tried to decide what to do. The last time I'd visited, I'd run into that sad, pregnant model with the red hair, and Stefan had been furious. It wasn't a place I particularly wanted to go back to.

On the other hand, I knew Stefan was at meetings all day and probably wouldn't even be at the office if I went. Surely there was no problem in just popping in to see some of the photographs Emzee had brought. Besides, Stefan had told me not to go to the KZM offices without being *invited*— and Emzee had just invited me. If I'd been officially and permanently banned, she would have been informed.

Finishing up lunch date with my dad, I texted her. *Should be over within the hour.*

Emzee sent me a thumbs up in response.

I hugged my father outside, promised to visit him soon, and hopped in an Uber to the Loop. I loved him as much as ever, but after I'd gotten married the distance between us had grown. Now I felt like a new person, and I wasn't so affected by the things he said. It wasn't that I didn't need him anymore, just that I needed him for different things. Marriage advice clearly wasn't one of them.

When I got to the KZ Modeling offices, I was told that Emzee had called down to put my name on a list and that security was expecting me—another good sign. My anxiety about visiting the building finally drained away.

The receptionist up on the twenty-ninth floor waved me away from the sign-in sheet on the clipboard and let me know that Emzee was photo editing in one of the executive suites a few floors up. I'd seen so little of the building that even though I tried to follow her directions, I found myself lost in the winding maze of hallways.

The floor itself was a puzzle, especially since it wasn't laid out the same way as the level where Stefan's office was. It was also mostly empty, and with everything so blank and grey, it was impossible to keep my bearings. Had I already passed that potted palm? Was that the same corner office I'd seen before? The doors weren't even numbered up here.

I realized I was getting nowhere. But when I pulled out my phone to text Emzee and ask her to rescue me, I saw that my phone had no service. Great. I'd apparently wandered into the building's Bermuda Triangle. My best bet was probably just to go back to the receptionist on KZM's main floor and ask for directions again—this time I'd write them down.

That's when I heard voices. Harsh, angry voices, sounding muffled behind a door.

I headed toward the sound, my steps barely a whisper against the thick carpeting, hoping I'd find someone who could give me directions. But as I was about to turn the corner, I finally realized who I was overhearing.

It was Konstantin and Luka.

I stopped in my tracks, ducking back around the corner. If they saw me, they'd definitely tell Stefan I'd been sneaking around. I was worried for a moment that my husband might actually be in there with them, but it became clear as I listened that it was just the two of them.

I didn't mean to eavesdrop, but they were so close, with the door cracked open by the sound of it, and talking pretty loudly. Clearly, they thought they were alone.

I told myself to leave, but I was too worried about getting caught, my feet frozen to the floor. Stefan might blow up if he knew I had come here, and it would undo all the good things that had been blossoming between us. I didn't want to lose that.

This had been a mistake. I needed to get out.

Careful to walk lightly so my steps wouldn't be heard, I began backing away from the office where Konstantin and Luka were talking. I was making progress when their conversation finally registered with me and I froze again, not sure that I was hearing them correctly.

"And you need to keep your greedy little hands off the KZM girls," Konstantin was scolding Luka. "They're not for you to play with."

"They clearly don't have a problem with it," Luka shot back.

I was shocked. Not that Luka had been screwing around with the KZ models; that was pretty obvious and not surprising at all. What was shocking was that Konstantin didn't approve. I'd seen the way the family patriarch looked at women—all women, not just the models—and he didn't seem like the type to care who they ran around with. In fact, I almost expected him to encourage his son to sleep with them as a sign of masculine virility.

I felt a twinge of respect for Konstantin.

One that immediately disappeared when he kept talking.

"Your actions are impacting our bottom line. You're distracting them from their work."

"It's harmless," Luka scoffed. "They have fun, I have fun. They know the rules."

"They might, but you don't," Konstantin said, his voice rising with impatience.

"What's the point of having beautiful women around if I can't get a piece of the action? There's plenty to go around. They're practically falling from the sky," Luka whined.

"You can have any woman you want in Chicago," Konstantin said, unmoved. "Wet your wick somewhere else."

Luka let out a sigh of frustration and Konstantin continued lecturing him.

"Our investors don't like getting your sloppy seconds," Konstantin went on, disgust obvious in his voice. "You need to keep your pants on around the merchandise."

Merchandise?

I got a sick feeling in the pit of my stomach. It wasn't just the way Konstantin was talking about the models, as if they were merely property, it was the way he had treated them on the night of the fashion show. The way he had spent the whole evening introducing beautiful young women to older men. Older men that looked as wealthy as Konstantin. And just as careless in the way they handled the women, in the way they dragged them out the door.

An awful thought crossed my mind.

Konstantin had called the models 'merchandise.' Surely he didn't actually mean...

"It's not my fault that they'd rather sleep with me than the men you introduce them to," Luka said.

"You think they like you? My son is an imbecile." There was a large slamming sound, as if Konstantin had dropped a heavy fist onto a table. "If you want to sleep with our models, you need to do what our other clients do," Konstantin said. "And pay for the pleasure of their time."

My blood ran cold.

"What?" Luka asked, the shock in his voice echoing the shock I felt.

I felt so naïve. So stupid. How had I not seen it? Not put the pieces together?

"Don't play the fool, boy." Konstantin's voice was vicious, full of contempt. "It's time you learned where our money really comes from. Those girls are our livelihood."

It made sense all of a sudden, the realization slamming into me like a car wreck. The introductions after the fashion show. The distant models who didn't want to talk to me. The crying redhead and her obvious disgust at leaving with the older man.

KZ Modeling wasn't just a modeling agency. It was a prostitution ring.

"They're *models*," Luka said weakly.

His father laughed. "And they're consummate professionals. But we both know they're not earning their keep on the runway—they earn it on their backs. Unless they want to hand over their work visas."

I didn't even wait for Luka to respond. I pressed my hand to my mouth, and then I ran. I didn't look back.

TORI

CHAPTER 30

I barely remembered stumbling back through the maze of the office layout, or passing the security desk, or even walking out of the building. I was halfway down the block when I realized I was outside, the cold November air finally shocking some reality back into me.

I didn't want to believe what I had heard. That the renowned and highly respected KZ Modeling—Stefan's family business, the one he'd given up everything in order to take over someday—was a front for sex trafficking. And since most of the young women that the company employed were from other countries, that meant it wasn't just local; it had international ties. Who knew how far the network reached? How many women's lives had been destroyed?

I felt sick, but I forced myself to keep it together and hailed a cab.

"Where you going?" the driver asked as I got in and slammed the door.

I was reeling. I needed to talk to my husband. But Stefan was in meetings all day, and I knew he wouldn't answer his phone. And how could I explain this? Would he even believe me when I told him about what his father was doing, all the dirty dealings KZM was up to behind the scenes? His agency was about to implode. His whole world was going to collapse.

I didn't know what to do.

"Excuse me? You have an address?" the driver prodded.

"Yes, sorry, hang on." I needed to come up with a plan.

I told the driver to take me to my father's office there in town. As we wove our way through the traffic in downtown Chicago, I texted Emzee with shaking hands. I told her I had to cancel my KZM visit and gave an apologetic excuse about my lunch not agreeing with me, promising we'd raincheck soon. Afterward, I texted Stefan just in case he checked his phone.

Something bad has happened, I said. *If you get this, I'm at my father's office*. I tapped out the address and hit send. Then I tried to make sense of everything I'd just heard.

For blocks I just stared out the window, hardly registering which streets we were turning onto, attempting to think straight. But every time I thought I had myself under control and ready to explain everything to my father in clear, simple words, I remembered Konstantin's words.

"You need to keep your pants on around the merchandise."

"If you want to sleep with our models, you need to do what our other clients do, and pay..."

"It's time you learned where our money really comes from. Those girls are our livelihood."

"They're not earning their keep on the runway—they earn it on their backs."

Every word I recalled sent a shiver of revulsion and disbelief down my spine. Konstantin was despicable. He needed to be stopped.

Thank god my father was in town. I felt a twinge of hope. He would know exactly what to do, and he would take action. Forced prostitution was an international crime, a crime against humanity. As a United States senator, my father would be able to pull in law enforcement and get KZ Modeling shut down. They'd rush in and save those girls—those *women*—and send Konstantin straight to the International Criminal Court to be tried. I hoped he'd rot in jail.

The only relief I felt was that Luka had seemed as shocked as I was at the information his father had just imparted. I couldn't imagine that Emzee knew, either. And there was no chance that Stefan knew about it. He couldn't. Even if he could be cold or callous sometimes, he wasn't the kind of person who would ever allow something like this. Or participate in it.

Konstantin was the creep of the family, but he was also the one in charge of KZ Modeling. The founder, owner, and C.E.O. All the criminal activity the agency was engaged in was clearly the reason he was so obsessed with maintaining control of the organization, not allowing any of his children to step in and take charge. The prostitution side-business he was running alongside KZM's legitimate work had to be his project. His and his alone.

I had to roll down the window, let the cold air shock my cheeks and ruffle my hair. Just thinking about Konstantin and the way he'd always looked at me—like his eyes were skinning me alive—nauseated me all over again. No doubt, he saw me the same way he saw his models: as a piece of meat. Something he could use to serve his purposes and then discard afterward.

I was desperate to talk to my father. Desperate to expose Konstantin—to bring him to justice. Jail would be too good for him, but at least if he was locked up he could never hurt anyone ever again.

Just imagining the way he'd tricked these women, lied to them, offered them work and a career and a chance to make a life in this country—only to force them into his service. He'd taken ownership of their bodies and used them, profited off of them in so many ways. Without a second thought. I needed him far away and out of my life. Out of Stefan's life.

Suddenly, I recognized the stone façade as we pulled up in front of my father's office building. I fumbled as I paid the cab driver and then bolted for the doors. I needed to see my father. I needed to see him now. He would fix this. He would make it okay.

I could feel my hair falling out of its neat twist as I crossed the lobby. If I'd looked prim and put together at lunch, I was sure I was a mess now. When I glanced up and saw myself in one of the floor-to-ceiling mirrors, I barely recognized myself.

Wide eyes, wild hair, no jacket. I must have left it in the cab. Or at KZM. I didn't care. The only thing that mattered was finding my father so he could deal with Konstantin.

In the elevator, I half-heartedly attempted to compose myself. I smoothed back my hair, re-twisted the knot and straightened my dress. My hands were still shaking, but I looked a little more presentable when I stepped onto my father's floor.

Taking a deep breath, I knocked on his door. I probably should have texted or called him to make sure he was actually in the office, but I hadn't thought that far ahead. I had barely been able to make it here in the first place.

Thankfully, I could hear a voice, mid-conversation, inside. It was likely my father was talking on the phone. I thought about waiting until he was done before trying again, but I didn't have that kind of time.

I knocked again. Harder.

"Dad!" I called out. "Dad, it's Tori. I need to talk to you!"

He would be furious at me for interrupting him on a work call, but once he realized why I had barged in like this unannounced—and that this was truly an emergency, with lives at stake—he would understand. He would be glad that I had come to him, that I had acted quickly. After all, my father had run all of his campaigns on the basis of family values. Of morality. Integrity. He would be horrified once he found out what Konstantin was doing.

There was only silence inside. Had he not heard me? Was he in his office, pacing back and forth across the rooms as he took the call like he always did? I kept knocking, feeling a little manic and a little desperate as my knuckles began to burn, the skin starting to break in some places. But I didn't stop. These women couldn't wait any longer.

Finally, I heard footsteps coming toward me. I felt like crying, I was so relieved. When my father opened the door, I practically fell into his arms. He stiffened, surprised. It was out of character for me—I had never really been raised as the hugging type—but I just needed to feel safe and held at that moment. I needed my daddy.

"Tori? My god, what's wrong? What is going on?" he asked, once I had pulled back.

"Something terrible is happening," I said, stepping into the suite.

This wasn't something that could be discussed out in the hallway, where anyone else could hear us. This was a crime and a scandal. Not just for KZM, but for my father as well. No one could know anything about it until we had figured out what to do next. I waited for my father to close the door, his expression still more bewildered than concerned.

"You know I'm very busy," he said. "Is this about Stefan? You two having problems?"

"No. Well, yes. Sort of. Look, I promise you, it's important," I said, my hands shaking, my head aching from the shock and stress of the whole afternoon.

I put a hand to my forehead, not exactly sure how to tell my father what had happened.

"What in the hell is going on?" he demanded, crossing his arms.

"It's not Stefan. It's Konstantin. He...I went to the KZM offices. I overheard him and Luka, talking about...they've been doing really bad things. Dad, you have to believe me... he's a bad person. He needs to be stopped." The words poured out of me, senseless and jumbled.

"You need to calm down and choose your words. Now one more time: What are you talking about?" His tone was placating, controlled as usual, but his body language was impatient. "You're not making any sense."

I took a deep breath.

"KZ Modeling," I said, trying to organize my thoughts. "It's not just a modeling company. It's an international crime ring. And we need to do something about it. You're a United States senator. You have connections. Power. You can get law enforcement involved and arrest him and take care of it."

It had all been there. All in the open. I just hadn't been able to piece it together fast enough. The horror and guilt washed over me afresh. No one else had figured it out either. What other horrible things were they missing? Was *I* missing?

I felt sick knowing that I was now, in some way, connected to what was happening behind the scenes at KZM. That by marrying Stefan, I was a part of his family, and would be associated with their activities and reputation.

And because of me, my father was a part of it too. He was implicated. It might even look like he'd had a hand in keeping it covered up. God, this could end his career. It would blacken his name.

The whole thing was a fucking disaster. Lives had been ruined, and the damage would keep on spreading like ripples in a pond. The fallout would be incredible. No wonder I could barely speak coherently about it.

"Those poor girls," I went on. "They didn't come here for this. They didn't deserve this. Someone needs to help them. *We* need to help them."

"The girls...?" My father was looking at me, clearly waiting for me to say more. Or to say something that made actual sense.

"The models! It's a sex trafficking ring," I blurted out. "KZ's models are sex workers. And I think it's against their will. That's coercion, right? Isn't that a felony? This is an international crime."

There was a long silence. I waited for alarm and disbelief to appear on my father's face, waited for his cry of outrage. I waited for...something. Any kind of reaction at all.

"Why are you bothering me with this?" my father finally said, his tone as cold as ice.

The floor dropped out from under my feet. With *this*?

I took a step back, studying his expression. There was nothing in his demeanor or body language to indicate that this was new or shocking information to him.

"*You knew*," I choked out, my throat closing up.

"Of course I knew." His tone was annoyed, as if we were talking about something as insignificant as my curfew, instead of the brutal, illegal dealings of the family I had married into. That he had coerced me into marrying into.

My stomach clenched, blood rushing to my ears. I backed further away from him, the room spinning.

He had known all along. This entire time.

Had that been the real reason he wanted me to marry Stefan? Some kind of insurance policy, to prove his loyalty to Konstantin? Or were they in this together? Associating with my father would have lent KZ Modeling an air of legitimacy, protected them against any accusations of wrongdoing. Meanwhile, the agency could return the favor by offering my father campaign money and a network of political support. My marriage would have sealed the deal.

But if this was all true, then...

I heard movement behind me and turned to find Stefan standing in the doorway, his jaw clenched. It was clear he'd just heard everything that had passed between my father and me. And even worse, I saw resignation on his handsome face.

No surprise, no disgust.

He had known about the prostitution ring, too. *He had always known.*

My father-in-law, my father, and my husband were all involved in exploiting vulnerable women for profit, for the pleasure of rich, careless men. As if their bodies were nothing more than shiny objects to play with, commodities to be bought and sold—and violated. And I couldn't stop myself from thinking about the whole reason they'd been victimized to begin with...it was the same exact reason I'd ended up involved in this situation myself. We'd all wanted a chance at a better life.

And we'd all been betrayed. Some of us had been hurt worse than others. I knew that, compared to them, I'd been handed what looked like a winning lottery ticket. But in the end, we'd all been forced into service, had been offered something that sounded like a dream come true and had instead found ourselves living in a nightmare.

I had never felt so deceived...and so trapped.

Just remembering the dirty money I'd spent on clothes and spa treatments made me sick.

I looked at the both of them, shaking my head. I had always known my father would go to any lengths to secure his legacy. His position of power. But I had never believed he would stoop to these levels to get what he wanted. I never believed he would be this corrupt.

And Stefan. The nights we'd shared together, the dreams we'd confessed. This was his dream? The company he'd spent years working himself to the bone to gain control of? The 'path' he'd self-righteously talked about forging?

I backed toward the door. I couldn't stand to be near either one of them.

I had believed that by marrying Stefan, I would be free from the control of men like my father. That I'd be able to make my own way, on my own terms. Instead, I found myself trapped in a marriage—in a life—defined by lies and corruption.

And the worst part was, regardless of everything that had happened, and despite everything I now knew about Stefan...I still loved him.

Our eyes met, and in his cold green gaze I saw nothing but walls. I had no idea what he was thinking. His face was impassive, and he still hadn't said a word. The man I'd give myself to, body and soul. The man I'd thought I would build a life with. This was the man I loved.

But I knew the truth now.

The question was—what was I going to do with it?

Tori and Stefan have had a rocky start to their marriage. Can they work through their latest challenge?

Find out in The Secret.

On the day I was married, I promised to love, honor, and obey my husband Stefan.

Little did I know how literally I would mean obeying.

Stefan tells me what to do, and I do it. There are questions asked, but I always submit in the end.

It would hurt less if I hadn't started falling for him.

It was supposed to be pretend. But the secrets we now share are too real, and they're crumbling every piece of who I thought I was.

If only Stefan was the man I thought he was.

If only I weren't so powerless.

But there's one thing I have that he wants.

My body.

And I'll do anything it takes to right the wrongs I've discovered.

The Secret

~

Dear Reader,

I can't thank you enough for reading The Deal. I hope you enjoyed this arranged marriage, romantic suspense as much as I enjoyed writing it. You can continue Stefan and Tori's journey in The Secret and concluding with The Choice.

Thank you again for your support and reading Stefan and Tori's story. If you enjoyed The Deal , I would greatly appreciate it if you let a friend or two know and leave a review. It's the best way to thank an author and just a few sentences is all it takes to show your support.

Sincerely,
Stella

~

Want to be up-to-date with all my releases? Sign up for my newsletter!

ABOUT THE AUTHOR

Stella Gray is an emerging author of contemporary romance. When she is not writing, Stella loves to read, hike, knit and cuddle with her greyhound.

Made in United States
North Haven, CT
04 September 2024

56934641R00178